The Lost Fleet

By Marvin Levine

Print ISBN: 979-8-9851999-9-4

Cover Design by www.coveredbymelinda.com

4

Contents

CHAPTER 1

Jack Abromski saw the first glint of gold in the faint sunlight reaching the ocean floor, far below his thirty-five-foot trawler. His heart skipped a beat. He had found the wreck, and now he had found its treasure. A quick check of his diving watch told him he had only fifteen minutes left to explore before running out of air. Jack snatched up two gold coins and pocketed them, then explored more of the wreckage. It was spread out over a wide area of the seabed. Rotted remains of the ancient ship's hull, masts, and decking lay scattered all around. Several rusted, barnacle coated gun cannons lay about in the sand — all of which would make for terrific exploration at some future date. Schools of fish served as the only guardians to the three-hundred-year-old ruins. For now, he focused on the real value the ship presented — its gold and silver.

Jack did what reconnaissance he could in the time he had left. Two spots held accumulations of coins and bars, and he knew there'd be plenty more nearby. If the ship was what his research said it was, the *Concepcion*, there'd be at least a hundred chests of treasure that went down with the Spanish galleon, whose grave now laid fifteen miles from Georgetown, off the South Carolina coast at a depth of eighty-five feet.

Jack glanced at his watch. It was time to head to the surface. He couldn't tamp down his excitement but forced himself to breathe steadily into his respirator. He had to remain calm and take his time without risking the bends. It had been a while since he dove at this depth, but Jack knew the procedure. He paused at sixty feet to avoid the decompression contamination of nitrogen in his bloodstream. Breathing slowly, he allowed the necessary changes to happen naturally while conserving his precious air.

Jack ascended toward thirty feet, unable to put the coins out of his mind. They were certainly gold, as there were no stains or corrosion of any kind. He recognized the imprint on the coin's head as a Jerusalem cross. And the date — the date was proof he had found what he was looking for — 713; common Spanish coinage indicating a mint date of 1713. It had to be one of the missing treasure ships from the lost fleet.

When he reached thirty feet, the surface came into view, and with it, the first sign of trouble. In addition to the hull of his trawler, the *Sunny Daze*, another hull floated next to it. Jack had company at the worst possible time. His first thought was maybe the Coast Guard, but that made little sense. Jack had told no one about his exploratory excursion today; not his partner Neil, not his fiancée Emmy — no one. Was he followed? Maybe it was another fisherman in the vicinity, coming to check why his boat was floating unmanned, stationary on the open sea. But the other hull didn't appear to be a fishing boat. It looked more like a speed boat of some kind with a large twin outboard motor.

Jack gave a brief thought to jettisoning the coins. If there was trouble on the surface, it'd be best not to have the evidence on him. But then he'd have to go back down to get them again, and he didn't have enough air in the tank for another dive today. Plus, with the hurricane bearing down, no telling how long before he could get back out. In one of those moments when the seemingly rational mind dismisses its own intuition, Jack proceeded to the surface.

He regretted it the instant he grabbed the ladder attached to the stern's gunwale and pushed his mask to the top of his head. When he looked up, he stared into the barrel of a handgun. Jack's eyes bulged. "Shit," he muttered, as the trouble he feared suddenly came to fruition.

"Come on up, Jack," said the man with the gun. "Let's see what you got."

Jack had no choice but to climb the ladder and step foot on the trawler's back deck. He kept his eyes glued to the man with the gun, but noticed an accomplice was also on his boat. He didn't recognize either of them. "Who are you, and how did you find me?" Jack demanded.

The man with the gun laughed. "Jack, we'll be asking the questions here. Now, take off your tank and fins, then we'll have a little chat."

Jack thought for a moment about jumping back into the ocean, but realized it would be a fool's choice. He'd be on the surface again within ten minutes and would have no choice but to return to his boat. It wasn't as if he could swim the fifteen miles to Georgetown, and even if he tried, they'd intercept him long before he got there. Just see this through, he thought, gritting his teeth as he removed the tank from his shoulders. Then he slipped off his two flippers, never taking his eye off the gun pointed at his chest.

Once he had only his diving wetsuit on, the man with the gun ordered him to the edge of the boat. Jack backed up to the gunwale with his hands raised, glaring at his captors. He turned his head and inspected the water all around. Nothing but sheer deep blue ocean butting up to an azure sky. Not a cloud in sight, nor any other boat clear to the horizon.

"Forget being rescued, Jack. There's not another boat within ten miles of here." The man took a step towards Jack. "Now, why don't you show us what you pulled up from that wreck."

Jack assessed the man again as he searched his memory for any connection. Well-tanned, he had a hard, chiseled look about him. Dark hair hung below his ears and a scrabble beard partially hid a scar that ran down the length of his right cheek. The man had a Spanish accent. His buddy, who hadn't said a word, was shorter and overweight. Jack tried to delay the inevitable.

"I didn't pull anything up. The wreck is just an old fishing boat, probably nineteenth century. Nothing much worth exploring."

"Ha," the man cackled. Then much more seriously, "That's bullshit, Jack, and you know it." He approached Jack and aimed the gun a few inches from his face, then turned to the other guy and nodded his head. "*Buscarlo*," he ordered.

The short, fat one, who obviously didn't understand English, moved toward Jack, and patted down his wetsuit. He found what he was looking for easy enough. The small zip pocket on the back of Jack's hip held the two gold coins. The man's eyes lit up when he unzipped the pocket and removed the coins. "*Mira monedas de oro!*"

"*Si, mi amigo — oro.*" The gunman smirked.

The short fat one handed over the coins. The gunman inspected them and nodded his head in approval. Then he took a closer look, and a wide grin broke out on his face. He turned his anger back at Jack. "Nothing to find, eh, Jack? I'd say you stumbled on quite the find here." He held up the coin's face to Jack. "Jerusalem cross. You know what that means?"

"It's Spanish," Jack replied with disgust, his upper lip curling.

"Yes — it's Spanish. But look at this." The gunman flipped the coin around. "This coin was minted in 1713." The man's voice deepened in anger. "What does that tell you, Mr. Jack Abromski? Mr. Wanna-be-treasure-hunter. Huh?"

Jack glared at his captor with even more antipathy. "The 1715 Treasure Fleet," he spit back.

The gunman laughed. "This is true. You know your history. And you knew there were three missing ships from that fleet, didn't you?

Congratulations on such a historic find." He examined the coins once again, his grin broadening even more, before placing them in his pocket. His attitude hardened again. "Too bad you won't be around to see the rest of it brought up." He lowered the aim of the gun to Jack's chest and fired three times.

Jack let out one scream that evaporated in the warm sea air. As he collapsed to his ship's deck, his last vision was of a seagull, witness to his brutal murder, flying over the top of the *Sunny Daze*.

CHAPTER 2

Amelio Santori glared down at Jack's still body, his blood oozing out onto the deck. He felt no remorse. Killing was simply a requirement of his job as a key lieutenant in the Constantine cartel. He'd learned over the years that guilt and regret were hazardous to maintaining a good standing in the organization. Destroying the enemies of the cartel and those who would stand in its way were necessary prerequisites. Amelio never shied away from a good fight and had his share of wounds to show for it. The five-inch scar flaring down his right cheek was the most enduring of these. A knife fight in a back-alley Miami barrio when he was a young rising star proved a constant reminder of the risks of the job.

Over the years, Amelio developed a hardened shell, protecting his emotions while providing ruthless muscle for the organization. For that, he'd been generously rewarded. Now a senior officer in the cartel, he spent most of his time shuttling drugs and other contraband from Miami to the Carolinas. Sebastian Constantine had moved his base of operations from Colombia to Miami several years ago and Amelio set his Carolina home in a secluded bungalow on a creek in McClellanville, a small village in Cape Romain not far south of Georgetown.

Drug smuggling wasn't the only source of revenue for the cartel. Mr. Constantine took a keen interest in sunken shipwreck treasure, plundering them and selling the illicit finds on the black market. Although Amelio had never been involved in one of these salvage operations, he knew the potential profits were enormous.

So, when he received intel of a possible find off the coast of Georgetown, Amelio was assigned the task of finding it and running an under the radar salvage operation. Amelio took pride in the faith the boss put in him. He had plenty of resources to draw on, but first the wreck had to be found. A fortunate twist of fate led to this Georgetown fishing boat captain, Jack Abromski. From there, a trap was set and this morning, Amelio and his assistant Enrico trailed Abromski out to sea. When he saw Jack dive, he moved alongside, then boarded his trawler. Sure enough, thirty minutes later, Abromski surfaced with the proof of the treasure. Now it was his.

"Let's sink it," he told Enrico. The two men left Jack's body on the deck and returned to their speedboat they had secured to the trawler. Enrico untied the ropes and eased the speedboat away.

"Seventy meters," Amelio told him. He grabbed the rocket-propelled -grenade launcher he used for sinking boats. Once a proper distance from the trawler, Amelio aimed and fired the missile. It struck the stern just above the waterline and blew the back portion of the vessel apart.

"*Buen tiro,*" Enrico told him, smiling a mostly toothless grin.

Amelio nodded. It was a good shot, and not the first time he'd used an RPG for this specific purpose. The two men watched in silence as the *Sunny Daze* took its last trip straight down to the bottom of the ocean.

"Our captain swims with the fishes now," Amelio told his friend. "His boat will rest with the *Concepcion.* The treasure of the lost fleet will soon be ours."

"*Si,*" Enrico nodded and smiled.

"Come, my friend. We have work to do." Amelio noted the GPS location they were at. He had to get back to shore and purchase a buoy, then attach a surveillance camera on top of it. Constantine had provided a contact in the Charleston area who could manage such a device. Now that the shipwreck had been located and verified, he could take no chances of anybody sniffing around looking for Abromski. If they did, they would soon meet the same fate.

Amelio couldn't wait to let his boss know the good news. He dialed his number on the satellite phone he kept for keeping in contact at sea.

"Yes, Amelio," Constantine answered. "I hope you have good news."

"Indeed, I do, Sir. The *Concepcion* has been located and its treasure confirmed. The fishing boat captain has been eliminated."

"Excellent, excellent! That is wonderful news, indeed. I knew I could count on you." Amelio sensed the joy in his boss's voice. Constantine was a man of few positive emotions. It felt good to hear.

"I have the shipwreck's location, and we're headed back to obtain the necessary surveillance tools. We should be able to begin salvage operations soon. However, there's a tropical storm headed this way in a couple days. I will keep you abreast."

"Understood. Again, good work, Amelio. The recovery of the *Concepcion's* treasure will be a magnificent addition to our assets. I look forward to further updates."

"Yes, Sir." Amelio ended the call and sped his way back to shore. A hurricane may delay things a few days, but nothing would stop him from completing his mission. Perhaps the most important mission of his life.

CHAPTER 3

Emmy Sweeney woke before the alarm Thursday morning, the day after Hurricane Kit barreled through the South Carolina low country. She'd hardly slept at all. Hadn't all week since Jack failed to return to the marina on Monday evening. At first, she was just mad at him, after his partner Neil told her he didn't go out on Jack's boat to fish on Monday. She couldn't for the life of her figure out why he'd go out by himself without telling anyone.

By Tuesday morning, with no word from her fiancée, Emmy began to fear the worst. That evening, she filed a missing person report, but with the hurricane approaching, the Coast Guard couldn't do a search. Her and Neil posted on social media and put up some flyers in the Georgetown historic district. She still held out hope, but it was fading quickly.

Then, yesterday, Emmy watched with shock and dismay as Kit decided at the last minute to hang a left twenty miles east of Georgetown and crashed down on her hometown. Thank goodness it didn't strengthen past the Cat 1 storm it had been all the way up the east coast from its origins south of the Bahamas. It had actually decreased slightly to a low Cat 1. Plus, it made landfall at low tide yesterday afternoon, further minimizing the potential damage. Still, there'd be a mess everywhere, both outside around Georgetown and inside her worried sick mind.

"Where are you, Jack?" she said out loud for the hundredth time, holding back tears. She reached out for Sandy, her three-year-old Golden Retriever, and held her tight. This time, the tears ran freely. She couldn't understand why he would take the trawler out by himself, something he never did. It didn't come back on Monday. She knew that the chances of him surviving at sea through the storm were slim. Emmy couldn't come to grips with the real possibility she would never see Jack again. It was just too much to bear.

Emmy let herself have a good cry, but at some point, had to snap out of it. She had a job to do today. Same as it was the day after every other hurricane or tropical storm that blew by the South Carolina coast. She'd need to make a damage assessment of the Barony property. Emmy enjoyed her day job as one of three of the Hobcaw Barony's Naturalists more than any other previous job. She loved interacting with the patrons, especially when the school kids took their tours. But the Barony would be closed today, and depending on what she and her coworkers found, more days to come before the place could get back to a presentable state.

She looked out the front window of her home in the historic section of Georgetown. The water had mostly receded after reaching a peak of about a foot on her street. She'd seen worse. Matthew in 2016 brought in two feet. She'd been told that Hugo in 1989 drenched her town with four feet of seawater. Emmy was just four years old when the Cat 4 Hugo blew in. But at that time, she wasn't anywhere near the coast, having spent her childhood well inland around Columbia, South Carolina. But she'd lived and worked in Georgetown ever since she graduated from the University of South Carolina in 2009.

Emmy sat down on the living room couch with her morning coffee and turned on the Weather Channel. As she suspected, Jim Cantore had landed in Georgetown and was now standing just three blocks away on Front Street, still in several inches of standing water. The heart and soul of historic Georgetown, Front Street always took the brunt of any tropical system. The sea would funnel into Winyah Bay, then up the Sampit River past Front Street like a flash flood pouring down into a Rocky Mountain town.

"C'mere Sandy. Let's see what the old blow-bag has to say about our poor little town." Sandy jumped up on the couch and watched as keenly as Emmy. She often wondered if her dog perceived information every bit as intelligible as humans did. More so for a lot of them.

Emmy sipped her Gevalia and watched the scene unfold in front of her. She'd have to check in with Tom at Coastal Catch and Neil again before she headed out to the Barony. Those two men were her bedrock, now more than ever. Neil was Jack's mate on the boat, and his best friend since college. He took Jack's disappearance every bit as hard as Emmy.

As if on cue, Jim Cantore walked over to a utility pole, one of the ones where she placed a missing person flyer. The TV camera zoomed in on it. Emmy's heart caught in her throat when she saw Jack's picture, the one with him smiling on the *Sunny Daze*. She'd taken it not even a month ago. Oh my God, she thought, her hand covering her open mouth. All of America is seeing this right now. Emmy raised the volume. Sandy yelped, seeing her dear friend on the screen.

"And on a sad note, all the folks here in the Georgetown area are still praying for the safe return of Captain Jack Abromski and his fishing trawler, the *Sunny Daze*, missing now for three days." Cantore spoke with all the sincerity and empathy of a seasoned correspondent, looking straight into the camera. It was as if he was talking directly to her. "We here at the Weather Channel give our best wishes to Jack's friends and family." Emmy sat stone still on her couch, not believing what she had just heard. Sandy sensed the emotion and laid her head on Emmy's lap. Sandy whined softly while Emmy gave her a hug and began to cry again.

******

Emmy needed to get to the Barony and begin her damage assessment. Seeing Jack's flyer on the Weather Channel brought her already raw emotions to the surface once again. Soon after Cantore's plea, Emmy received several calls from friends offering their continued condolences while still offering prayers for Jack's safe return. She let their empathy soak into her and thanked them for their support.

The last call came from Jordy Gorman, her boss, and managing director at the Barony. "Emmy," he said emphatically, "when are you coming in? We need to get started on the damage assessment as soon as possible."

Emmy looked at the time and realized she'd spent too long on the phone. "Shit," she cursed under her breath. "Be there in twenty minutes, Jordy. Sorry."

Before she let Sandy out the front door, Emmy paused and sighed. She let her sights wander down the street, searching for answers. Searching for Jack. "Where are you, Jack? Where in the world are you?" She refocused on what was real, which meant getting to work.

Emmy's first look at the hurricane impact came as she drove over the bridge crossing the Waccamaw river. The immense Hobcaw Barony laid out to her right, sixteen-thousand acres of low country pristine wetlands. Many of the lowest lying areas were still under water, like what they normally experience during the semi-annual king tides. The green marsh shimmered in the late August heat, the sun already well up in the southern sky. Sandy and she would be down on that shore in her Jeep Wrangler within the hour. A quick glance indicated at least some trees were down. She'd have a ground view soon enough.

Emmy greeted Jordy in the Barony's main office as soon as she parked the jeep out front. He gave her a smirk that both admonished her tardiness, but also showed understanding for why.

"Catch the Weather Channel this morning?"

"I did," Emmy replied, emphasizing the second word. She pasted a smile on her face. "Did you see the sign someone held up behind Jim Cantore?"

Jordy laughed. "Yeah, Jim Cantore please go home. It's a meme now. He always goes to the hardest hit spot." Then more serious, "Nice plug for Jack, though. Nothing else new there?"

Emmy just shook her head no. She didn't want to talk about him. "Um, so where do you want me to start?"

Jordy came right back to business. "Take Hobcaw Road out to the end. See what we might have to clear to get the tour bus back on the road. Then hike around the point to the inlet. You know what to look for. This ain't your first hurricane rodeo."

No, it wasn't, not nearly. "Got it, boss. Come on, Sandy. Let's go exploring."

"Got your radio?"

"Always, Channel 5." Emmy held up her two-way. "I'll let you know what I find." She pushed open the screen door and made her way to her jeep.

Hobcaw Road was the main road out to the southern boundary of the Barony. It started as a two-lane paved road, but soon became a gravel road. At its end, four miles out, stood the Georgetown Light, a still operating lighthouse, keeping watch over the tricky currents of Winyah Bay. The lighthouse marked the beginning of one of the hiking tours the Barony offered. Emmy would walk that route today, around the point marking the mouth of the Waccamaw River and the end of Collins Island. From there she'd hike the beach down another half mile before cutting back on a trail through the marsh grass. That trail may likely still be too wet to trek, and the Barony couldn't reopen the lighthouse tour until it was passable.

Emmy's drive out was uneventful through the woodland section. Each time her mind wandered toward Jack, she forced herself to snap out of it. It proved to be a task too difficult. Perhaps the physical exertion of the hike would help her focus on her task. Several smaller pines had fallen across the road, which would need to be cleared, but she negotiated them easily in the jeep. At the edge of the woods, Emmy received her first shock. The enormous live oak, known affectionately as Big George, had been uprooted and laid full across Hobcaw Road.

"Oh, no," Emmy lamented, turning to Sandy. "Big George is gone." The tree had been a landmark in the Barony ever since it opened in 1935. Estimated at 350 years old, the oak had stood guard overlooking the wide span of marsh south to the bay beyond. As sad as it was to see him fall, the team knew Big George was on his last legs as several large limbs had broken off in recent storms, revealing internal rot. Kit appeared to be George's last stand. Could it be symbolic of Jack's last stand as well? Emmy shook her head with vigor, again straining to rid her mind of such awful implications.

It was also the end of the road for the jeep, as the massive oak blocked any path around. She let Jordy know by radio, then proceeded on foot. Ten minutes later, Emmy and Sandy arrived at the Georgetown Light. The old tower survived yet another hurricane, looking hardly worse for wear than she did when she was rebuilt 212 years ago. East of the lighthouse began the beach portion of Collins Island, with the inlet just a quarter mile ahead.

Emmy took in the vast seascape the view offered. She always marveled at its beauty and serenity. Layers of green and yellow marsh grass blended effortlessly with the shimmering blue waters of the bay. The bay also seemed to have completely ignored the fact another hurricane had come and gone. The sun shone bright and hot with barely a light breeze to break it. "Come on, girl," Emmy told Sandy, "Let's see what treasures the storm washed up."

Sandy barked with delight and ran ahead along the beach. After another ten minutes, the two rounded the point and started the hike to the north, now alongside the glistening Atlantic. With it came a change in landscape. Emmy noticed right away the storm had eroded much of the beach. What was normally a fifty to sixty-foot-wide beach at high tide, today was more like thirty. Mother Nature at work, surmised Emmy. The beach had been here for a millennium and had seen countless storms before it. She knew what was lost today would slowly grow back over time before giving back again to the sea in a never-ending cycle. Just like life — and death. Jack flashed in her mind again. Emmy paused to reflect. He was out there, she thought gazing out over the sea. Just three days ago. Where is he now? What happened to him?

Emmy refocused on her beach assessment. What the ocean took away, it also replenished. Once around the point, Emmy began to see what she had become accustomed to after such storms. A treasure trove of seashells. They littered the beach, thousands of whole pristine shells unearthed from their homes on the ocean floor. Dredged up by the churning currents, they were deposited all along the South Carolina beaches. Emmy knew many a beachcomber would scour the shoreline today from Pawleys Island to Myrtle Beach and haul away a year's worth of shell trophies. But not on her beach. The beaches on the Barony were strictly off limits to the public, except for the daily organized tours. Emmy knew the beachcombing hiking tours would quickly fill up after the storm. Serious shell collectors loved an unpicked-over trove.

Even by Emmy's experience, the pickings today were superb. It must have been the turn the storm took, she mused. When Kit made an abrupt turn to the west, the shells on the continental shelf were ripe for uprooting. Emmy walked over the layers of them piled on top of each other all along the beach. Highly sought Striped Tulips, Lightning Whelks, the prized Venus, or Pawleys Island shell, Scotch Bonnets, Checkerboard Clams, and Calico Scallops were mixed among the more common clams, quahogs, and pen shells. What a beachcomber's delight, Emmy thought, contemplating the thrills awaiting the beach hike tours soon. She hoped the tours would start up again on Saturday, the day after tomorrow, and then right on through the Labor Day weekend.

Lost in her speculation over the reopening of the Barony, Emmy saw a quick flash of light coming from something on the shell strewn beach. It caught her eye, as even the shiniest shell didn't reflect the sun like that. Only metal did. The object that sparkled turned out to be a fairly large whelk, maybe three inches long. But it wasn't the shell itself that gleamed. She picked up the whelk and immediately gasped. Stuck in the shell's hollow midsection was a coin. A gold coin. Emmy picked it out of the shell and almost lost her breath. "Oh my God," she whispered. "Oh my God, I don't believe it." Emmy stared at it, unblinking. The coin had a square-looking cross on the front and some other detail she didn't recognize. But when she turned it over and saw the number 713 imprinted, she knew she had found something very special. 713 was meant as a date — 1713. This coin came from somewhere over three centuries ago.

As Emmy gazed at the best beach treasure she'd ever seen, Sandy suddenly gave a sharp bark and took off further down the beach.

"Sandy," she shouted after her, "What is it, girl?"

Sandy continued to sprint down the shore. Emmy tucked the coin in her khaki shorts pocket and began to jog after her. A minute later, Sandy stopped and barked loudly, nonstop. Emmy felt a sense of fear run up her spine. As she neared Sandy, she saw something lying on the sand. At first, she thought it was a piece of dark driftwood. Sandy kept yelping at a high pitch. Emmy felt her lips begin to tremble. Whatever Sandy found had to be more ominous than driftwood.

When Emmy got within twenty yards of her irate retriever, the object took shape. She first noticed the glistening reflection of a wetsuit. Moments later, she realized what lay on the beach was a body, a man's body, lying face down. "Oh no, oh no," she muttered, her whole body now trembling. Sandy continued her hysterics. Emmy knelt next to the body. She recognized the wet suit, the man's broad shoulders, and the dark curls on the back of his head.

"Oh no. Please, God, oh no." Emmy swallowed hard and gently turned the body over. When she recognized the bloated, distorted face of her fiancée, Emmy screamed hysterically, "Noooo! Nooo! Oh no, oh no." Sandy kept barking. Emmy turned to the side and vomited violently in the sand. When everything in her stomach had emptied, she curled herself into a ball and sobbed, heaving huge breaths, shaking as if she were freezing. Sandy sat right next to her, whining and licking her face. Emmy's entire body was numb, her mind blank. She felt weak and dizzy, unable to comprehend the horror of her discovery.

Lost in the isolation of the beach, the warm salt breeze coating her saline tears, Emmy cried herself out and eventually came to her senses. She crawled back toward Jack and examined the rest of his body, shielding her sight from the hideous, swollen face. Her heart froze. Three holes had torn through the wetsuit in Jack's chest. Another wave of shock tore through her. She had to get a grip. She needed help. Emmy turned on the radio and screamed, "Jordy, Jordy, are you there?"

"Go ahead, Emmy," he replied. "What's up?"

Emmy heaved in a couple more deep breaths before she answered in a shaking voice, "Call the Sheriff, Jordy. I found Jack. He's dead!"

CHAPTER 4

Emmy saw Jordy round the point, jogging slowly towards her. At the same time, she noticed a patrol boat with red flashing lights make its way to her position on the beach. It had been forty-five minutes since she radioed Jordy. The worst forty-five minutes of her life. Emmy alternated between periods of sobbing while holding Sandy tight and outbursts of anger. She screamed at the passing gulls and pelicans, demanding answers, and cursing her fate, and that of Jack's. Nagging questions remained unanswered. Why did Jack go out on the *Sunny Daze* alone on Monday? Why hadn't he told either Neil or herself? Obviously, he'd gone out somewhere to dive. Did it have something to do with the gold coin she found? Did he, in fact, find sunken treasure and was diving for it? She prayed for Jack, and she prayed for answers.

Emmy stood and greeted Jordy. The man had to be flirting with a heart attack. He looked breathless and ragged as he approached. Gray strands of thinning hair plastered his forehead with sweat. He was sixty years old and sixty pounds overweight — and looked terrible.

"Emmy, Emmy," he cried out as he embraced her in a smothering bear hug, drenching her with his sweat. "I'm so sorry. So sorry."

Emmy let him squeeze her for a few seconds, then broke his hold. She looked up at him, her eyes puffy and red. "Thanks, Jordy. Looks like the sheriff's here. Thanks for coming out all this way. You really didn't have to. I mean, look at you, you're a mess."

Jordy continued to gasp for air, eventually regaining his breath. "Too important, too important. Let's greet the sheriff."

The two made their way to the shoreline, where the patrol boat slid its flat hull onto the beach. Three men exited the boat. Emmy recognized the tall, bald, muscular Black man as Sheriff Leroy Keating. She'd met him a time or two, under more pleasant conditions. The two others she didn't know. The five of them formed a circle on the beach, ten yards down from Jack. Sandy stayed close to Emmy's side.

Jordy began the introductions. "Sheriff Keating, I believe you've met Emmy Sweeney before."

Emmy shook Leroy's hand. "Yes, I have. Thank you for coming out like this."

"Miss Sweeney," said Leroy in his booming baritone voice, "this is Detective Tony Meacham, and our Medical Examiner, Murrey Freeman. We're very sorry to meet under these circumstances."

Emmy shook the other two men's hands. She saw all three look over at Jack. Emmy had moved a good thirty feet away, and upwind. The stench of Jack's body was too much for her to bear.

"Let's start with Jack," Leroy stated solemnly. "Why don't you two stay here for a few minutes while we examine the body and then we can talk."

Emmy covered her mouth and nodded. She and Jordy walked to the back edge of the beach and took a seat on a piece of driftwood. They watched as the ME inspected the back side of Jack, then turned him over and did a complete examination of his front. Sandy yelped again, seeing Jack's bloated face.

"It's ok, girl. It's ok." Emmy stroked the retriever's neck, trying to calm her and herself as well. She sniffed and wiped her nose on her sleeve. Her breathing continued to heave. At least she had others around now to support her. She knew she'd have nightmares of the time she was alone on the beach with only Sandy and her deceased fiancée.

Jordy kept his hand on Emmy's forearm. "We're going to figure this out, Emmy. You know we will."

Emmy turned her soft brown eyes, still moistened with tears, towards her boss and whispered, "I hope so, Jordy."

Leroy approached Emmy and Jordy while Tony and Murrey continued to work on Jack. He turned to Jordy.

"Mr. Gorman, I'd like to talk with Miss Sweeney alone, please."

Jordy nodded his understanding and walked back to the shoreline. Emmy stood and faced the sheriff.

"Jack was shot, Miss Sweeney. We're treating this as a homicide."

Emmy nodded her head and said with her voice cracking, "I know." She kept her hand over her mouth, and her eyes wide open.

"Why don't you tell me what you can, starting with the last time you saw Jack?"

Emmy gulped. As difficult as it was, she knew she needed to tell her story. First, she took a few deep ragged breaths. "Yes, so, the last time I saw Jack was at dinner this past Sunday night." Emmy had to pause as she caught herself starting to cry again. She looked at the sheriff, whose face radiated empathy and patience.

"Take your time, Miss Sweeney. There's no rush."

Emmy nodded as she took another deep breath and exhaled, then regained her composure. "We went to the Coastal Catch, one of our regular places on the waterfront. We've known the owner, Tom Boswell, for some time. It was a typical dinner. Nothing unusual came up that I recall. The normal excellent Lowcountry food we both love." Emmy paused for a second, remembering holding Jack's hand across the table, seeing his signature smile while she felt the warm blush on her cheeks.

She caught her breath, then remembered something else. "There was one thing, though. When dinner was over, before we paid, Jack left the table and went with Tom back to his office. They were gone for less than five minutes. When I asked him what that was all about, Jack dismissed it, said, 'Nothing, just some fishing business.' I thought nothing of it." Emmy noticed Leroy make a note on this pad. They'd certainly follow up with Tom about that conversation. She'd like to know herself.

"After dinner, Jack drove me back to my house, only three blocks away, and we kissed and said we'd get together again soon." Emmy caught herself in a moment of emotion. "That was the last time I saw him." Her voice cracked again.

Emmy could see the compassion on the sheriff's face. Leroy asked, pointing to the driftwood, "Miss Sweeney, would you like to sit down here?"

Emmy caught herself and shook her head. "No, no, I'm fine."

"Go ahead then. What happened on Monday?"

"Well, I thought Jack was going out fishing that day, a normal workday. Usually, he calls when he gets back to the dock, but I didn't hear from him. When I couldn't reach him by phone at, I guess, around five that afternoon, I called Neil, his partner, and Neil told me they hadn't been out fishing that day. Jack had called off the trip that morning and he hadn't heard from Jack all day either. That's when I started getting worried." Emmy put her hand on her forehead. She took a couple more deep breaths before continuing.

"So, I picked Neil up at his house and we went over to the marina where Jack keeps the *Sunny Daze* in dock. It wasn't there. The dock master told us Jack took it out that morning by himself. I couldn't for the life of me figure out what was going on. Monday night, we started making calls to his friends, his customers and suppliers and no one had a clue where he was or why he would have gone out to sea by himself. I mean, he's never done that to my knowledge. No one takes a fishing trawler out to sea alone. And he would never dive by himself. It's against everything he knows as a sailor and a diver."

She noticed the look of mounting concern on Leroy's face.

"On Tuesday, we searched all over Georgetown. No sign of him. That's when the hurricane turned toward us. As you probably know, I called in Jack as a missing person at that time, then posted on social media and made some flyers. Neil helped me put them up around town. Wednesday, we hunkered down with the storm and today I'm out here."

Leroy pinched the bridge of his nose and frowned. "What about the wetsuit, Miss Sweeney? What can you tell me about that?"

Emmy took a deep breath and exhaled. "Well, Sir. Yes, Jack liked to dive in his spare time. We both did. There are a couple of Civil War era wrecks around the bay where we liked to dive. He was always looking for fresh places to explore. He'd tell me someday he'd find something really valuable, like some lost treasure or something. I always laughed it off. So, obviously, he was diving somewhere out there on Monday. I don't have a clue as to where."

Emmy stuck her hand in her pocket and felt the coin. She'd already decided not to share the coin with the sheriff. It was the best lead she had and knew the sheriff would confiscate it if she showed it to him. Always keep your best cards in your hand, Emmy, she smirked to herself, recollecting one of Jack's euphemisms.

"Anything else, Miss Sweeney? Anything that might help us in the right direction?"

Emmy shook her head. "No, Sir. Not at this time." She glanced over at Jack's body. It appeared the ME and detective were finished with their examination. She could feel the emotional toll catching up with her. It was already past two in the afternoon and the August heat on the beach felt brutal. Suddenly, all she wanted to do was go home and crash. She looked back at Leroy. "I'm not feeling well, Sheriff. If there's nothing else, I'd like to get off the beach as soon as possible."

"I understand. Just a minute, please." Leroy walked over to Tony and Murrey and had a brief discussion. When he returned, he told Emmy, "Our business here is finished. We'll be glad to give you and Mr. Gorman a ride back to your vehicles. Just tell us where they're at."

Emmy smiled to herself. The worst part of the worse day of her life was over. All she wanted now was a cool shower and sleep. Tomorrow, the sheriff's investigation would continue — and her own investigation would begin.

******

Emmy felt lost in grief during the brief boat ride back to the lighthouse, recollecting the many times she had sailed into Winyah Bay with Jack on the *Sunny Daze*, pointing out to him the landmarks on the pristine shoreline of her beloved Barony. For four miles the bay stretched in from the Atlantic without any signs of civilization; the lighthouse being the only structure visible until the bay narrowed into a channel before reaching the bridge. The geography changed from protected wetlands to the bustling seacoast town.

When they reached the lighthouse, Emmy, Jordy, and Sandy disembarked the patrol boat and made their way down the road to their vehicles at the spot where Big George had fallen. Emmy thought about the eerie metaphor the ancient tree now represented. Seeing its demise, just minutes before finding Jack, sent a chill down her spine. Emmy shook it off. She didn't believe in superstitions or any dark connections like that. That being said, she lived in an area with a deep legacy of ghosts and unexplained phenomena. Seeing is believing, she always told herself. She'd seen nothing supernatural in her thirty-four years.

"Come on, girl," she said to Sandy when they arrived back at her jeep. Sandy jumped in the passenger side. Emmy turned to Jordy, her emotions still raw on the surface. "Thank you again, Jordy," she said, as they embraced. She separated and realized again that tears were running down her cheeks.

"We're going to find out what happened, Emmy. You can take that to heart. I promise."

"I know we will," she answered, making herself believe the words. "I, I need to go home and crash. There are some things that I need to do tomorrow morning. Would it be alright if I come in later in the day?"

Emmy saw Jordy look at her with a mix of shock and perplexion. It wasn't the look she expected. He cleared his throat and declared, "Emily Sweeney, you need to put the Barony out of your mind. You need to recover and take care of your personal business before even thinking about coming back to work. You have three workdays of grievance benefits, and I don't even want to see you back here until next week at the earliest. Now, you need my help with anything, you just let me know. Do you understand me, young lady?" The tone of his voice left no misunderstanding.

Emmy stared at Jordy as if in a fog. Yes, he was right, she needed rest and time to take care of her personal business. So much would need to be done. Her exhaustion had caught up with her. She cracked a wry smile and thanked Jordy again for his understanding and compassion. "Come on, Sandy, let's go home."

Twenty minutes later Emmy pulled into her driveway. All attempts of rational thought and reason were futile. She was so fatigued by the day's events, she had to force herself to stay awake on the drive home. There will be much to do tomorrow, but now she needed sleep.

Once in her house, she fired off a single text to Neil.

Let's meet tomorrow at noon at my house. Much to discuss.

Once sent, Emmy powered down her phone. There would be no interruptions until she could put herself together in the morning. Then she stripped off her sweaty clothes and took a brief cool shower. She popped an Ambien, then crashed on her bed and was asleep as soon as her head hit the pillow.

CHAPTER 5

Fifteen hours later, Emmy woke from her deep slumber when the early morning sun filtered through her bedroom shades and fell on her face. Even though she slept soundly, a variety of disturbing dreams haunted her night. A compilation of Jack, and Neil, and the *Sunny Daze*, and shipwrecks and pirates played out in her subconscious a harrowing version of what may have or could have happened out at sea last Monday.

When Emmy shook loose the cobwebs from the Ambien and her nightmares, the cold grim reality of yesterday's events hit home. Jack was still dead. The sheriff's investigation had begun, and so would hers. She wondered if Sheriff Keating had already made an announcement of Jack's death. If so, she imagined her voice mail inbox would be overloaded by now. As she dragged herself out of bed and went to make her first cup of coffee, Emmy powered on her phone with more than a shade of dread.

She held her breath as the text and voice mail icons appeared. Fifteen texts and five voice mails. A quick check showed them mostly from Neil, questioning the cryptic text she had sent. There were brief texts from her parents and Tom, and one from Sheriff Keating. The voice mails shed more light on where things stood that morning. The first two were from Neil, again questioning what was going on. The third, also from Neil, cast an entirely different tone. He wailed about Jack's death and how he had just been wrung through the wringer at the police station.

"Well, that answers that question," Emmy said out loud to Sandy. The last voice mail was from Sheriff Keating. Could she please come to the station at her earliest convenience and answer a few more questions. Emmy smirked to herself. She had more questions for him than he had for her. But she knew she'd need to uncover the answers to her questions on her own, if they could be resolved at all.

When she dressed, Emmy examined herself in the mirror. She put her shoulder length straight auburn hair in a bun, then placed some Visine drops in her still red eyes. A blue striped button-down short-sleeve shirt hid her expansive bosom. Emmy looked closer in the mirror. Did she appear gaunt, her high cheeks showing some signs of hollowness? She'd hardly eaten since Tuesday and the continuing stress seemed to be taking a physical toll. She added a touch of blush and finished getting ready. Emmy fixed herself a simple breakfast of toast and fruit, fed Sandy, then sat down with her second cup of coffee to plan the day.

First order of business was to visit Dick Robbins, the Dockmaster at the Georgetown Landing Marina where Jack kept the *Sunny Daze*. She was almost certain the police had already met with him yesterday and wouldn't be sharing anything confidential with her. But she knew Dick well and knew he'd share any key information from Monday. Then she'd pay a visit to the Rice Museum on Front Street and talk with Theresa Jenkins about the gold coin. Theresa had a PhD in History from UNC Chapel Hill and knew more about the history of the southeast coast than anyone else Emmy knew. Emmy had worked with the Rice Museum on several historical projects at the Barony. She could confide in Theresa, who would keep a secret when she needed to. After that, she'd meet with Neil, then she had to break the news to her parents. After that, she reckoned she'd check in with Sheriff Keating.

It will be a busy day. Thank goodness Jordy was understanding and didn't expect her back at work anytime soon. There was so much to do it made her head swirl. Also, Jack's family would soon come south for a funeral. She needed all her strength to get through the next few days.

And she needed all her intuitive strengths and determination to find out for herself the mystery of the gold coin and her lover's untimely death.

The phone rang. It was Neil. Emmy took a deep breath before answering. Neil was such a worrywart. The man needed babysitting on a good day. And today wasn't a good day. But it was time to face her new existence. She'd do it head on.

"Hello, Neil," she said in a dead tone voice.

"Oh, Emmy," Neil's voice cracked. Then the sobbing began.

******

Emmy parked her jeep in the marina's gravel lot and strode down the entrance pier to meet Dick Robbins. There was some light activity in the marina area, a couple of boats getting ready to sail. Seagulls squawked, looking for any free handouts. Emmy noticed the other two trawlers who used the marina were back out to sea.

Dick was waiting and met her outside his office. Just like Jordy, he approached and gave her an enormous hug, apologies spilling out of him. Emmy had known Dick ever since she was thirteen when her parents bought their first yacht and moored it at the Georgetown Landing. Jack had been a regular customer since he became a commercial fisherman seven years ago.

"Sheriff Keating and some detective were here yesterday," Dick told her after he broke their embrace. "Come on into my office. I have the security footage from Monday ready to review. There're some interesting things on it. I hope it'll help."

Emmy raised her eyebrows at hearing this. "Interesting things, you say. Did you see Jack on Monday before he left?"

"I did, actually. I remember asking him where Neil was. Jack told me he wasn't fishing today. Secret mission, he said. You know how he could be. Always hyping the ordinary. Thought nothing of it then."

She simply nodded and said, "He did do that — a lot."

Emmy and Dick entered his modest office. His desk was piled high with folders and various nautical devices sat scattered around. Plenty of boat and fish pictures hung on the paneled walls. Emmy got the feeling Dick only used a computer by necessity and preferred written records.

"Here, Emmy, have a seat. I'm sorry the place is a mess."

Emmy took a seat in a creaky, folding metal chair next to Dick's worn reclining office chair so they could both see his computer screen. A wave of anxiety washed over her as she fiddled with her engagement ring. She knew in time she would need to remove it. For now, though, it was just another way of coping with her grief. She wondered again what Dick meant by interesting things.

Dick went through some menu options and loaded the security footage. "I'll start at 6:00 AM Monday morning. I checked and didn't see any activity the night before." Emmy saw that Dick had two cameras. A split screen on the monitor showed both at once. The first was outside the office with a view of the pier and the parking lot. The second was on the west end, closest to the bridge, facing east out to the bay. It had a view of the entire marina.

The two watched as the first activity showed Dick opening the marina. About ten minutes later, a Chevy Silverado pulled into the parking lot. When the driver exited the truck, Emmy gave a quick gasp.

She cut her eyes at Dick. "That's Dr. Morgan. He's a friend of my parents. Or, I should say, used to be a friend. He's one of their neighbors in DeBordieu."

Both were familiar with DeBordieu, the gated enclave for the rich, located just north of the Barony.

"Yes, it is," answered Dick. "Keep watching."

Emmy felt her heart rate jump and her anxiety rise. What did that mean? She crossed her arms and leaned in towards the monitor.

Dick fast-forwarded the tape. During the next two hours, several others entered the marina. A couple of them, Emmy knew, and a few others she didn't. Dick identified each as they entered, and within fifteen or twenty minutes, also identified their boats as they left the marina. Emmy paid particular attention to Dr. Morgan's splendid fifty-foot sportfishing yacht, *Doctor's Orders*, still moored in its spot.

At 9:15 AM, Jack's Ford pickup pulled into the parking lot. Emmy caught her breath, seeing her fiancée on the screen. He looked so full of good cheer, smiling all the way past the camera. Then at 9:36 AM, Jack's trawler backed out of its dock. It was in the easternmost row of the marina, first in from the bay where Jack and the other two commercial fishing boats moored. They, as well as the other boat owners, preferred this setup, given the fish stench that usually accompanied the trawlers.

On any given fishing day, Jack would bring his catch to one of two seafood retailers on the Sampit River, shortly before the historic Front Street section of town, then sail back out and around the point at East Bay Park back to the marina. But this wasn't a fishing day for Jack. The two watched as the *Sunny Daze* made its way out of the dock and headed into the bay. Less than five minutes later, *Doctor's Orders* pulled out and also made its way out towards the sea.

"What the hell!" Emmy jumped to her feet and pointed at the monitor. "Is he tailing Jack?"

"I don't know, Emmy. He might be."

Emmy stayed on her feet and fidgeted as the footage continued. She fought to control her breathing. For the next twenty minutes, nothing else happened. A few more boat owners arrived, but no others launched. By now, the *Sunny Daze* would have been close to the mouth of the bay, and out of sight of the marina.

"That's all the relevant video to see from Monday morning," said Dick. "I've already looked ahead and can tell you that Dr. Morgan's yacht returned at two-thirty that afternoon. Obviously, the *Sunny Daze* never returned." Dick closed the video feed and pushed his chair back.

"I know there's history with Morgan and your dad, Emmy. But I don't pry. I really don't know what significance any of this may be."

Emmy took a ragged breath and pinched the bridge of her thin nose. This wasn't good news. But it was a lead, and that's why she was there. Her memories took her back many years. A happier time when she was a teenager and dad and Dr. Morgan were close friends. She'd been on *Doctor's Orders* several times. But that all suddenly ended in 2008. And she clearly remembered why.

Emmy snapped out of her recollections. "Yes, yes, there was history with them. You said the sheriff and detective were here yesterday. And they saw the same footage, I assume."

"They did."

Emmy nodded and pursed her lips. She glanced back at Dick with a determined look. "Well, alright then. I so appreciate you sharing this with me. Thank you, Dick. Really — thank you," she said, extending her hand. "I need to talk with my parents."

"Any time, Emmy. I hope you sort this out soon. Let me know if there's anything else I can help you with." Dick shook her hand, then embraced her again.

Emmy let him hold her for a second, then broke it off. "I will. Yes, absolutely. Thank you again."

As she walked back down the pier to her jeep, the implication of what she saw swam through her mind, while the anger inside her swelled. If that fucking doctor had something to do with Jack's death, there'd be hell to pay.

CHAPTER 6

It was a short five-minute drive from the marina to the Rice Museum. Before Emmy went in, she called Sheriff Keating to tell him she would come into the station at two that afternoon. The sheriff told her that would be fine.

"When do you plan to make an announcement about Jack?" Emmy asked nervously. She bit her bottom lip as the sheriff paused before answering.

"We still haven't determined that, Miss Sweeney. There are some issues we're dealing with this morning. Perhaps I can update you more when we meet this afternoon."

Emmy bit down harder as she tried to regain her composure. Did she really expect the police to be up front with her? She wasn't exactly telling them everything, either. "I see. Very well then. I'll see you this afternoon." She ended the call without another word.

Emmy sat in her jeep for a few more minutes until she calmed down. One thing at a time, she reminded herself. There's still a lot to get done today.

She entered the small museum, located on the north end of Front Street. Built in 1842, the brick and stucco structure, originally the Old Market Building, which also housed the Town Clock, became the Rice Museum in 1970. Theresa Jenkins was curator for all but the first ten years. With her PHD, she was a virtual encyclopedia of Lowcountry knowledge. At seventy-five, the petite Black woman with her tight wavy perm of grey curls neatly pulled back in a bun, came across as physically unimposing. But when she opened her mouth, she oozed southern charm, while also projecting herself as the unabashed authority in the room.

Theresa's eyes brightened when she saw Emmy enter the museum. "Why, Miss Emmy Sweeney, what a surprise. To what do I owe the privilege of your company this morning?" Emmy could tell, behind Theresa's bright smile, was concern. "Have you heard anything else about Jack?"

Emmy opened her mouth but froze. This was suddenly more difficult than she envisioned it would be. She gulped, then took a deep breath. She could feel her jaw shimmer. "Jack's dead, Ms. Theresa. I found him on the beach on Collins Island yesterday."

Theresa's hand shot up to cover her gasp. "Oh, my Lord. Oh my. Emmy, I am so sorry."

Emmy tried to fight back the tears but failed. "I know, I know," she said, now crying. "Yesterday was so bad." She let Theresa embrace her while she once again cried herself out. When her tears dried, Emmy said, "Ms. Theresa. This is confidential for now. The sheriff hasn't released the news yet. But there's something else that I think you can help me with."

"I'll certainly do my best. Come into my office and let's sit." Theresa put her hand on Emmy's back and led her into a small office off to the side of the museum. When settled, Theresa handed Emmy some tissues and said, "Now, dear, tell me what's going on. You know I'll help you any way I can."

"Thank you, Ms. Theresa." Emmy dotted her eyes and put the tissues in her shorts pocket. "I do truly appreciate your kindness and understanding." She reached inside her other pocket and put her hand on the coin, hesitating before pulling it out. She knew she was about to cross a threshold, one that couldn't be taken back. But it was a gamble she had to take.

Emmy removed the coin, first holding it up and then giving it to Theresa. "I found this, on the beach yesterday, close to where I found Jack. It was lodged inside a whelk. What can you tell me about it?"

Theresa took the coin and put on the reading glasses she kept draped around her neck. She examined the coin's head, then the tail side. At first, her expression was of curiosity. But an instant later, she gasped again. "Oh, my Lord!" This time disbelief broke out on her face as her mouth went slack.

When she looked back at Emmy, Emmy could tell the coin had hit a very sensitive nerve.

"You said you found this in a shell? On the beach, near Jack? This is — this is —"

Emmy looked in awe at Theresa. She'd never seen the woman at a loss for words like she appeared now.

"This is unbelievable!" Theresa practically shouted her enthusiasm. "Do you *know* where this is *from*?"

"Uh, no, Ms. Theresa. That's why I'm here."

Theresa gawked at Emmy. She took a deep breath. "This is from the 1715 Treasure Fleet."

Emmy shrugged. "I'm guessing that's —"

"The most important shipwreck of the New World!" Theresa completed Emmy's sentence. "But," Teresa shook her head, the wrinkles on her face deepening in concentration as she continued to examine the coin. "But this can't be. That fleet wrecked off the coast of Florida. Unless, unless — I don't believe it, but it has to be. It has to be."

"It has to be what, Ms. Theresa? Tell me. Tell me the story of this treasure fleet."

Theresa set the coin down on her desk and relaxed in her chair, her reading glasses set back on her chest. Theresa's eyes glazed over. "Well dear, it's not a story for the faint-hearted, but I'll do my best."

Emmy leaned in with anticipation. She'd often seen the same sort of wonder in her tourists at the Barony when she began one of the many tales she gave on her tours, especially stories of pirates and treasure.

"Go back to the early eighteenth century," Theresa began, now in her lecture voice. "Spain was at the height of their power. They controlled much of the Caribbean, Mexico, and the northern parts of South America. As I'm sure you're aware, the Spanish stole countless tons of silver and gold from the Aztecs, Mayans, and Incas. These ill-gotten treasures supported much of their economy back home, as well as financing the various wars they entangled themselves in with the English, the Dutch, and the French. Much of this transport was interrupted for a period by the War of Succession, which ended in a treaty with England in 1715. Spain desperately needed to refill their coffers and had spent three years stockpiling silver and gold in Havana before setting the fleet home in the summer of 1715."

Theresa paused for a moment. Emmy sat with her hand on her chin, transfixed by the story.

"Talk about putting all your eggs in one basket. The Spaniards put together a fleet of twelve vessels, laden with over thirteen hundred chests of silver coins and pieces of eight, as well as countless gold coins and bars, emeralds, and pearls. At the end of July, they set sail in good weather. It lasted a week. On July 31, a vicious hurricane off the coast of Florida rocked the ships. The entire fleet sank, except for the lone French vessel in the fleet, the *Griffon*, which broke off early and made it back to France unknowing what had happened to the rest.

It was an unmitigated disaster for Spain. Over twelve hundred sailors perished. But, because they wrecked close to the coast, several hundred survived. It proved a Pyrrhic victory for most. They found themselves stranded in an inhospitable landscape in the middle of the brutal heat of a Florida summer, without food, water, or medical supplies. The survivors faced disease carrying mosquitos, rattlesnakes, wild animals, and hostile Indians. The nearest settlement was St. Augustine, two hundred miles away. It took over three weeks for the first relief expedition to arrive."

Theresa paused again to let the gravity of the scene set it. Emmy sat there with her mouth stuck open. She proved to be an attentive student.

"Soon afterwards, however, a full-scale salvage operation went into effect. In the end, by 1718, they recovered over half the lost treasure. But only eight of the original eleven Spanish ships were ever located. Modern salvage recovery efforts began in 1960, recovering more of the treasure in the deeper waters further offshore. You've heard of the Treasure Coast of Florida, dear, haven't you?"

Emmy nodded her head. "Yeah, I guess so."

"From north of Ft. Pierce to Melbourne, the remains of the Treasure Fleet found their last home. Sometimes after hurricanes, coins still wash up on their beaches."

"Ok, so what does that have to do with this coin?"

Theresa looked Emmy in the eye and broke into a wide smile. "Why, my dear, isn't it obvious? This coin was minted in 1713. The number you see on the coin is 713. They didn't use the one in front back then. The Jerusalem Cross you see on the coin's face was one of the standard designs used by their mint in Mexico City. There's no doubt it belonged to one of the missing ships of the 1715 fleet. Now, the bigger question is, how did it find its way into South Carolina waters? Here's one theory."

Emmy sat still, completely transfixed by Theresa's story. She thought about how much more interesting college would have been with Theresa Jenkins as one of her professors.

"We don't know the exact path of the 1715 hurricane. They didn't have The Weather Channel back then, you know."

Emmy had a brief image of Jim Cantore posted up on a Ft. Pierce beach giving a play-by-play of the Spanish galleon going down. She quickly snapped out of it.

"But, we know the storm came from out of the Bahamas and headed north up the coast. It's possible one of the missing ships broke off from the main fleet, like the *Griffon,* but instead of heading east out of the storm, it tried to outrun it to the north. Assuming this ship was east of the eye of the hurricane, the storm's currents and winds of its outer bands would have forced the ship even further north and faster. Look at the map. Georgetown lies just over three-hundred miles due north of the Treasure Coast. It's not inconceivable that the missing ship rode the storm north for a day, before eventually being overtaken by it and sunk.

Here's another little-known fact of the Treasure Fleet. Virtually all the coins found in the known wrecks were minted in 1711, 1712, 1714, and 1715. They never found any coins minted in 1713. It almost goes without saying that the 1713 minted coins were on one of the three unaccounted for ships. And here it is — holding it right there in your hand. Utterly amazing, my dear. Utterly amazing."

"And there's something else I need to tell you that's even more disturbing." Emmy braced herself before she divulged the rest of Jack's discovery. "I found Jack wearing his wetsuit. He was shot to death."

"Oh, my heavens, no!" Theresa gasped, her hand covering her mouth. "So, do you think —"

"That Jack found this treasure in a wreck? Yes, yes, I do. And someone discovered him and did that to him. Now they know where it is. And whoever it is, doesn't play by the rules."

Theresa frowned. "I'm afraid so, dear. I'm afraid so."

"Tell me, Ms. Theresa, how much is this worth? Can you give me a ballpark figure? And who owns the treasure? Can anyone just claim it?"

"Hmm. Good questions, both of them. Let me see the coin again, please."

Emmy handed Theresa the coin. She held it in her open palm and raised it a few times, getting a sense of its weight, then gave it back to Emmy.

"I'd say it weighs about two ounces of solid gold. Most likely 18 or 22 carats. You could melt it down and get over four thousand for it at today's prices. But I know gold coins from the Treasure Fleet sell on eBay, or other open market sources, for between thirty and fifty thousand dollars. A coin like this, from a newly discovered wreck, could fetch twice as much."

Emmy felt her eyes pop out of her head. "For one coin!" she shouted. "Oh my God, there could be —"

"Thousands of them in that wreck." Theresa completed her sentence. "An entire year's minted production, like you said. You're talking millions, hundreds of millions in value, maybe more."

"And what about the salvage rights?"

"Well, dear. For the Florida wrecks, the rights belong to Brent Brisben and his company, the 1715 Fleet Queens Jewels. Has been for many years now. But that's for wrecks in Florida waters. Should this new wreck stake a claim," Theresa paused and chuckled. "Well, let's just say there'd be quite the legal brouhaha over it. I'm sure Spain would want it returned, as would be their right, if proven. Of course, that's just on the open market. Many sunken treasure finds never make it there. It's estimated between twenty-five and fifty percent of all recovered treasure gets bought and sold on the black market." Theresa folded her hands and looked straight at Emmy. "When this gets out, my dear. You're going to have one hell of a story to wrestle with."

CHAPTER 7

Emmy checked her watch, realizing she was running late and needed to get home for her noon meeting with Neil. She bid goodbye to Theresa, thanking her again for her help. Theresa insisted on supporting Emmy any way she could.

Five minutes later, Emmy had just entered her house when Neil tore into the driveway and slammed his Subaru to a stop. Sandy yelped as Emmy greeted him at the screen door.

"I can't believe it, Emmy. I can't believe it." Neil was out of breath and had that frantic look in his eye. Typical Neil. The man got emotional at the slightest inconvenience. She knew the news of Jack's death would hit him hard, almost as hard as it hit her. He hugged Emmy briefly, then entered her home and paced the living room, unable to sit. "I was afraid something like this might happen."

This was news to Emmy. She cut him short earlier this morning when he called. Told him to hold it until they met later. Now, hands on her hips, watching Neil pace, she wanted answers. "What are you talking about, Neil? What do you know? Tell me," she demanded, lowering her voice and drawing her eyebrows in.

Neil kept pacing. He slapped his hand to his forehead. "Ever since he bought that damn sonar, he'd been acting crazy. Wouldn't tell me anything, but I knew something was up. Just knew it. Damn crazy fool."

The only one acting crazy to Emmy was the guy who couldn't stop pacing her living room. "Neil!" she shouted at him, loud enough for him to stop. "Sit down," she ordered. "Can I get you anything to drink?"

After looking at her as if he'd been slapped in the face, Neil sat on the couch as instructed and shook his head. Emmy sat down next to him and held both his hands in hers. She needed him to calm down. When she gazed into his hazel eyes, partially covered by his light brown hair that always seemed to be in the way, he started to tear. As if on cue, Emmy cried as well. Sandy approached and leaned her head in. Neil released one hand and patted the retriever's head, which seemed to soothe him a bit.

"I know this is hard on you, Neil. I'm devastated as well. We'll get through it though — we will." Emmy lifted his chin with one finger and raised her eyebrows. "Ok?"

Neil nodded, then pulled away to wipe his tears. "I don't know, Emmy. I hope so."

Emmy needed to move the conversation forward. "You've talked with the sheriff, right? You told him everything you know?"

Neil nodded in agreement.

"And did he tell you how I found Jack? With his wet suit on, shot to death?"

"What? No." Neil pulled back, astonished. "He just said you found him washed up on the beach. He was asking the questions, not me. His wet suit? That means he went diving on Monday."

"Yes, and he probably found something, and I think I know what it is. But first, you're going to tell me everything you know. What about this sonar? How has Jack been acting strangely? Go ahead. Then I'll show you what I found."

Neil narrowed his eyes. "What's that? What do you have? Did Jack give you something?"

Emmy gritted her teeth. He wasn't making this easy. Neil had to get a grip, starting now. "Just begin, Neil," she said in as stern a voice as she could muster. "Tell me what you told the sheriff."

Neil took a few deep breaths and seemed to calm down a bit more. "Ok, it started back in July, shortly after the Fourth. At first, Jack just seemed preoccupied. Wasn't as focused on fishing as he always was. Then, toward the end of July, I go in one morning and he's installing this new sonar system. I asked him what was wrong with the old system. I mean, it wasn't like we were having any trouble finding fish. It'd actually been a great year for our yields. He told me he wanted the best. That this new system could identify species. I never heard of anything like that. Then I did some research.

He bought a Furuno Omni system. You ever heard of that? It's at the top of the line. The freaking Navy uses it on their submarines. You know what those things cost?"

Neil had Emmy's full attention. She shook her head. "No."

"Over a hundred grand, Emmy." Neil raised his arms in exasperation. "Jack bought a freaking hundred-thousand-dollar fish finder. You know how many freaking fish he'd have to catch to pay for that?"

Emmy didn't think there were that many fish from here to Maine. She kept shaking her head. "Why would he do that? He had to have told you something."

"I told you, the only thing he said was to find better fish. And we did. That thing worked amazingly well. We could pick out a Snapper from a Grouper. But in the end, we basically caught the same number of fish. When I asked him how he paid for it, he told me to mind my own business. This wasn't the Jack I knew, Emmy."

"So, how do you think he paid for it?"

"No clue. He must have got financing from somewhere. But I couldn't see a bank loaning him that much money just to catch more fish."

"No, I don't either. And I don't know who would have lent him that much. But Neil, I think I know why he got that sonar."

Emmy saw the light go on in Neil's eyes.

"Why? Tell me. What do you know?"

"Ok. But what I'm about to show you must remain under wraps. You promise? I haven't shared this with the police. At least not yet."

Neil's eyes narrowed. "Yeah, sure. What is it?"

"You promise. You swear to keep this between us?"

"Yes! I promise." Neil's hands again went up in the air. "What the hell is it?"

Emmy reached into her pocket and pulled out the coin. Like Theresa, Neil's reaction was immediate and shocking. His eyes and mouth both popped wide open.

"What the hell is that? Where did you get it?"

"This is a gold coin, Neil. It's from the lost Spanish fleet of 1715. I just learned a lot about it from Theresa Jenkins at the Rice Museum. I found it on the beach, close to where I found Jack."

Neil took the coin and continued to stare at it. "You have got to be kidding me," he muttered.

"Jack was diving on Monday. He had to have been looking for this wreck. That must be what he wanted that sonar for. Don't you see?"

Neil sat back on the couch and looked at the ceiling, taking several deeper breaths. He turned back to Emmy. "It makes sense, but I can't for the life of me fathom how he found out about the wreck. But if he knew he was on to something like this, I could see how he might have gotten someone to fund the sonar." He paused for a second, nodding his head. "There's something else that fits."

"What? What now?" Emmy's head was still spinning with the revelation about the sonar, and the mystery of how Jack could have found out about the wreck.

"After Jack installed the sonar, we started fishing differently. It was almost like he was marking off a grid, you know. We'd go east to west for several miles, then go back. He was constantly checking his GPS coordinates. If we found fish, we'd catch them, but it seemed like Jack was looking for something else. Now it looks like we know what. But not where."

"But you know the area Jack was tracking, right? You know the GPS coordinates?"

"Well, I mean yeah, roughly. But over the two weeks he had the new sonar, we must have covered at least fifty square miles."

"But you know the general location, then?"

"I suppose so. We were between ten to twenty miles out, sort of east to northeast of Georgetown."

"He must have found it last Friday, the last day he went fishing. Do you remember where you were then?"

"Um, no, not specifically. Same general area. Don't forget, Emmy, I didn't know what was going on. I was just out there to catch fish, you know."

Emmy nodded as the thoughts raced through her mind. After the meeting with Theresa, she realized the wreck would be of enormous historical importance. Jack's killers now knew where it was located and would undoubtedly desecrate the site as soon as possible. With the hurricane now passed, it was up to her to find the site and alert the authorities. With any luck, they could protect the site and also catch Jack's killers. And she knew who could help her.

She turned back to Neil. "Neil, do you think you could find the wreck site with regular sonar if we got close enough to it?"

Neil frowned and wrinkled his forehead. "I don't know. Why, what are you thinking?"

"You said Jack was searching ten to twenty miles out, east to northeast. He was diving with his normal scuba gear, so that means the wreck had to be in water less than a hundred feet deep, because that's the limit for the gear he has. We'll look at an ocean depth map. That should narrow the search area." Emmy could feel the adrenaline pump through her as her plan came together. "I need to talk with my dad and get an expedition together. You're coming as well."

"Whoa, wait a minute there, hotshot." Neil raised one arm with his palm facing out. "Do you hear what you're saying? Don't you think we should leave this to the police and the Coast Guard?"

Emmy nodded, but she was already three steps ahead. "Yes, yes, they'll be involved." She rose and strode to the kitchen. Sandy yelped, sensing something was up. She returned with a Diet Coke and a map. Emmy spread the map out on the coffee table. It showed the ocean depths off the South Carolina coast.

"Emmy, are you sure you know what you're doing?"

Emmy looked up and stared Neil directly in the eye, then gave him a wry smile. "Absolutely, Neil. We're going on a treasure hunt."

CHAPTER 8

Emmy braced herself before she exited her jeep in her parent's driveway. Once again, the grief of Jack's death would wash through her and her loved ones. She had phoned her mother as soon as she ushered Neil out of her house and told her she'd be there in twenty minutes and needed to talk with her and dad. It was important.

Her mother, Maureen, and dad, David, were waiting at the front door of their enormous six-bedroom DeBordieu estate when Emmy walked up the entrance steps. Normally, she'd have liked to have their conversations on the wide wraparound veranda, but even with four broad ceiling fans circulating the air, the heat and humidity of a late August afternoon was too much.

Her grief seemed to precede her, as she could tell by the look in her mother's eyes that she suspected bad news. Emmy trembled, then gulped, then just spit it out. "Jack's dead, Mom. I found his body yesterday morning on Collins Island." As soon as mom opened her arms for an embrace, Emmy broke down again and sobbed into her mother's arms. Dad moved in for a group hug as well.

After a minute, when Emmy composed herself, she broke from the embrace and said, "Come, let's go inside. A lot's happened since then."

"Can I get you anything to drink or eat, dear?" Mom asked.

Emmy realized it was almost one in the afternoon, and she hadn't eaten since a light early breakfast. "Sure, Mom. What do you have?"

"Why your favorite dear, chicken salad croissant and half-sour pickles. And sweet tea, of course."

"Love it." Emmy smiled, knowing that would make her feel a little better.

While mom fixed lunch, Emmy sat down in the spacious great room to bring dad up to speed. Mom didn't need to hear the gory details, anyway. Looking around the immaculate home, she recalled how she always felt awkward, surrounded by her parents' wealth. They weren't that wealthy when she was young, and it certainly wasn't how she lived her life now. But dad had built his career as a successful banker in South Carolina's capital, Columbia, and invested well over the years.

He set up his own financial advisory shop in Pawleys Island almost twenty years ago and reaped the fruits of his labor when they bought into Debordieu, then later, his yacht, the *Fair Allowance*. She was happy for them and glad they lived as close to her as they did. But she never asked for financial assistance, except the one time they insisted on helping her when she bought her home in the Georgetown historic district. It wasn't like their wealth turned her off exactly, but there always seemed to be some unspeakable edge she felt, as if she didn't somehow measure up to their expectations.

Dad leaned in and listened with keen interest as Emmy recounted the events of yesterday, up to finding Jack and the sheriff's men arriving by boat. But she saved the story of the coin and what she had seen at the marina until after lunch, along with the real reason she was there.

Emmy paused her story and joined mom and dad at the dining table where she polished off mom's homemade chicken salad but passed on the fudge brownies. The discussion veered to whether Jack's family had been informed and what funeral plans she had in mind. Emmy told them the sheriff was breaking the news to Jack's folks up north and she hadn't a clue about funeral details. Dad offered to help in any way he could.

An awkward pause ensued. "Let's go back to the living room," Emmy said. "There's something else I need to talk to y'all about."

"Of course, dear," mom said, cutting her eyes toward her husband. The three took seats around the large, white leather sectional couch.

Emmy took a deep breath, shuddering as she inhaled. "So, Mom and Dad, there's more to the story, unfortunately."

Dad leaned in with his full attention. "Tell us, Emmy. What else is it?"

"Um, so, um, are you still on the outs with Dr. Morgan?" Her brow wrinkled, bracing for his possible reaction.

Dad stiffened. "What does he have to do with this?" His tone was gruff to the point of threatening.

"I'm going to take that as a yes."

"That's correct. The man's a drug addict and a crook. So? What does he have to do with Jack's death?" Obviously, the mention of Dr. Morgan rubbed her dad the wrong way. The old conflict still simmered.

"Ok, so I went to Georgetown Landing Marina and talked with Dick Robbins. He showed me security footage from this past Monday. Please Dad, this is confidential. You can't let anyone know about it."

"I understand. Go ahead."

Emmy explained the footage, keeping a close eye on her dad, whose face deepened several shades of red. When she finished, he exploded. Dad always had a short fuse.

"I'll cut that bastard's balls off if he had a hand in this."

"David!" Mom scolded her husband. "Would you listen to yourself? Get a grip, for God's sake." She turned toward Emmy. "Forgive your father, dear. Dr. Morgan is not a name we like to bring up around here."

Emmy had predicted a less than enthusiastic response, but this was over the top. She remembered the last time she brought his name up and the subsequent admission from mom about Dr. Morgan's drug connection. But her dad's reaction made her even more determined to find out about Morgan's nefarious dealings.

"What's his connection, Dad? I've heard the rumors. Tell me what it is about this guy you hate so much?"

Dad rose to his feet and paced the living room but remained silent. Emmy could tell he was forcing himself to remain calm. Finally, he faced Emmy and took a deep breath.

"Back in 2004, not long after we moved down here, and I set up my company, Paul invited me to sail on his yacht. I gladly accepted, and we had a terrific day deep-water fishing. It was on the way back in that he offered me some cocaine. I politely declined, but he was so arrogant, he boasted about how his connections could get him whatever he wanted. For the next few months, he asked again a few times, but I turned him down.

Then, one day I got a call from an FBI agent in Charleston who was trying to track down a money laundering operation and guess whose name comes up — Dr. Paul Morgan. Told him I knew the good doctor, and I'd be glad to help. It turned out they suspected Morgan of having connections to the Constantine organized crime family out of Miami. They ran drugs out of Colombia and have runners up and down the east coast. They also have a sophisticated money laundering operation, of which Morgan allegedly played a small part. But they covered their tracks well and, in the end, I couldn't get enough hard proof for anything to stick."

Emmy listened, awestruck. This was way more than she'd known or had bargained for.

"However," Dad continued, "the FBI also told me they suspected Morgan was one of the runners in the South Carolina area, and if I had any inside information, would I please pass it along. Apparently, their MO is to have their runners meet on the water at a designated GPS location outside the territorial limit and bring the drugs in to wherever their front operation was located. To my knowledge, they never caught Morgan. He certainly continues to run his obnoxiously large yacht out of Georgetown Landing. I try to avoid him as much as possible."

Emmy absorbed the information while feeling her blood boil inside her. She hadn't mentioned the gold coin yet and debated when to bring it up.

"You mentioned you found Jack with his wet suit on, and Neil said they didn't fish on Monday. Do you have any idea what he was diving for?"

"Actually, Dad, I have a hunch —"

Dad interrupted her. "Because, besides drugs and money laundering and prostitution, I've heard rumors the Constantine family is involved in black marketing shipwreck treasures. I wonder if,"

"What?" This time Emmy interrupted her dad.

Dad looked at Emmy with a shocked look on his face. "Shipwreck treasures, but that's down off the coast of Florida. There aren't any shipwreck treasure ships off the South Carolina coast, at least not to my knowledge."

Emmy smirked and shook her head. "Me neither, Dad, until yesterday." She pulled out the gold coin and handed it to dad. "Right before I found Jack, I found this washed up on the beach. It's from the 1715 Spanish Treasure Fleet that sank off the coast of Florida. I just came from a meeting at the Rice Museum with Theresa Jenkins, the curator there."

Emmy then told her parents about the history of the coin. They sat there in complete amazement. A few times, dad interjected, "That's unbelievable" or "That's incredible."

When she finished telling them about the high-priced sonar Jack bought and the importance of protecting the wreck, dad turned out to be an easy sell. "You're right, Emmy," he said, nodding his head. "We need to find that wreck before any more damage is done. Do you think we can find it with just my regular sonar?"

"I hope so. Between what Neil remembers from the last day fishing with Jack and the ocean depth map, I think we can narrow it down pretty close. So, you're in?"

"You better believe I'm in. When do you want to go?"

Emmy smiled. Nothing was going to bring back Jack, and she would mourn him for days to come. But this brought her hope that something good might come of it. And she'd be right where she wanted to be — smack dab in the middle of it. "How about tomorrow?"

CHAPTER 9

At noon on Friday, Tony met Leroy in the sheriff's office to bring each other up to speed in the Abromski investigation. Since returning from the beach with Jack's body the previous afternoon, Leroy had interviewed Dick Robbins and reviewed the security footage from the marina and conducted his interview with Neil Goodsen. Tony talked with Tom Boswell from the Coastal Catch and spent most of the rest of his time tracking down Jack's family up north. They would both be visiting Dr. Morgan's home next, followed by their meeting with Emmy Sweeney back at the station at 2:00 PM.

Tony settled his long lanky body into one of the sheriff's comfortable office chairs around a small oval conference table. Leroy came from around his desk and greeted his detective.

"So, where are we at currently? Let's start with the family notification. Are we done there yet?"

"Just about, Sheriff. Jack's immediate family includes his mother and father out of North Kingstown, Rhode Island, and two brothers, one in New Jersey and one in Massachusetts. We've informed everyone except the one in Massachusetts — Robert Abromski, currently unemployed and hasn't been home since no one can remember. The dad, Scott, made some derisive comments about how Bobby was probably out on one of his binges and would disappear for weeks at a time. The other brother, Rick, backed up the dad's assessment. So, we may hit a roadblock there."

"Ok, that's fine. I'll prepare the press release for four-thirty this afternoon. After our interviews today, I don't want this dragging out any further. Now, are you ready to see the lead I told you about last night?"

"Like a kid in a candy store with a ten-dollar gift card. Let's see."

Leroy chuckled at his eager detective and selected the icon on his phone with the marina security video. He turned it on speaker and placed the phone on the table. "So, here at 6:45 AM this past Monday morning, we have one Dr. Paul Morgan entering the marina making his way to his rather impressive yacht, *Doctor's Orders*."

Tony stifled a laugh at the yacht's name.

"Yeah, you won't be laughing in a minute."

Both men watched the scene play out with Jack's arrival, then departure, then Morgan's yacht following the *Sunny Daze* out of the marina.

Tony's expression changed to a frown, and he sat still with his arms crossed. "And what do we know about this Dr. Morgan?"

"He's a Pulmonologist at Georgetown Memorial Hospital, has offices here and Pawleys Island and Murrells Inlet. Lives in DeBordieu. No record, but a call to the FBI came back with some interesting tidbits. Seems the feds investigated his involvement with a money laundering operation through a drug cartel about fifteen years ago. And who do you think played a part in that investigation? None other than one David Sweeney, also of Debordieu."

Tony's eyes popped open wide. "Sweeney? As related to our Emmy Sweeney?"

"Yup. Her father. Turns out they couldn't prove anything against Morgan, so they dropped the investigation. Morgan's stayed off the radar ever since."

Tony rubbed the stubble on his face. "What drug cartel was involved?"

"Constantine family, originally out of Colombia, now based in Miami. They run drugs throughout the Southeast, plus the usual mob activities, except for this. They like to get their hands dirty with black market shipwreck treasure finds. Mostly out of Florida. Which leads me to the next talk I had, with Jack's shipmate, Neil Goodsen."

Tony sat back and stretched his hands behind his head. "I got a feeling, boss. I know where you're headed."

Leroy scoffed. "You think so, huh? Yah, well, after I broke the news about Jack's death to Neil, I practically had to mop him off the floor. Took ten minutes for him to talk coherently. Then he tells me about this special sonar Jack purchased a few weeks ago. Jack told him he wanted to find more and better fish. But when Neil saw what Jack had installed, it was some state-of-the-art sonar the Navy uses. Cost over a hundred grand. Neil didn't know how Jack could afford it and didn't buy his reasoning of catching better fish. In the time since Jack had the new sonar, Neil said they basically caught the same amount, but their fishing patterns seemed to change. As if —"

"As if they were looking for something at the bottom of the ocean, like some kind of shipwreck." Tony finished Leroy's sentence.

"Exactly!" Leroy pointed his finger at Tony.

"And it ties in neatly with what I found out from Tom Boswell at his restaurant."

Now Leroy folded his arms. "And what was that?"

"Well, Tom knew about the sonar Jack wanted to buy, and through some of his associates, put together the financing. But he was coy when I asked him why Jack wanted this special sonar. Said he didn't know for sure, but it was definitely more than just catching fish. There was something on the ocean floor off the coast of Georgetown that needed to be found. And when he did, the return on his investment could be astronomical. He didn't *say* shipwrecked treasure, but I think we can put two and two together. Special sonar, fishing in a pattern, and now our Captain Abromski washes ashore, shot to death with his wetsuit on."

"Yeah," Leroy replied, nodding his head, "he found something alright. But what did he find, how did he find it, and how did someone else find out about it?"

"All good questions. So, what's the plan?"

"We're both going to pay a visit to this Dr. Morgan. Then we'll talk with Emmy Sweeney. She's due in here at two. In the meantime, see what else you can find out about this Constantine organization. I'll tell the press there'll be a news release later this afternoon. Maybe by then, we'll yield some results."

Leroy rose and was ready to see Tony out when Murrey knocked and entered the office.

"Hello, Sheriff, Detective. I'm glad I caught you both."

"Come on in, Murrey," answered Leroy. "We were just getting ready to head out, but I take it you have some news for us. Here, have a seat." The three sat back down at the table.

"Yes, I do. The autopsy is complete with no real surprises. I've determined the time of death to be between 9:00 AM and 3:00 PM this past Monday, so that fits the timeline. But the surprise, to me at least, was the type of gun used to kill Jack."

This was what Leroy really wanted to know. He inched forward, anticipating the news.

"It was a FN 57. Not a gun you normally see in your average street crime."

Leroy glanced over at Tony as they both frowned. This wasn't good news. "No, no, it isn't," said Leroy.

"It's a weapon commonly used by the military. Known for its high velocity. If it wasn't for the strong fabric of Jack's wetsuit, the bullets probably would have gone straight through him."

"It's not only the military who likes that gun," offered Tony. "It's pretty common knowledge the FN 57 is the handgun of choice with the drug cartels."

All three slowly shook their heads, understanding the significance of this assumption.

"If that turns out to be the case," continued Tony, "we have a much bigger problem than the murder of a local fisherman."

Leroy bit his lip and continued to stay silent, still shaking his head.

"We're talking Coast Guard, DEA, maybe FBI involvement and —"

But Leroy had lost his patience. "I get it, Tony. I get it! Fuck! That's all we need." He took a deep breath and regained his composure. "Thanks, Murrey. Anything else at this point?"

"No, boss. I'll have the written report to you later today."

"Thank you, that's all."

Murrey took the cue and left the office without another word.

"Well, Detective," Leroy looked across at Tony with a disgusted look on his face. "Let's find out where this mess is going to lead."

CHAPTER 10

Amelio knocked on the ornate mahogany door of the main building in the Constantine compound. The heat was insufferable, and he couldn't wait to enter the air-conditioned mansion. The limo had whisked him from the private airport in Miami, after his flight from Charleston, to the secure enclave the Constantine family maintained on the western outskirts of the city. Two machine gun wielding guards with expressionless faces greeted him. One of them opened the door without a word.

Amelio entered the lavish foyer, the marble sunlit floor decorated with towering palms. An escort led him to his boss's main office down a long hallway. Amelio brimmed with confidence. Today's update was some of the best news he had delivered in some time. The boss liked to hear good news. Amelio knew from experience it was the only news Constantine ever wanted to hear. He was well prepared and ready to take the next steps. Sebastion Constantine didn't like surprises, and Amelio wasn't about to give him any reason to doubt him. He knocked on the door.

"Come in, come in, Amelio," Constantine's baritone voice boomed throughout the spacious office.

Amelio entered and took a seat in the opulent Italian leather armchair in front of his boss's enormous desk. All around were the trappings of the ultra-rich. Elaborate Oriental tapestries draped the bay windows overlooking the eastern edge of the Everglades. Turkish carpets spread over a wide area of the floor and original Impressionist oils decorated the walls. Constantine always surrounded himself with the finest things money could buy.

"Tequila, yes?" Constantine asked.

"Yes, thank you." Amelio knew his boss only served the highest quality tequila. He'd never been disappointed.

Once the drinks were served, Constantine offered a toast. "To the *Concepcion*, my trusted friend. You are sure you have found the missing ship of the lost fleet?"

Amelio tipped his glass. "Salud," and downed the shot. It went down like silk. He felt the tequila warm his body at once while feeling the scar on his face flush. "We believe so, Sir. You've seen the coins we recovered. We checked our research again and believe no other ship from the 1715 fleet carried the 713 mint. We'll know more when we send our dive team to the site."

"Yes, yes, and when will that be, Amelio?"

"We are hoping for early next week, Sir. The hurricane up there put us behind a few days."

Constantine chuckled. "Yes, a minor inconvenience today. Not like the hurricane that greeted the lost fleet. And this fisherman, Abromski, is dead and will not be found?"

"He swims with his fish, Sir. According to my people, the authorities only know he is missing and presumed dead. The authorities have not issued any official notice."

Constantine nodded his approval. "Let's hope it stays that way. What precautions do you have to protect the site?"

Amelio grinned. He'd done his homework and had come prepared. It was a prerequisite for the job. "Yes, Sir. We have secured a buoy above the site with a 360-degree motion detection camera. Any vessel that gets nosy will get a rude greeting soon afterwards." Amelio saw his boss nod again. The meeting was going flawlessly.

"This is a very big deal, Amelio. The recovery of the treasures of the *Concepcion* will net our organization many millions, perhaps even a billion dollars. I want complete security over this operation. Are you sure you have enough resources at your disposal?"

"I do, Sir. We don't want to flood the area with too much attention. We'll operate only at night and should have the bulk of the treasure brought up within two weeks. I am confident of this."

"Very well, then. Now, on a different subject, we have a shipment of cocaine ready to offload to the Carolina market. Forty kilos. Are your contacts ready for this?"

Amelio smiled to himself again. Forty kilos will net the organization around three million dollars, allowing for his two percent cut of sixty thousand. Not bad for placing a few discrete phone calls and a boat ride back to McClellanville. "They will be, Mr. Constantine. They stand ready at a moment's notice."

"Good, good. Your pickup contact, Morgan, is it?"

"Yes, sir."

"He played a role in finding the treasure wreck, did he not?"

"Yes, sir. He alerted us when Abromski left the port by himself and gave us his heading."

"That's good. And he partakes in the powder, does he?"

"Indeed, he does."

"Then give him my personal thanks. With a fifty-gram bonus."

Amelio raised his eyebrows. It was seldom the boss was this generous with his most profitable product. But even the sale of cocaine might be dwarfed by the revenue he'd receive from the black-market receipts of the wreck's treasure. He salivated the fortunes his own cut would bring, assuming the boss continued to show his generosity to his most trusted lieutenant. "I'm sure the good doctor will be most grateful for this offer, Sir."

"Hmm, yes, as he should." Constantine's tone became serious. "Back to the *Concepcion*. Security is paramount. If word of this gets out, we're going to have the US Coast Guard, the FBI, the fucking Spanish government and who knows who else snooping around. We need to secure this treasure before anything goes on the black market. Once it does, the shit is going to fly. I want that gold in our safes first. I ask you again. Have you taken all the necessary precautions?"

Amelio gulped and gritted his teeth. His facial scar flared once more. Did the boss doubt his ability? Has he ever disappointed him before? No, he hasn't, and wouldn't this time, either. "I am positive, Mr. Constantine. All necessary precautions have been taken. Once I complete this cocaine run, I will devote all my efforts up there to the salvage operation. By this time next week, you should begin receiving shipments from the missing ship of the lost fleet. You have my word."

"I hope so, Amelio. I certainly hope so. For your sake."

CHAPTER 11

Leroy and Tony stopped at the security gate at the DeBordieu front entrance. Leroy lowered the driver's side window and presented his badge.

"Good afternoon, officers. How may I help you today?" the ill-informed guard asked.

Leroy cracked a wry smile. "I am *Sheriff* Leroy Keating, and this is *Lieutenant Detective* Tony Meacham. We're here on police business. Now, if you would please open the gate, we'll be on our way."

The guard, obviously new on the job, stood in his guardhouse and paused for a second with his mouth open. Then he stuttered, "I , I'm supposed to ask all visitors who they're here to see."

Leroy couldn't believe it. Short on patience, he glanced down at the guard's nametag, then looked up and stared him straight in the eyes. "Mr. Lewis," he stated in a snort, "If you would like to continue this charade, we have an open jail cell in Georgetown right this minute, of which we'll be glad to place you in for impeding an official police investigation. Now you can either open this God-damn gate or I'll place you under arrest. Is that clear enough for you?"

Lewis opened his mouth again, but this time, nothing came out.

Leroy gave him five seconds.

On the fourth, Lewis muttered, "Yes, Sir," and opened the gate. "Have a nice day."

As Leroy pulled away and began driving down Luvan Boulevard, he shook his head in disgust. "Where's the respect, Tony? Tell me that."

Tony chuckled and said, "Honestly, I'm not sure he even knows what a sheriff is. But to answer your question, no. There isn't the respect there used to be. This ain't Mayberry, Leroy. It's the 21st century."

Leroy grumbled about something unintelligible. They drove down the oak lined divided boulevard in silence. About halfway down the four-mile road leading to the development, Leroy asked, "You been in here much?"

Tony smirked. "Yeah, sure. Plenty of times. Why the wife and I are building our dream home right down the road from here."

Leroy shook his head. At times, his detective's sarcasm could be over the top. They took a left onto Bonneyneck Drive and entered the subdivision. The homes were massive cathedrals of wealth. Most had multi-car garages, manicured deep-green front lawns and towering white pillars guarding the front of the house. Leroy winced, thinking they looked more like plantations from the Old South. As they drove deeper in, the mansions got even larger.

"How much you think these places go for?" Leroy asked, still shaking his head at the display of affluence.

"Three to four mil, at the low end. These here, I bet up to ten."

"You'd have to be a pretty successful doctor or lawyer to afford that," quipped Leroy.

Tony nodded. "Or a crooked one."

"With a little drug thing on the side."

"Perhaps, maybe we'll find out soon enough. Here it is. 1256 Bonnyneck. Conveniently near the clubhouse."

"Yeah, does our doctor also play golf?"

"I don't know. Maybe we should ask him."

Leroy and Tony parked in the semi-circle front driveway and assessed the enormous mansion of Dr. Paul Morgan. The wide wraparound veranda had multiple hanging ferns and large ceiling fans, bracketed by four enormous white pillars. A black Porsche 911 Carrera sat out front, next to a manicured rose garden, implying the doctor was home. Leroy had called his office before they left, and they confirmed he wasn't in the office, it being Friday and all.

When they rang the doorbell, the chimes sounded like Westminster Abby. A Black maid answered the door. Her eyes popped seeing the two law enforcement men.

"Good afternoon, Ma'am," said Leroy. "Is Dr. Morgan in?"

Leroy saw the maid gulp hard, then say, "Yes, Sir. I'll go get him. Please come in and have a seat in the receiving room."

"Thank you, Ma'am." Leroy looked at Tony and whispered, "Receiving room? Good grief."

They took seats in a couple of overstuffed armchairs in an ornately decorated room off the foyer. If the opulence of the room was any example of the rest of the home, then Leroy's idea of wealth would have to be upgraded.

A couple of minutes later, Morgan entered the room and greeted Leroy and Tony. Leroy sized him up with a quick first impression. Medium build, in good shape, tanned with piercing blue eyes and thin greying hair. When he smiled, his white teeth practically gleamed.

"Hello, Officers. To what do I owe this unexpected visit? Here, let's take this conversation to the living room." Morgan led Leroy and Tony to his enormous great room. It was much like the greeting room, but on steroids. On the mantle above a gigantic fireplace sat a wide screen TV the size of a movie screen.

"I'm Georgetown County Sheriff Leroy Keating and this is Lieutenant Detective Tony Meachem. We'd like to ask you a few questions related to a recent crime we're investigating."

"Sounds serious," answered Morgan, raising his eyebrows. "Do I need to contact my attorney?"

Leroy grinned. Morgan sounded like he was only half kidding. "That is, of course, your prerogative, Dr. Morgan. But we're just looking to gather some preliminary information. You're not obligated to answer questions at this point."

The three took seats around the giant glass coffee table. Leroy glanced at the rug underneath. Had to have come straight from Turkey and guessed it cost at least twenty grand. Leroy focused all his attention on perceiving the first impression Morgan gave when he asked his initial question. He knew Tony would do the same.

"Do you know Captain Jack Abromski?" Leroy asked, starting straight at Morgan.

Morgan blinked but kept a deadpan face. He paused for two seconds. "Abromski?" he asked, again raising his eyebrows, "the fishing boat captain? I know of him. Can't say I've ever met him."

"Where do you buy your fish, Doctor?" Leroy segued straight to another topic. This caught Morgan off guard.

"Excuse me, Sheriff? Where do I buy *fish*? I normally don't buy any groceries myself. I have hired help to stock my kitchen."

Leroy cut his eyes at Tony. "Do you like seafood, Dr. Morgan?"

Again, Morgan seemed shocked at the direction of the questioning. "Of course I do. I beg your pardon, Sheriff, but you mentioned you're investigating a crime. I'm not sure how my taste in seafood is of any relevance."

Leroy chuckled and glanced at Tony, who also laughed. Then Leroy's tone changed to serious. "I'll get to the point, Doctor Morgan. As I'm sure you're aware, Captain Abromski and his trawler, the *Sunny Daze*, have been missing since he left the Georgetown Landing Marina on Monday morning. You yourself sailed on your yacht Monday morning. Why don't you tell us what you did Monday, starting with when you arrived at the marina?"

It was then that Leroy saw the brief glint in Morgan's eyes. A kind of subtle change in facial expression that showed the slightest tinge of fear. Leroy never took his eyes off Morgan's, whose appearance adjusted to one of steely determination.

"I'm sorry, Sheriff. I wasn't aware Captain Abromski was missing. Has he turned up anywhere? Has his trawler been located?"

Leroy gave a slim grin. "Not yet, Doctor. There's an ongoing search underway."

"I see."

Leroy glanced sideways at Tony, then stared back at Morgan. A pregnant pause ensued as Leroy's impatience grew. "I'm waiting, Doctor."

"Excuse me?" Morgan answered.

Leroy found the feeble attempt at diversion unamusing. He felt his blood pressure climb.

Tony took over the questioning. "Monday morning, Dr. Morgan. Tell us what you did Monday morning."

"Ah, yes. Monday. Well, it sounds to me you already know what I did Monday morning. I went to the marina early, not long after six. I had breakfast on the boat, something I often do, and then sailed later that morning. Once at sea, I fished for an hour or so, then made my way down to Murrells Inlet where I had a business lunch appointment. I believe I made it back to the marina sometime before three and then went home. Is that all you're interested in knowing?" Morgan ended his answer with a barely disguised sneer.

"Tell me, Dr. Morgan," Leroy resumed the questioning. "Did you see Captain Abromski's trawler when you pulled out of the marina at 9:16 AM Monday morning?" Leroy saw Morgan shift his eyes between himself and Tony. He's squirming now, Leroy thought. Let's see if he's going to hang himself.

Morgan cleared his throat. "Well, Sheriff. To be honest with you, I don't remember. There might have been a boat ahead of me. It wasn't anything I was paying attention to. Now, I'm getting the impression that I'm being treated as a suspect in this captain's disappearance, and I don't appreciate the tone of your questioning. So, if you have any further questions for me, I'm going to have to insist on calling my attorney."

Leroy chortled softly, then sucked in air between his teeth. "I think that's all the questions I have for now. Detective, anything you want to add?"

"No, Sheriff. Not at this point."

Leroy and Tony rose to their feet. Just then, a phone pinged from another room. Leroy looked down on the coffee table and saw what appeared to be Morgan's iPhone. "Sounds like you have a text message on another phone. Who's might that be?"

For a split second, Leroy saw fear in Morgan's eyes, but it was gone in an instant.

"That would be my pager. I'm on call today at the hospital." Morgan stared at Leroy with his lips pursed, exuding contempt.

"Hmm, I see." Leroy nodded. "One last question, Doctor. The person you met for lunch on Monday in Murrells Inlet. Would you mind telling us who that was?"

Morgan widened his eyes. Leroy could tell he'd be blocked again.

"Actually, Sheriff, I would mind. Like I said, I'll be glad to call my attorney if you have any further questions."

Of course, thought Leroy, so he can advise his client not to answer any. But he'd get his answers alright. And he'd be getting them right soon. "I understand. We'll be in touch. However, I recommend you don't go on any extended fishing trips anytime soon." He turned to Tony. "Detective, shall we?" Then back to Morgan. "Thank you for your time, Dr. Morgan."

Morgan remained silent.

Once outside the front door, Leroy released his built-up steam. "Son of a bitch is lying through his teeth. Son of a mother —. I've seen plenty of rich, arrogant men in my time, but that guy takes the cake."

Tony nodded in agreement. "I concur, Sheriff. So, what's your plan?"

Leroy stopped outside the patrol car. He looked around the property once more, disgusted at how the rich could flaunt their wealth and through it, exert their power. Well, he thought, two can play that game. He turned to Tony and said, "I want a surveillance camera with GPS placed on the bow of that yacht of his. He goes anywhere on it; I want to know where."

Tony grinned and nodded at the sheriff's assertiveness. "You got it."

"Today. Understood?"

"Yes, Sir."

"Good. Let's get out of here. This place makes me sick."

******

Back inside the house, Morgan raced to the bedroom and grabbed the burner phone he kept solely for his clandestine business. Of all the poor timing, he thought, this had to be the worst. At least they didn't insist on seeing the burner. Pager, he chuckled to himself. Good save there.

When he called up the text, Morgan swore under his breath. This was the last thing he needed right now, with the damn police breathing down his neck. It was from Amelio's number, as was almost every text he received on the phone.

New package pickup, tomorrow at 9:00 AM. Lat 32.6378 Long 78.3543

Morgan plugged the coordinates into his iPhone. Looked to be about fifteen miles southeast of Georgetown. Telling him no wasn't an option. Reluctantly, Morgan sent a reply.

I'll be there

CHAPTER 12

Emmy drove straight from her parent's home to the Georgetown Police Station. She debated what and how much to tell the cops. The gold coin would continue to be off limits for them, at least until she could find the wreck and verify where it was and what it contained. But she decided it would be safe to tell them about the marina and Dr. Morgan, and what her dad had told her about him. Let the cops chase down Morgan while she and dad and Neil were busy finding the wreck.

She arrived right at 2:00 PM and found the sheriff and detective waiting. They ushered her into a small room with a single window, blacked out, and one rectangular table with four chairs. The walls, floor, and ceiling were all a dull, flat gray. Florescent lighting seemed abusively harsh. Must be the interrogation room, she thought with a frown, her shoulders sagging. Yes, I am being interrogated. Maybe they haven't even ruled me out as a suspect yet.

"Thank you, Miss Sweeney, for coming in to see us," Leroy said with what seemed to Emmy as forced politeness. "Please have a seat."

Emmy squinted up at the fluorescent. "Any way to tone that light down?" she asked.

Leroy and Tony both chuckled. "I'm afraid not. Standard protocol."

"And that window is one-way, I assume?"

"Again, standard protocol."

Emmy settled in her seat and forced herself not to cross her arms. It's their meeting. Let's see how it unfolds. She smiled at them across the table.

The sheriff smiled back. "I meant to ask you yesterday, are you any relation to Dabo Swinney?"

Emmy raised her eyebrows. Obviously, they wanted to start the meeting with some pleasantries. She could play that game as well. "Well, no, Sir," she replied, feeling some of the tension ease. People often asked her that question, ever since Dabo became the Clemson football head coach and made the Tigers perennial national contenders. "He's from Alabama. I'm a Carolina girl. Plus, it's spelled differently." Emmy forced a smile. She watched both men nod their head.

"I see," said Leroy. He now appeared ready to begin the business part of the meeting. "Miss Sweeney, first, I want to bring you up to speed on several developments from our end."

Emmey perked up. That's a good way to begin.

"We have contacted Jack's immediate family members. I'm sure they'll be getting in touch with you soon to discuss funeral arrangements."

This wasn't a complete surprise. On the way over, she saw a text from Jack's brother, Rick, but hadn't had time to reply. She knew Jack's family would arrive in the next few days. They were a lot to deal with on a good day. Typical New Englanders — terse, abrupt, aloof. And the way they talked sounded like fingernails scraping on a chalkboard, especially the parents from Rhode Island. Half the time she couldn't even understand them. Jack had lost a lot of his harsh New England accent since he moved south. She and Jack had visited his family twice before. Although she loved the scenery up there, both times she couldn't wait to get back home.

Emmy nodded. "That's good to hear."

"And I'll be issuing a press release at 4:30 PM this afternoon. It will be brief, but I will state that we are treating this as a homicide. You're welcome to attend if you'd like. I'll hold it here out front of the station."

Emmy gulped. This news hit her harder. Her breathing deepened. "I think I'll pass. I'll watch it on TV at home."

"Understood," replied Leroy, more softly. "Now, Miss Sweeney, we've been able to gather some initial information since yesterday and would like your input as well. We reviewed the security video from the Georgetown Landing Marina from last Monday and found something suspicious. Do you know a Dr. Paul Morgan?"

Emmy gritted her teeth and stared straight into Leroy's eyes. "Yes, I do," she said flatly. "I also went to the marina this morning and met with Dick Robbins. I saw the surveillance video as well."

Leroy widened his eyes and turned to look at Tony, who also seemed surprised. "I see. Alright then. Would you mind telling us what you know about him?"

Emmy resisted the urge to cross her arms, knowing it might send the wrong message. She'd never been in an interrogation room before, assuming that's what this was. She wanted to know everything they knew, but realized, like with Neil, that she was there to be questioned, not to ask questions.

"I just know there's some bad blood between him and my dad. I wasn't privy to what the details were, other than dad had alluded to some kind of previous illegal activity on Dr. Morgan's part."

"Do you have any reason to believe Dr. Morgan had anything against Jack? Did he hold a grudge or have any kind of leverage over him?"

Emmy shook her head. "No, Sir. Not that I'm aware of."

Tony took over the questioning. "Miss Sweeney, you told us yesterday that Jack had met with Tom Boswell privately after dinner at the Coastal Catch this past Sunday. What kind of relationship did Jack have with Tom?"

Emmy took a deep breath and exhaled slowly. Where was this going? "Umm, well, I'm not sure what you mean. They were friends. We were friends. Had been for several years. Jack supplies them with fish sometimes when he has a surplus catch. We've socialized before with his wife Katie."

"Did Jack have any other financial relationship with him, other than what you just mentioned? Did Jack ever borrow money from him?"

Emmy squinted and pursed her lips. Is that what he's after? Could Tom have lent Jack the hundred grand for the sonar? She knew Tom was well off and had lots of money besides the income from the restaurant.

"I'm not aware of Jack ever borrowing money from Tom. Then again, I wasn't aware of much of Jack's financial activities. It was something we were going to discuss further after we were married. Could I ask why this is relevant?"

Leroy changed the subject, ignoring her question. "What can you tell us about Jack's business relationships?"

"Umm, what do you mean?"

"Who did he deal with? Who else were his customers, his suppliers, how were their relationships? How did he get along with them?"

Emmy took another deep breath. She fidgeted in her seat and licked her lips, now feeling the strain of the interview. And it didn't look like it would end anytime soon. "Well, his primary customer is Sonny Petrino. He owns the Atlantic Seafood fish market in Georgetown. As far as I know, he gets along fine with him. If he had extra fish, he'd sell it to Tom at Coastal Catch, and also the River Run and Root restaurants here in Georgetown. Occasionally he'd sell some in Pawleys Island at a seafood shop there."

"So, you're not aware of any problems Jack had with Mr. Petrino recently?"

Emmy paused and tried to remember. There was something Jack had mentioned a few weeks ago. Some kind of argument he had with Sonny about. What was it? She couldn't remember. Jack wasn't specific, he just grumbled to her about it. "Well, Sheriff, I don't recall anything specific. He'd gripe about Atlantic, and all his customers, about the selling price. You know, it was always negotiable in that line of work. But no, nothing out of the ordinary as far as I could tell."

"How about his suppliers?"

Emmy shook her head. "I had nothing to do with his suppliers. He dealt with various businesses for his boat and gear supplies. I couldn't even tell you who they were."

Tony took over the questioning. Emmy felt like she was in a tag-team wrestling match. "Have you talked yet with Jack's partner, Neil Goodsen?"

Emmy sat stunned by the switch in questioning. Now she felt sweat forming on her brow, along with a rising level of discomfort. She imagined what a real criminal might feel like sitting in this chair, then gulped again.

"I have, earlier today."

"And what did he tell you? About Jack and the *Sunny Daze*, specifically."

Emmy tried her best to maintain steady breathing. It was obvious how one-sided the conversation was. Best to just answer their questions, for now.

"Well, he told me about this expensive sonar Jack purchased. Ostensibly for catching more fish."

Emmy saw Tony and Leroy glance at each other and nod.

Tony continued the questioning. "And were you aware of this sonar purchase?"

"I was not."

"Do you have any idea what he might have been looking for, other than fish?"

Now Emmy shrugged her shoulders. "I really can't say, Detective. I'd imagine he'd be looking for some kind of shipwreck. He always talked about discovering new wrecks. I believe I told you yesterday we liked to dive together around the Civil War wrecks in the Georgetown area."

"Miss Sweeney, I'll be blunt. Do you have any reason to believe that Jack had found a shipwreck recently that may have contained some kind of treasure?" Leroy's eyes bored directly into Emmy's.

Now Emmy felt put on the spot. She didn't want to relay the information about the gold coin until after she had the chance to look for the wreck the next day.

"Is that what you believe happened?" Emmy asked with her eyes wide open.

"Please answer the question, Miss Sweeney."

Emmy now felt sweat run down her spine. "I do not." She blinked a couple times and wished she hadn't. The two men looked at each other and she could tell right away they didn't believe her.

"Are you're sure Jack didn't mention anything out of the ordinary he may have found in the week before he went missing?"

Now Emmy bit her lip. She needed this to end. With probably more emotion than needed, she raised her voice and stated emphatically, "I told you; I know nothing about what Jack may or may not have found. Please, I've told you everything I know."

Leroy glanced at Tony as Emmy held her breath. "Miss Sweeney, I want to assure you we are doing everything in our power to find who killed your fiancée. We ask if you have any new information that may be relevant to the case, to please forward it to our attention."

Emmy sensed the meeting was almost over. She breathed a little easier. "I will, Sheriff, I promise."

"Very well, then. Anything else Detective?"

"Not at this point, Sheriff." Emmy couldn't help but notice the smug look on Tony's face.

"Then you're free to go. Again, let us know if anything else comes up." Leroy paused for a second. "Or if you can recollect any further details about Jack."

Emmy rose and headed for the door.

Leroy had one last comment. "And Miss Sweeney."

Emmy turned and stared at Leroy. "Yes, Sheriff."

"I strongly advise you don't go around sticking your nose where it doesn't belong. That wouldn't be a good look."

Emmy tried to swallow, but her throat was dry. "Yes, Sir," she croaked and headed out the door.

CHAPTER 13

Emmy had one more stop to make before she headed home for the day. She needed to face Sonny Petrino at Atlantic Seafood and find out what the disagreement with Jack was all about. Her mind swirled as she made her way back across the historic district from the police station. When she passed Coastal Catch, she almost stopped to talk with Tom, but knew he normally didn't come to the restaurant until after five. She figured he'd know more about this sonar than Neil, and certainly the police led on. But she didn't consider him completely trustworthy and wasn't ready to divulge the gold coin to him, either. She'd go to Coastal Catch after she watched the press release on TV, have dinner, then talk with Tom.

Atlantic Seafood sat on the east end of the historic district, directly on the Sampit River waterfront, where the *Sunny Daze* and the two other trawlers could dock almost up to the back door. Emmy had known Sonny for all four years she'd been with Jack. A burly, short, muscular man of Italian descent, with a deep baritone voice, Sonny knew his fish inside and out. Jack would gripe about how Sonny would constantly bicker about the price for Jack's catch, but in the end, Jack always said he was a fair and honest businessman.

The front doorbell chimed when Emmy entered the shop. She found Sonny behind the counter, busy with another customer. The place had that familiar smell of fresh seafood, a sort of briny scent, but not at all fishy. The display of seafood was impressive, as always. Bins of freshly caught snapper, grouper, and flounder sat on ice together on one side of the store, while piles of oysters, blue crabs, and several varieties of shrimp were on display on the other side. Emmy caught Sonny's eye, and he broke into a wide grin, holding up one finger, signifying he'd be with her in just a minute.

Emmy bid her time thinking about all the fish Jack had sold to Sonny over the years. Sonny would need a new supplier now, in a time when commercial fishing was stretched to the limit. Already at sky-high prices, she imagined an even tighter supply would drive the cost of his fresh seafood even higher.

As Sonny finished with his customer, it dawned on Emmy that he didn't yet know about Jack's fate, and that she'd have to break it to him. Like the others before her, she braced herself for another emotional shock.

"Emmy Sweeney, how are you?" Sonny said when he had finished his sale. His accent was an odd mix of Italian mixed in with a little Southern. Emmy was glad to see him remove his apron, knowing it would be coated with dried fish guts. Sonny came around from behind the counter and held out his arms for Emmy.

"I've been better, Sonny," was all she said as she let him embrace her. The familiar smell of fish was never far from Sonny, much as it was never far from Jack.

"Tell me, what do you know about Jack? Any news?"

Emmy broke the hug and held his hands in hers. Just tell him, she thought, but the words stuck in her throat. Tears formed before she could speak. "Jack's dead, Sonny. I found him washed up on Collins Island yesterday afternoon."

Emmy could see how Sonny was thunderstruck by the news. For a moment, he stood there speechless with his mouth open. "Oh, my God! Oh my God!" he finally spit out. "This is horrible. Oh, Emmy. I am so sorry."

She let him hold her again; her tears flowing freely once more.

After a minute, Sonny said, "Come, let's go back to my office. Tell me what you know." Sonny first went to the front door and changed the sign from open to closed. Then he led Emmy back behind the counter to a small office on the right. She glanced out back to the dock and the long open tables where Sonny cleaned the hauls that came in.

When settled, Emmy recounted the events of the day before, leaving out the gold coin and the other evidence she'd collected earlier. But she wanted to see his reaction to the way Jack was found.

"Someone murdered Jack? In his wetsuit?" Sonny's astonishment appeared genuine. "Oh my God, Emmy, this is so horrible. Any idea why this happened?"

"I have some, Sonny. What about you? Do you have any idea why someone would want Jack dead?"

Now Sonny appeared defensive, as if he were being accused of being complicit in some way. "Of course not, Emmy. This is a total shock to me." He held up his hands and waved them back and forth, emphasizing his denial.

To Emmy, it seemed almost too vigorous. She reminded herself; he *is* Italian and prone to showing a physical display of his emotions. But she wanted to see if Sonny knew about the sonar.

"Tell me, Sonny. Did Jack ever mention buying a new high-tech sonar for the *Sunny Daze* recently?"

The glint in Sonny's eyes set her off immediately. She knew he knew something, and he'd better fess up about it.

"So," now Sonny's mood became somber, "You know about that, do you? From Neil, I presume?"

"That's right."

Emmy watched as Sonny's dark eyes seemed to look straight through her. Then he remade eye contact. "Yes, he told me. 'Catch more and better fish', he said. I told him he was wasting his money. 'Unless,' I asked him this, yes, 'unless you are looking for something other than fish.'"

Emmy waited for Sonny to finish, but that was it. "And did he say what he was looking for?"

Sonny rolled his eyes. "No. No, he didn't say. But I was suspicious, Emmy. Something was not right about this."

Emmy sighed, and she narrowed her eyes. Was Sonny leveling with her? Was he hiding something about the sonar, or something else about Jack? She couldn't tell, so she moved on. "There was something else, Sonny. Something that Jack complained to me about you back in July. When I asked him, he was evasive. He didn't like to talk about his business with me. I asked Neil, and he knew nothing about it. What did you argue with him about then? Please tell me."

Sonny again had a look in his eyes, like he was off somewhere else. It looked to Emmy like he was trying to come up with some cockamamie story to placate her. Again, he returned his gaze to her eyes.

"Yes, Emmy. I remember having an argument with Jack in July. It was over a fish. You understand something about my business, I'm sure. Every catch, every shipment, the price is negotiable. I evaluate the quantity, the species, the variety, and especially the size of the fish, based on my knowledge of what I can sell them for. To Jack and the other captains who supply me, my price is always too low. But I have a business to run, as do they. I honestly always try to be fair."

Emmy felt like she could do without the mansplaining, but knew Sonny would arrive at his point at his own pace.

"So, back in early July, maybe just after the Fourth, Jack brings in a massive size grouper. I mean, it would have been close to a record in these waters. Three hundred and seventy-five pounds it weighed on my scale. A huge prize and it would feed many mouths with succulent meat over the next week or so. Obviously, such a fish would generate a lot of business for me and deserved a high price for Jack. I offered him an even thousand dollars for it. He laughed and spit on the ground. Told me I'd get five times that in retail sales and wouldn't take less than three thousand, or he'd take the fish elsewhere."

Emmy listened with interest. Jack never mentioned such a large catch. Again, she thought about just how many things Jack kept from her knowledge. They were piling up. "But you reached a deal, right?" she asked him.

Sonny nodded, then chuckled. "We did. I paid him two thousand. I knew he wouldn't get more than that at Georgetown Seafood, and it was too large for any of the restaurants. Jack was bitter, but in the end, it was a good deal for us both. So, I imagine that is what you mention."

Emmy bit her lip and nodded, digesting the story. It made sense. Still, she resented Jack for not telling her about it. First the solo dive on Monday, then the sonar, now this. How well did she really know Jack? But she had to move on.

"Thank you for your help, Sonny. There'll be a press conference announcing Jack's death in a couple hours. Things are really going to get crazy after that." Emmy rose and walked to the front door. Sonny followed.

At the entrance, Emmy stopped and turned toward Sonny. "I'm sure the police will want to ask you some questions pretty soon."

"I understand. I have nothing to hide."

Emmy again looked at Sonny with a touch of caution. "We'll be in touch. Please let me know if you come across any new information." She gave Sonny a brief hug and turned and left the store.

******

Once Sonny saw Emmy drive away, he returned to his office and pulled out the burner phone he kept locked in a drawer. This was trouble with a capital T. The news of Jack's demise was a surprise all right, but it wasn't completely unexpected. Sonny knew all about the sonar and what Jack was after. This news confirmed the best and the worst-case scenario. The treasure of the lost fleet had to have been found. But it wasn't Jack who controlled it.

Sonny hit the button to speed dial the only number the phone had ever called. It answered on the second ring.

"This better be good," came the rough Spanish accented reply.

"I just found out, Abromski has been found, shot to death."

The line paused for a second. "Where did you hear this from?"

"His fiancée, Emmy Sweeney, just left. The police are going to announce it later today." Silence on the line. Sonny became agitated. "This isn't what we discussed, Amelio."

"Shut up," came the forceful reply. "This was always a possibility. Nobody knows anything."

"What are you going to do about it?"

"That is not your concern."

"The police are going to be calling me soon, Amelio. They already know about Ambroski's sonar. What do you want me to say to them?"

Sonny could hear Amelio grumble on the other end of the line. "You tell them nothing, you understand, you fool. Nothing that will lead them anywhere close to that treasure. You screw it up and you'll be joining your Captain Ambroski. Understand?"

"Perfectly. I know nothing."

"And it better stay that way. Now listen. I was going to call you soon, anyway. Expect another shipment, forty kilos, around noon tomorrow. Morgan will bring it in. Follow the usual protocol."

Sonny pinched the bridge of his nose. This was all getting to be too much. Why couldn't he just go back to selling fish? Maybe one day. One day, when his bank account is stuffed to the brim and he's back with his family in Salerno. "I understand. I'll be waiting."

Sonny heard the line click, ending the call. He sighed, then walked to the front door and changed the sign back to open.

CHAPTER 14

Leroy braced himself before he opened the station's front door. The crowd appeared to be even larger than he had estimated. Never one who was comfortable around large crowds, the circumstances of this presser made him ever more anxious. Still, it was part of the job, and he never shied away from the requirements of his position, as unpalatable as they were. Funny how looking at a mutilated dead body hardly fazed him, but staring at a set of microphones in front of hungry reporters left him breathless.

He stepped out the door and headed to the podium at the edge of the top of the steps. In front of him were maybe thirty reporters. He recognized most of them, ranging from Wilmington to Charleston. A few he didn't, but guessed the sensationalism of the case could have reached as far as Charlotte and Savannah. There had certainly been a buzz around the South Carolina coast the past few days. It began with the flyers and social media posts. Then, since the hurricane passed, the rumors had spread like wildfire. Seemed everybody wanted to know what happened to the good-looking sea captain from Georgetown.

Leroy gripped the edges of the podium and took a deep breath. "Ladies and gentlemen of the press, I'm going to give a brief statement on some facts we've learned about Captain Jack Abromski, then I'll take just a few questions. Yesterday, the 29th of August, the body of Captain Abromski was found on the beach on Collins Island on the Hobcaw Barony property. His body washed ashore. We have reason to believe foul play has been involved and we're treating this as a homicide. We have found no evidence of his fishing vessel, the *Sunny Daze*. We know that Captain Abromski left the Georgetown Landing Marina alone on Monday, August 26th and had not been heard from since. Georgetown

County law enforcement is currently following several leads, and we hope to make an arrest in the case as soon as possible. That is all I have for you at this point. As I mentioned, I'll take just a few questions today."

Leroy scanned the audience. He knew his politics well and would need to call on at least the *Myrtle Beach Sun Times*, the *Charleston Post Courier*, and the *Georgetown Times*. Maybe one or two others. He pointed to Charles DePont, from the *Post Courier*, whom he knew was trustworthy.

"Sheriff, do you have a motive for Captain Abromski's murder at this point?"

Fair enough, thought Leroy. "We're working on a couple of angles but cannot yet divulge them." He pointed next to Lisa Kendricks of the *Sun Times*. "Go ahead, Lisa."

"Sheriff, is it true that Jack's fiancée, Emmy Sweeney, found Jack, and that he was wearing a diving wetsuit when he was found?"

Leroy blinked twice as tried to digest how this information got leaked. It was one complication which came from delaying breaking the news. These damn reporters had been snooping around for the past twenty-four hours talking to God knows who. He cleared his throat. "I can confirm that Miss Sweeney found Captain Abromski while she was doing post hurricane damage assessment as part of her job at the Barony. I won't comment otherwise."

Leroy was already tired of the questioning and debated the wisdom of even having a Q & A at this point. "I'll take one more question. Julie, go ahead." Julie Reardon was a respected crime reporter for the local *Georgetown Times*. He felt sure she wouldn't throw him a curveball.

"Sheriff, are you investigating the possibility that Jack discovered a shipwreck off the coast, was pursuing its treasure, and was murdered for it?"

Leroy stood behind the microphones, flabbergasted. So much for the integrity of the reporters he thought he knew. The rest of the crowd gasped at the question. Julie stood staring at Leroy, expecting a straight answer.

"Miss Reardon, I don't know how or where you received the information to make such an accusation. I'll not comment on any part of it." That was it for Leroy. He wanted out of there as soon as possible. He gazed out at the crowd. They looked like a pack of hyenas smelling a fresh kill — waving their hands, no doubt with a follow-up question to piggy-back on the treasure hunt / murder angle, now spreading like a match to a puddle of gasoline. Leroy's mind turned to who may have leaked it. It had to be Neil, that whiney ass little wimp. Several of the other reporters were already asking Julie where she got her lead. Leroy focused back on the frenzied crowd.

"That's all the questions I'll take for the day. As more information becomes available, I will pass it along." Amidst continued questions launched his way, Leroy abruptly turned around and marched back into the station.

******

Emmy sat on her living room couch, glued to her TV, with Sandy curled up by her legs. As expected, the 4:30 PM News led off with the sheriff's press conference. Emmy felt her breathing deepen and her chest tighten. However mentally prepared she was for this, it wasn't enough. Thank goodness she chose not to be there. That would have been a disaster.

There was Sheriff Keating. Emmy wondered how many reporters had shown up for the event. The statement was brief and to the point. That was good. The picture of Jack in front of the *Sunny Daze* made her heart ache. Sandy whined. Emmy patted her head. She must know that Jack is gone, she thought. When the second reporter's question mentioned her name, Emmy winced. At least the sheriff dodged the part of finding Jack in his wetsuit. She recognized Julie Reardon, the reporter from the local Times. Her question about the shipwreck and treasure hit her like a bombshell. "What?" she screamed at the TV. Sandy yelped. She could tell the question had caught the sheriff off guard as well.

Then she thought, did the police suspect Jack had found a shipwrecked treasure? Did the police find evidence of the wreck that they were concealing? And how did this reporter have enough information to even ask that question? There were only two people other than herself that could provide it: Theresa and Neil. Emmy was certain Theresa wouldn't give out that kind of sensitive information, plus no one would even know to ask her about it. But Neil? Emmy fumed when she recalled how Neil indeed knew enough about what was going on, and he would be just the kind of person to blab to a pretty redhead reporter asking hard questions with a smile on her face. She'd pull it out of him in the morning when they went out on the *Fair Allowance.*

Emmy worried about the gold coin. If they didn't find the wreck tomorrow, she'd have to let the police in on it. That wouldn't be a good look. Much better if they could bring the authorities into it with information about the wreck's GPS coordinates. She didn't give a fleeting thought that the criminals behind Jack's murder had found the wreck and may even be watching it. She simply pictured herself finding and securing the site of the wreck and then stepping away. It was the least she could do for Jack.

The press conference had ended, and Emmy's phone began to ding and ring. She looked down at Sandy and said, "Everybody's going to be calling me now, girl. I don't think I'm ready for it yet." She'd read the texts and listen to the voice mails later, then respond to those she wanted to. Emmy powered down her phone and grabbed a beer. Her stomach growled, and she knew exactly what she wanted to eat. An oyster po'boy like only the Coastal Catch could make. That and a conversation with Tom Boswell.

CHAPTER 15

Emmy arrived at Coastal Catch shortly after five. She quietly took a seat at the bar and greeted Suzanne, the bartender, who gave her condolences.

"Emmy Sweeney, my God," Suzanne said, a look of disbelief on her face. "We all just watched that press conference. It's all so terrible. We're so sorry for you."

"Thanks, Suzanne. It's been rough."

"I bet, darling. What can I get you?"

Emmy gave a slight smirk. Yah, you bet all right. "I'll have a pale ale draft, and the Oyster Po'boy. Been thinking of one all afternoon." This was partially true. Emmy tried anything as a diversion from thinking about Jack.

She glanced around the place, just filling up on what would be another busy Friday night. Was it really less than a week since she and Jack were here last Sunday? Felt like at least a month.

Suzanne poured Emmy a beer and entered her order.

When she returned, Emmy asked, "Is Tom in yet?"

"No, not yet. But he should be in any time."

"Ok, thanks." Emmy would have liked to enjoy her beer and wait in private, but Suzanne was more inquisitive. Some bartenders preferred to mind their own business, while others liked to talk. Suzanne was a talker.

"Did you really find Jack on the beach? That must have been awful."

Emmy looked up. Suzanne was all ears. "I guess you saw the press conference," Emmy stated flatly.

"Oh, yes. We all did."

Emmy looked around, picturing the entire staff glued to the TV screen over the bar not forty-five minutes earlier.

"Why did that reporter ask if Jack had found shipwrecked treasure? Do you think he really found something like that?"

Emmy glared at Suzanne, trying to determine the politest way to tell her to fuck off. "I don't, Suzanne. Really. I don't want to talk about it." She pursed her lips and stared straight into the bartender's eyes. Suzanne got the message.

"Gotcha, I understand." Suzanne nodded and went to make another drink.

Emmy sat and sipped her beer. A couple of the wait staff came up to her and offered their condolences without asking any nosy questions. She thanked and hugged them both.

When her dinner arrived, she devoured it, surprising herself at her level of hunger. The Catch made the best Po-boys in town, and the crispy sweet potato waffle fries were the bomb. Did grief make you hungry, she asked herself. She thought about the lavish spreads they normally have at wakes and funerals, at least in the South. Shifting her mind to Jack's impending funeral had the opposite effect. She pushed away the last few waffle fries.

Just as Emmy wondered when Tom would arrive, she heard the front door open and turned around to see the Coastal Catch's owner walk in. He caught her eye immediately. The slight eye widening before he flashed his signature smile told Emmy he was unprepared to see her. Or maybe he just didn't expect to see her. But he turned on his charm as he approached the bar.

"Emmy Sweeney, it's so good to see you. How are you holding up?"

Emmy stood from her barstool and hugged Tom. "I'm ok, considering. Listen, can I talk with you for a few minutes — in private?"

Tom looked into Emmy's eyes without emotion. Again, she tried to read something that may or may not have been there.

"Absolutely. Here, come back to my office."

"All right, let me settle the bill first." Emmy reached in her purse to pull out her Visa card.

Tom gave her a backhanded wave. "What? No way. On the house." He caught Suzanne's eye, pointed to Emmy's plate, and nodded. Suzanne understood. Emmy gave Tom a friendly smile and put her Visa back in her purse, then followed Tom to the rear of the restaurant and took a seat in his small office.

Tom leaned back in his reclining chair and put his hands behind his head. "So, what's this all about?"

"I'm trying to piece together what could have happened to Jack, and I'm finding out things about him I didn't know before."

Tom remained silent and emotionless as he listened.

"And it's not all that endearing — to me."

"For instance?"

"Well, for instance, this expensive sonar he bought for some unknown reason."

Tom raised his eyebrows. "He didn't tell you about that?"

To Emmy it sounded like a fair question, and not a statement.

"He did not. Perhaps you can."

"So how did you learn about the sonar, then?" Tom asked, avoiding the question.

Emmy nodded slowly, sensing Tom's reluctance. But she needed information, so she played along. "Neil told me earlier today, after he had told the police about it. He didn't know how Jack financed it, but he said maybe you did. So, tell me. Did you help Jack get this sonar?" Emmy ended her question in an intentionally stern manner.

Tom took a deep breath, then relaxed. "I did, Emmy."

"And why did he want it? I don't buy what he told Neil. Some bullshit story about finding better fish."

"So, you don't know then?"

"I have a pretty good idea, but what I want is for you to tell me." Emmy's voice deepened in agitation.

"Emmy, forgive me for being evasive, but the subject is extremely sensitive. I think Jack's unfortunate murder is proof of this. So, before I say anything else, tell me why *you* think Jack bought this sonar."

Emmy could tell she wasn't getting anywhere, and she wasn't about to tell Tom about the coin quite yet. But she gave him a little more rope. "I think he was looking for some kind of shipwreck off the coast. A wreck that maybe held some kind of treasure. And he found it and was killed for it." She stared at Tom for several seconds, waiting for his reply.

Tom sat silent. To Emmy, it was obvious he was debating what to say. Finally, he said, "So then, you know about the coin."

Emmy blinked once, then twice, then froze stiff. I know about *a* coin. The coin *I* found, but that couldn't be what he's talking about, which means. Shit! That means there's a second coin. Emmy's brain went into overdrive over this stunning news.

"What coin?" she asked as calmly as she could.

The cat-and-mouse game continued. "Then you don't know about the coin?"

"I'm asking you again, Tom. *What coin?*"

"Then why would you suggest Jack was after treasure if you didn't know about the coin?"

Emmy lost all patience. Both arms went up, hands flailing in the air. "Jesus Christ, Tom. Stop playing games with me. Whatever coin you're talking about, I know nothing about. So, please, just tell me. What *fucking coin?*"

Tom pinched the bridge of his nose and looked down. Emmy continued to stare at him, waiting for his answer. When he looked up, he appeared resigned.

"All right, I'll tell you. But you must keep this confidential. I didn't exactly tell the police about it. I just told them that Jack was searching for something on the ocean floor, which could be very valuable. There is this coin, this gold coin, that Jack showed me, shortly after the Fourth of July. It's a Spanish coin minted in 1713. He said it had to come from a shipwreck that nobody knew about. From a fleet of Spanish ships that went down off the coast of Florida, except this one apparently made it to the South Carolina waters."

Emmy continued to stare at Tom as she listened. She knew the history but couldn't for the life of her figure out how Jack could have found another coin like hers. She fumed internally again at Jack, keeping another secret from her.

Tom continued, "Jack said he knew roughly where this wreck was located but needed a much better sonar to find it. I didn't pry at first, but when I did some research on this fleet, the treasure that it carried was enormous. A single gold coin from one of these ships could fetch tens of thousands of dollars. A whole chest, or multiple chests — I mean, just thinking about it blew my mind."

"So what kind of deal did you make with him?"

"He offered me five percent of whatever he could recover. If he didn't find the wreck, he'd pay off the loan over time. But he seemed confident to me. I guess he had his reasons."

"And did you know that he had found something? Neil believes he found it last Friday, the last day he fished. Then you two met after our dinner last Sunday."

Emmy became increasingly agitated over how much both Tom and Jack had left her out of the picture. Had she known about it, she could have gone out with Jack on Monday and possibly saved his life.

"Yes, Emmy, I did. Looking back, I'm sorry we kept it a secret from you. But the information was so sensitive, Jack didn't want anyone else in on it. Not you, not Neil. Nobody else knew about it."

"And look where it got him," she said caustically. "So, you don't know where this —" Emmy paused for a split second as she almost said, 'other coin', "coin came from, or how Jack found it?"

"No, other than he told me it wasn't his to keep. Someone had leant it to him to secure the financing he needed. That's really all I know, Emmy. I'm sorry I can't tell you anymore."

Emmy realized he was being far more forthcoming than Jack had been to her. Her temperament softened. Rising to her feet, she said, "Thank you, Tom. I appreciate your information." She shook his hand and was about to turn to leave.

"My pleasure, Emmy. Again, I'm so sorry for what happened. We'll all miss Jack terribly. Are there any funeral arrangements set yet?"

"No," she replied, her shoulders sagging. "But I expect to be in touch with his family soon. I'll let you know."

"And what about you, Emmy? What are you going to do next?"

Now a wry smile broke out on Emmy's face. "Right now, I'm just trying to function. But I have a few ideas. Thanks again for dinner and the info. I'll keep in touch." Emmy turned and left the office, then went to the bar to give Suzanne a five-dollar tip and say goodbye before walking out the front door. The blast of heat and humidity didn't faze her one bit. She lost herself in speculation about where that second coin came from and how Jack had come across it.

CHAPTER 16

Emmy finished loading her jeep with all the equipment she'd need for the day of diving. It was only 7:20 AM, and the temperature was already 83 degrees. Sweat began to form under her armpits. At least the sea breeze on the boat would cut the heat a little. Her mind continued to swirl at the rapid development of information from the previous day.

After returning from Coastal Catch, Emmy began the tiresome task of returning calls and messages. She had put it off as long as she could, and didn't want to appear ungrateful. But it meant repeatedly reliving the emotional grief. That, and lying about how much she knew, yet held back.

Jack's parents were the hardest. They kept badgering her for information. Between the mom's shrieking and the dad's obvious displeasure that his son's murder had yet to be solved, all Emmy could tell them was that they'd know more when they came down. And when will that be? Not long enough for her, but they were shooting for Sunday. Emmy offered for them to stay at Jack's house, which they readily accepted. Rick would join them. Nobody could get in touch with Bobby and Emmy got the impression they wouldn't want him around, anyway.

By eight o'clock last night, she'd had enough. She had reached out to her closest friends and relatives. The rest she'd get to later in the weekend. Emmy retrieved her diving suit and equipment and made sure everything was in working order. It had been June since her last dive with Jack, a day trip to the Civil War wreck of the Harvest Moon, one of their regular haunts. Even then, Jack kept talking about finding something new and exciting. But that was before the sonar purchase. Did he already know something then?

Now, with her equipment loaded in the jeep, Emmy left Sandy food and water for the day and gave her a good pat. "You hold down the fort, girl. Mama's going treasure hunting today." Then she pulled out of the driveway and drove the short distance to the marina. She saw her dad's Mercedes and Neil's Subaru already in the parking lot. When she saw the Silverado pickup parked near the Mercedes, Emmy's blood ran cold. She recognized it from the security footage yesterday, belonging to Dr. Morgan.

"Of all the people here," she muttered.

"Emmy! Over here," she heard coming from the direction of the *Fair Allowance*. Neil was on the front deck, waving to her. "Do you need a hand?"

"That would be nice. Thanks," Emmy called back. She set her equipment down on the boardwalk outside of Dick's office. Between the tank, flippers, and wetsuit, she needed two trips, but didn't want to catch Dick's attention if she could help it. Too late. Dick appeared out his office door and greeted Emmy.

"Good morning, Sunshine," he said with a toothy grin. "Going diving today, I see."

"Brilliant deduction, Sherlock." Emmy beamed in return. "Yeah, going to check out a couple of fresh places."

"Uh huh, with Neil, I see."

Emmy detected his suspicion and changed the subject. "I see Mr. Nosy is here this morning." She pointed her head toward Morgan's yacht.

"Yes, not unusual for a Saturday morning."

"Yeah, well, I better not see him tailing the *Fair Allowance* out of here."

Dick folded his arms and nodded. "Hope not too. Well, have a good day out there. Be careful."

Emmy smiled. "Thanks, Dick. And thanks again for your help yesterday."

Neil approached and grabbed Emmy's tank. She followed him down the pier towards the *Fair Allowance*. Once on-board, Emmy gave her dad a hug and stored her dive equipment in the cabin. "You happen to see the good doctor this morning, Dad?"

"I did, briefly. All I could do not to give him the finger."

"You don't suppose he's going to follow us out of here, do you?"

"Not if that bastard knows what's good for him. I keep a 12-gauge in the cabin. You never know what kind of funny business goes on out at sea."

Emmy pinched the bridge of her nose and shook her head. She certainly didn't want any kind of trouble today. It was risky enough as it was, she thought, again debating the wisdom of keeping her mission hidden from the police. She had determined that whatever happened today, regardless of whether they found the wreck, she'd let the police in on the gold coin. She'd just have to come up with some excuse why she didn't tell them about it earlier.

As the three continued to prepare the *Fair Allowance* for sailing, Emmy kept one eye on *Doctor's Orders,* three docks down. She didn't see Morgan or any other sign of activity on his yacht.

Twenty minutes later, they had the *Fair Allowance* ready to go. Dad eased the boat out of its mooring and backed into the channel leading to the bay. Emmy stood next to him on the flybridge and felt a warm breeze blow against her face. A wave of exhilaration washed over her. It had been some time since she had sailed with dad, and never with Neil. The grief of Jack's death was still fresh, but now, two days on, the shock had eased just a bit.

Today's mission, she thought — that's what this is, right — a secret mission, could go a long way toward retribution for Jack's murder. She wasn't particularly concerned about finding and catching Jack's killers. That's the job of the police. But if she could find the wreck and the treasure, she somehow felt that Jack's death would not have been in vain.

Dad put the *Fair Allowance* into forward drive and started moving out into the bay. Emmy gazed east into the haze toward the ocean and thought about Jack again: the *Sunny Daze*, which she would never again see, the dive trips they would never take again, and the lingering smell of fish, which never seemed to leave Jack's surroundings.

Lost in her musings, Emmy heard a sound from behind her. She snapped back to reality and turned to look over the stern. She gasped, not believing her eyes. Not one hundred yards back was Morgan's yacht, chugging down the channel behind her. Just like she saw on the security footage when he tailed the *Sunny Daze*.

"Dad," Emmy hollered, "look who's behind us."

Dad turned and grunted when he realized it was Morgan's yacht directly behind him. "Why that son-of-a-bitch."

"Do you think he's tailing us?"

Emmy could see the fury mount in her dad's face. "If he is, he's going to get a rude welcome." Dad turned to Neil, who had joined the two at the helm. "Neil, take the wheel."

"What are you doing, Dad?"

Dad turned to go below deck without answering. Neil, unaware of the significance of *Doctor's Orders,* looked puzzled. "What's all that about?" he asked Emmy.

"I didn't tell you yesterday. That's Dr. Morgan's yacht. He lives down the street from dad. I looked at the marina's security video from last Monday, and his yacht tailed Jack out of the bay."

Neil's eyes popped. "No, shit! Do you think he's tailing us now?"

"If he is, he's going to be sorry," shouted Dad as he climbed back up the ladder holding his 12-gauge shotgun.

"Dad!" screamed Emmy. "What the hell do you think you're doing?"

The three of them huddled around the helm, looking back toward *Doctor's Orders*. They could see Morgan at his helm, paying no attention to the boat in front of him. Emmy saw her dad seething. She'd never known him to be violent in any sense of the word. But she didn't know just how deep his loathing for Morgan ran. An armed confrontation with the man was the last thing she needed now. She could just picture how that sheriff and his smug detective would see it if things got out of hand.

"If he follows us out of the bay, there's going to be trouble."

"Why would he do that, Dad? I mean, really. Nobody else knows what we're doing today."

"Then tell me this, my darling daughter. Why did he tail Jack out of the bay last week?"

Emmy sighed and shrugged. "I don't know. I really don't. But please, Dad. Let's not shoot anyone today. Ok?"

Dad scoffed and turned to face forward. "We'll be out of the bay in another ten minutes. Then we'll see."

Morgan kept his distance as the two yachts made their way past the lighthouse and headed to the ocean. When they breached the bay opening, Emmy held her breath.

"Give us a heading, Neil," Dad said.

"Let's try eighty degrees, east, northeast," Neil replied.

"You got it."

Dad turned the wheel to the left and set the course. The *Fair Allowance* began its trek into the open ocean. Emmy turned around and anxiously waited to see where Morgan was headed. In another minute, she breathed a sigh of relief.

"He's headed south, Dad. He's not following us."

The gap between the two boats widened as they sailed in different directions.

"Goodbye and good riddance!" Dad shouted into the ocean breeze, shaking his fist. He turned to Emmy and Neil and smiled. "Now, let's go find some treasure."

******

Tony's phone buzzed, waking him out of a hazy morning sleep. Figures, he thought, ruining the one day of the week he got to sleep in. He rolled over, trying not to disturb his wife, who would continue her slumber. He picked up the phone and saw the alert came from the surveillance app he had just installed on Morgan's yacht the previous day. The doctor was on the move.

Tony rolled out of bed and took the phone to his study. He turned on the light and opened the app. It showed a wide-angle view from the bow of the yacht. Real time updates of the boat's GPS location flashed at the bottom of the screen. Tony nodded his approval of the first sight he had using the app, along with the acknowledgement that today's technology could really do amazing things. Initially, the view was of the marina, panning from north to south. *Doctor's Orders* was backing out of its moor. A minute later, it headed directly to the east as it began its passage out of the bay.

What was Morgan doing this morning? Nothing unusual about hitting the water early on a Saturday. Could be headed out fishing, or just going on a leisure ride. Or maybe he's meeting someone. Someone who the sheriff's department would be very interested in learning about.

Tony debated calling Leroy, but given the early time of day, decided to let it ride unless something more interesting appeared. That happened a minute later. There was another boat in front of Morgan's, also heading out of the bay. At first, he couldn't read the boat's name on the stern, but he upped the magnification the camera allowed, and when he could read it, his heart skipped a beat. The *Fair Allowance* sailed just ahead of Morgan. Yikes! The research he did yesterday showed the *Fair Allowance* belonged to Emmy Sweeney's father David, who also kept it at the Georgetown Landing Marina. Now it was also heading out to sea.

There were three people on board the *Fair Allowance*. Tony zoomed in some more, trying to see who they were. When they turned and faced *Doctor's Orders*, Tony caught his breath. He assumed the man at the helm was David Sweeney. The other two he recognized straight off. Emmey Sweeney and Neil Goodsen were on board, and they were being tailed by the same man who had tailed Jack Abromski on his last sail just five days ago. Tony mumbled, "Son of a bitch," then speed-dialed Leroy's number.

CHAPTER 17

Morgan arrived at the marina at six-thirty Saturday morning. He planned to complete the cocaine pickup, deliver it to Atlantic Seafood, and be back to DeBordieu by noon. The Gamecocks were playing their opener today, and it was on ESPN at 12:30 PM. Morgan gave generously to the USC alumni organization and went to as many games as possible. But today was an away game in Atlanta against Georgia Tech, and he decided earlier not to make the trip. It turned out to be a wise decision.

He boarded *Doctor's Orders* and prepared his usual breakfast of scrambled eggs, toast, and coffee in the galley. This had been his routine for several years now, ever since his divorce. Morgan cleared his few dishes and went topside to prepare for today's mission. Like many before, it was a simple task of heading out to sea to a designated GPS spot, always outside the twelve-mile international water limit. Then pick up the load of whatever contraband Constantine moved that day. He'd bring the load back to the Georgetown marina and deliver it to Sonny Petrino at Atlantic Seafood. He wished he could pull his yacht right up to Petrino's back dock to unload, but Amelio shot that down a long time ago. It would raise suspicion, he had told him with no further discussion. The burden of risk fell solely on Morgan.

Where the illegal supplies went from there, he neither knew nor cared. He electronically transferred the funds he earned to his offshore account in Grand Cayman, where he could make withdrawals at his leisure, outside the peeping eyes of the IRS. In the ten years he'd been Constantine's ocean errand boy, Morgan had accumulated five million dollars in the Cayman account. Today's task will net him another twenty grand. Last Monday's assignment of mere reconnaissance earned him 10 K.

When he arrived at the console to start the engine, he looked across the pier and froze. There was activity on board David Sweeney's yacht. Morgan recognized David and knew the woman was his daughter, Emmy, Jack Abromski's fiancée, or former fiancée now. He thought the other guy was Jack's shipmate but couldn't be sure. Of all the bad freaking timing, he thought. What the hell are they doing out here this morning? Did it have something to do with Jack's disappearance? The last thing he wanted was to be seen tailing the *Fair Allowance* out of the bay. Bad enough, the cops picked up on the recon mission last Monday. But he couldn't wait either. He definitely didn't want to risk being late for his rendezvous pickup.

Reluctantly, Morgan eased his vessel out of his moor, and, going as slow as he could, couldn't help but follow the *Fair Allowance* out. He tried to look like he wasn't paying them any mind, but it was obvious he had their undivided attention. At one point, David came up from his cabin with a shotgun. He knew Sweeney detested him, ever since he had offered him that cocaine on a trip back when they could be considered friends. After a while, through his contacts in the organization, Morgan learned the FBI had contracted David to snoop into his money laundering escapades. They kept their distance from each other after that. Occasionally, they'd cross paths at the marina, but never spoke. Now, it seemed David so despised him; he was ready to take violent action against him. This had to have something to do with Abromski.

After a tense twenty minutes sailing out of the bay, Morgan was relieved to see Sweeney take a heading to the east, northeast. Interesting, he thought, the same heading Jack took last Monday. Coincidence? He couldn't worry about it now. Morgan veered his boat to the east, southeast and headed to his GPS location.

An hour and ten minutes later, Morgan approached the position. He was fifteen miles out of Georgetown, due east of McClellanville. That was Amelio's home port. Amelio kept a quiet bungalow deep in one of the many creeks feeding in from Cape Romain. He owned one of the fastest speedboats on the east coast, which he kept secured in a locked boat garage when it wasn't in Miami. Morgan had been invited to his remote outpost once, a couple of years ago, after one of the larger deliveries he had made. From the outside, it was a humble looking creekside home. But it had a security system that rivaled Fort Knox, and a luxurious interior which exceeded even his own high standard of living.

Normally, Amelio would escort the shipment of drugs, or whatever contraband they were moving, on his speedboat from Constantine's enclave in Miami up the east coast, well outside the territorial limit. After the delivery, Amelio would take his boat to his McClellanville home, clean, while Morgan risked the US controlled waters under the watchful eye of the Coast Guard.

Morgan slowed *Doctor's Orders* as he pinpointed the exact GPS spot. He was ten minutes early, so seeing no other boats in sight didn't alarm him. Amelio was usually punctual to a T, but occasionally would be a few minutes late. Only once was he more than a half hour late. Didn't matter. Unless he heard otherwise, Morgan wouldn't leave the rendezvous spot for as long as it took.

At 9:05 AM, Morgan saw a boat approaching from the south. With his binoculars, he recognized it as Amelio's speedboat. All seemed good and he shouldn't have any problem completing his tasks and getting home in time for kickoff. Sometimes, Amelio would offer a free bonus besides the funds, usually some surplus cocaine. Morgan broke into a wide grin, thinking about this possibility, and turning this Saturday into something truly special.

******

Tony kept his eyes glued to the video on the surveillance app. After he informed Leroy what was going on, the sheriff told him to stay on it and keep him updated. Tony felt relieved when he saw the *Fair Allowance* turn towards the north when it reached the open ocean, while Morgan took a more southerly heading.

"Now, where do you think you're going?" Tony said out loud as the view changed to all ocean to the horizon and blue sky above. There wasn't much of anything on the coast to the south until you reached Charleston. Murrells Inlet, where he said he went last Monday, as well as the Myrtle Beach area, laid to the north. Maybe he was visiting contacts in the Charleston area. This idea soon made little sense either, as the GPS coordinates showed Morgan headed east, away from the coast, and not southeast where he'd head if he were sailing to Charleston. Is he just looking for fish, Tony wondered, or is he after something else, perhaps less noble?

He received his answer an hour later. Morgan's yacht slowed, then stopped. The video feed showed nothing but open ocean. Tony checked the coordinates to the map he had spread out in front of him and pinpointed his position to be fifteen miles east-southeast of Georgetown. Maybe he's just fishing for trophies, he thought. That would make this whole morning nothing but a fishing expedition. Tony smiled to himself at the weak pun. But the smile wiped from his face when the video feed showed another vessel approaching.

"What do we have here?" he said, staring at his phone's screen. Within a couple minutes, what looked like a high-power speed boat approached Morgan's yacht. As it got closer, Tony could make out two men on board: a tall one with long black hair and a shorter, stocky one. Tony wished he had audio on the feed, but at least was relieved to know he could retrieve the video later. He'd love to make a positive ID on those two.

The speed boat eased past *Doctor's Order's* bow and out of sight from the camera. Tony watched and waited for the next move. Nothing more happened in the next ten minutes. Then Morgan turned his boat around. As he pivoted to the east, Tony could make out the speed boat moving away from Morgan. It appeared to be headed east, back to the shore. The video continued to show Morgan turning, then speed off in a heading which looked to be the reversal from where he came.

This was no fishing trip. This was a rendezvous, a pickup of some kind. And Tony would bet anything that whatever Morgan had picked up was highly illegal. And he had every intention of setting up his own rendezvous to intercept him. But where would that be? Either back to the Georgetown marina, or some other spot. Tony thought it through before he placed a call to Leroy. If Morgan headed back to the marina, it would be easy enough to be there waiting for him. Anywhere else would be a little trickier, but the GPS app gave real time location. He knew his patrol car could get anywhere on land faster than Morgan's boat, so Tony felt like Morgan was as good as caught.

Tony once again dialed Leroy's number to update him. He grinned and chuckled as he shook his head. This was turning out to be one fine day.

CHAPTER 18

Now clear of the bay and out in the open ocean, Emmy took a seat on the bow and gazed out to sea. It had been a while since she'd been on her dad's boat, and she missed the speed and agility the *Fair Allowance* had over the *Sunny Daze*. Her trips out with Jack always smelled of fish and they never ventured too far from the mainland. But today wasn't a pleasure trip either. She had a purpose and an agenda. Whatever secrets Jack had kept from her no longer mattered. Emmy was determined to find the truth and find a resolution to this tragedy which so viciously interrupted her orderly life.

They had an hour before they arrived at the area Neil thought would be a possible general location for the wreck. After a few minutes of quiet contemplation, something the warm, salty sea breeze made incredibly easy, Emmy switched gears and decided it was time to have it out with Neil.

She rose and climbed the ladder to the flybridge where dad and Neil were talking. "Neil, may I have a word with you?" She paused and watched Neil's face show surprise, with maybe a hint of concern. "In the back, please." The concern on his face grew.

"Sure, what's this about?" Neil followed Emmy down the ladder to the stern and they both took seats in comfortable swivel chairs facing each other.

"Catch the press conference on TV yesterday?" Emmy saw right away the anxiety grow on Neil's face. The man was as transparent as a sheet of plastic wrap.

"I did," he answered with a slow drawl.

"Anything surprise you?"

"Like what?" Neil narrowed his eyes. "What are you getting at?"

Emmy exhaled through her nostrils. For all she knew, there may have been steam coming out of them. "What I'm getting at, Neil, is Julie Reardon's question to the sheriff. Why would she ask about a shipwreck and treasure? How would she know anything about that, unless *you* talked to her?"

Neil stared at Emmy with a blank expression while he licked his lips but said nothing.

Emmy felt anger flush her face. "Did you, Neil? Did you blab your big mouth to that reporter?" The words came out just short of a shout. It caught her dad's attention.

"Everything ok down there?" he hollered from the bridge.

"Fine, Dad." Emmy called back, diverting her attention from Neil. "Just drive the boat." Then back to Neil. "Well, tell me. What did you tell her?"

Neil gulped. He should have thought this would come back to him. But Emmy wasn't certain about anything Neil did or didn't understand. He could be as naïve as he was skittish.

"Well, ok, yes, I talked with her yesterday. She came by the house, and I let her in. We talked about Jack, you know, what he was like, what he liked to do outside of fishing. She's very nice."

Emmy rolled her eyes. "Sure, Neil, she's very nice, and very pretty, and very good at what she does, which is to extract confidential information from gullible goobers like you."

"That's not true."

"So then, what did you tell her? How did she know to ask about shipwrecked treasure?"

Neil twitched his mouth back and forth, a telltale sign of his squirming. "Sooo, I might have said how you and he liked to dive the wrecks around Georgetown, and —" Neil paused.

"And, what?"

"And I might have said something like he might have found something new, something — uh — valuable."

"Oh Christ, Neil. Valuable? Really? Did you tell her about the coin? Maybe you should have just invited her to come along on our trip today! You freaking idiot."

"No, Emmy, that was all I said. Nothing about the coin, I swear. I guess she just kind of figured it out from there."

"Yah think!" Emmy slapped her hand on her forehead. This wasn't going anywhere. Don't cry over spilt milk, mom always said. She rubbed her head, trying to avoid an impending headache, while she took some deep breaths and calmed. "Do me a favor, Neil. Don't talk to any other reporters, Ok?"

"Yeah, sure, Emmy. I'm sorry. It won't happen again."

"It better not. Let's go up top and see what kind of progress we're making." Emmy bolted to her feet and climbed the steps to the bridge. Neil followed in tow.

"You two playing nice now?" Dad asked sardonically.

Emmy knew he heard every word, and no doubt would probably speak with Neil about it later. She ignored the question. "How far off the coast are we, Dad?"

Dad checked his coordinate reading. "We're about seven miles east of the bay. When do you want me to slow down?"

"I think we said about ten miles from shore, right Neil? That's as close as Jack came that last day fishing, when you said he was in that grid pattern."

Neil looked at her with a rigid face. Emmy could tell his feelings were still hurt. Come on, Neil, time to move on. "Let's have a look on the map again," he said, devoid of emotion.

"Yeah, sure." Emmy reached in her handbag and removed the ocean depth map she had printed out from Google, then spread it across the console. "Here's the area we think Jack was looking in." Emmy pointed to a Sharpy drawn rough square beginning about ten miles from shore and ending where the water depth exceeded a hundred feet. "And we are, where, Dad?"

"Right here." He pointed to a spot short of the northwest corner of the marked off square. "So, we'll be at that square in about fifteen minutes. How do you want to go about it?"

Emmy shrugged. "I don't know. What do you think, Neil?" Neil gave her that poor-puppy look as if saying 'Oh, now you're going to play nice?' "We'll do like Jack did. Start at the north corner and go in a grid. How wide will your sonar scan, David?"

"Not much, maybe a couple hundred feet."

Emmy groaned. "That's all! We could be out here all day and not cover half that square."

"Noone said it was going to be easy, darling," said dad. "We'll do the best we can. We can always come back out another day."

Emmy sighed. She knew this was a possibility, but she always looked on the positive side of things. That and her undying belief that no matter what, things always had a way of working out. She walked down from the bridge and stood on the bow, taking in the warm ocean breeze.

Somewhere out there lay the shipwrecked treasure of the lost fleet. And with it, probably the remains of the *Sunny Daze*. She thought again about Jack. How mere days ago, he was in these same waters, diving for treasure. What a risk he was taking. Diving by himself, out of sight from land. Not knowing in the least what he was getting into. Why didn't he tell her? Why didn't he let her in on it? She thought they were a team. A team that did everything together. Trying to deal with the secrets Jack kept from her was almost as difficult as dealing with the loss of him.

Emmy remembered she wanted to tell her dad about the other key bit of intelligence she had gathered. The conversation with Tom and this second coin. But she had no intention of letting Neil in on it. How to be discreet without being obvious? Emmy thought about it for a moment, then shook her head. She didn't know how to do one without the other. "Aw, screw it," she whispered to herself, then joined the two men back on the flybridge.

"Neil, would you excuse us for a minute? There's something I need to talk with Dad about."

Neil stood there, motionless, without saying a word.

Clueless, flashed in Emmy's mind. "Confidentially," she said, raising her eyebrows, "Please."

Once again, Neil had the hurt puppy look. "Fine," he said, then turned his back and headed back down to the seats in the back.

Dad gave Emmy another concerned look. "What's this about?"

"I need to tell you something else, Dad. Something I found out last night at the Coastal Catch."

"Ok, what'd you find out?"

"So, you know about this new sonar Jack bought last month. When I asked Tom Boswell about it, he admitted he financed the sonar for Jack.

When I asked him why he did that, knowing it wouldn't be worth the money just for more fish, he balked at first, then told me there was a reason he did it. Jack showed him a gold coin. The way he described it was exactly like the coin I found on the beach. So, it must have been from this same wreck."

Emmy saw her dad's eyes bulge with astonishment. "So there's a second coin?"

"Apparently." Emmy compressed her lips. "Tom said Jack was only borrowing it, so he could get the financing."

"Where do you think it came from?"

"I have no idea. I don't know if we'll ever know. But somebody else besides Jack knew about it. The wrong somebody."

Dad looked back out over the ocean. The two remained silent for a few moments. "When are you going to tell the police about this coin, Emmy?"

Emmy debated how to answer. "After this trip, Dad, I will; one way or another. I hope I didn't make a mistake not being up front with them. But I'd be less than honest if I told you, it hasn't bothered me. So. Yes. Whatever we find out today, I'll go to them tomorrow. Plus, Jack's family is coming in later Sunday, and I still haven't planned the funeral."

Dad nodded some more. "You know your mother and I will do anything you need to help."

Emmy placed her hand on her dad's arm. "I know, Dad. Thank you for everything you've done."

Dad checked his coordinates and pulled back on the throttle. "We're here, at the edge of your search area. You ready for Neil?"

"Yeah, sure." Emmy turned back to the stern to see Neil slumped in the chair with his arms folded. Has he been like that the whole time? "Neil," she shouted. "Come on up. We're in the search area."

Neil snapped out of his trance and bounded up the ladder to the flybridge. "Where are we?"

"Right here," dad said, pointing to the corner of the black square drawn on the map. "Heading due east from here for about three miles. Right, Emmy?"

"I believe so. We'll watch the sonar and let you know if anything pops up." Emmy kept her eyes on the sonar screen, which showed nothing at all. She resigned herself to the fact that this entire trip would amount to the same thing. Nothing at all.

******

For the next two hours, the *Fair Allowance* crisscrossed an area of the Atlantic Ocean with nothing showing on the sonar. They were out of sight of land, with only GPS coordinates telling them where they were. For all Emmy knew, they could have been halfway to Portugal. Dad made half a dozen turns back and forth and told the others he had enough fuel to go another hour before they needed to head back. That would only cover maybe a third of the area marked off on the map.

Emmy frowned, feeling the stress of the impending failure of their mission. If they found nothing and she reported the coin to the police, her dream of finding the wreck and the treasure herself would be over. Even if she didn't tell the sheriff, she couldn't waste another day on a goose-chasing mission with Jack's family coming into town. She gazed out at the ocean once more, enjoying the salt sea spray on her face, trying to avoid thinking about their inevitable lost cause.

From her right, dad suddenly shouted out, "What the hell is that?"

Emmy turned around and saw her dad pointing to something ahead of them on the starboard side.

"Do you see that?" dad asked.

"I do," Emmy replied. "It looks like some kind of buoy."

"It does. Let's check it out." Dad veered the *Fair Allowance* to the right and headed straight for the object bobbing on the water's surface. The three of them stared at the buoy as they approached.

As they neared within a hundred yards, Neil said, "That sure is some kind of buoy. Why would there be a buoy this far out at sea?"

Dad shook his head. "Got me."

Then Emmy glanced down at the sonar and couldn't believe her eyes. "Holy shit! Look at the sonar."

The other two looked at the sonar screen and were equally amazed. Background noise lit up the display, and in the center of it was the unmistakable outline of a boat. To Emmy, she recognized the familiar pattern of a fishing trawler. She covered her mouth as she let out an audible gasp. "That's got to be the *Sunny Daze,*" she said as she stared at dad and Neil, her brown eyes as big as boiled eggs. Emmy peered at the image on the sonar again. There was no mistaking what she saw.

Dad said, "Well dear, I think we found what we're looking for."

CHAPTER 19

Amelio was most of the way back to his bungalow in McClellanville when an alarm went off on his phone. He grunted before looking, fearing that the quiet afternoon he had planned would be interrupted. Colombia was playing Mexico in a FIFA World Cup preliminary game, and he'd been looking forward to it all week. The trip up from Miami was long and tiresome, but the rendezvous happened without incident and now all he wanted was to make it home and enjoy some good food, beer, and tequila.

He closed his eyes and said a quick prayer to St. Cajetan, the saint of good luck. But when he opened them and saw what the alarm alerted him to, Amelio cursed, and realized in an instant there would be no good luck anywhere today. The warning came from the GPS camera on the buoy he had secured at the wreck site. Incredibly, the buoy had detected a visitor. Amelio switched to the video feed from the attached camera and immediately saw the yacht which had invaded his most secret of sites.

He turned to Enrico and said in Spanish, "It looks like we have an intruder at the wreck site."

Enrico gave his boss a disgruntled look. "This means trouble, yes?"

Amelio sighed, "It appears so." The boat he saw had come to a stop. His anticipation of the football game had wiped away, leaving a sour aftertaste. He checked his gas, further disappointing him. "We'll have to get to town and fill up before we go pay a visit to our intruders."

The two men rode in silence for a minute. "Who do you think it is, Amelio? Is it the fish boat captain?" Enrico asked.

Amelio stared at his friend. Enrico had been his trusted assistant for over four years. He had proven himself both capable and loyal. But his mind was that of a child, and he relied on Amelio's brains for all operational matters. Enrico's naivety was never far from the surface. Neither was his belief in ghosts and other supernatural phenomena.

Amelio grinned to himself. "I don't know who's there, my friend. But no. It is not the fish boat captain." He thought again about the message he received last night from Petrino. They found Abromski's body, washed up on a beach near Georgetown. There had to be some connection between that and the boat now moored at his buoy.

He peered back at the camera view. It was a private vessel, not the police or Coast Guard. There appeared to be three people on board, two men and a woman. Why were they there? Amelio wracked his mind with possibilities. Were they out for a pleasure ride and just happened to come across the buoy? That couldn't be. Perhaps they were out deep-sea fishing and picked up a school of fish near the wreck site. This was a remote possibility, but it didn't last long.

His worst fear came to fruition a minute later when he saw the woman putting on diving gear. Whoever came to his precious shipwreck was there for one reason only — to claim his treasure. And this would not stand.

Amelio felt the anger well up in his throat. He had yet to update Constantine about Ambroski's body. Now he had a new situation he'd have to report. This upset him far more than the three new bodies and a new sunken ship that would join the *Concepcion* and the *Sunny Daze* at the bottom of the ocean.

Running as fast as he could negotiate the creek, the McClellanville marina soon came into view. Twenty minutes to refuel. Then race back to the wreck site. He'd be there in less than an hour. Then he'd wipe this untimely disturbance clean from the face of the earth.

******

Morgan was in high spirits as he approached the entrance to Winyah Bay. He had now long forgotten the disturbing incident of David Sweeney giving him the evil eye while holding a shotgun on the way out of the bay. What *was* on his mind, as well as swirling around in his brain, was the bonus sample of cocaine Amelio gave him at the rendezvous site.

He had hoped such a gratuity might be on the docket, but fifty grams — wow! Now that blew him away. And the full gram he indulged himself as soon as the two Colombians were on their way would keep him high as a kite, well into the Gamecock's first half. The other forty kilos of coke were safe inside his extra-large Yeti cooler and would be off his hands minutes after he docked at the marina. Atlantic Seafood was mere blocks away, and he knew Sonny Petrino would be there waiting for it. In this line of work, you never missed an appointment.

Morgan slowed to ten knots inside the bay area. He had no qualms about sailing high on cocaine. Drunkenness was riskier, and you never knew when the Coast Guard may want to have a look see when you were near the shore. Especially since he had to sail past the Georgetown Coast Guard station, located directly up from the marina. But Morgan could have brought *Doctor's Orders* in blindfolded, if need be, and being high to him only made him feel more at one with his yacht.

He thought again about the current state of his life. Successful beyond his wildest dreams, he still never seemed to be satisfied. He could leave his practice at any point in time and sail the world. That's what he really wanted to do. But what about Amelio? Quitting the role he played in the Constantine organization would probably amount to a death sentence. And quite a distasteful sentence at that.

Morgan tried to clear his intoxicated mind of all negative thoughts. The rest of the day should be wonderful. Kickoff in a couple hours, then his son Mark and the kids were scheduled to come over later for a lobster fest. There'd be beer, margaritas and more coke (for him). No one else knew of his habit. Well, his ex-wife did, but that was ancient history now.

But business came before pleasure. Morgan scanned the marina area carefully as he pulled *Doctor's Orders* into its mooring. The coast looked clear. The parking lot was full, not unusual for a summer Saturday, especially on a holiday weekend. A couple of boats were leaving. No one would suspect a thing. Just before he was ready to exit the yacht, Morgan succumbed to his weakness and snorted another fat line.

His brain raced again. Morgan gathered his belongings and grabbed the handles of the Yeti. This was the one tricky part of the operation. Vacuum-sealed packs of cocaine filled the cooler to the rim. Even though he kept himself in shape, it was still a struggle to lift the ninety-pound Yeti from the door on the gunwale to the pier. Once there, it was a simple task to roll it out to his truck, then one more lift to the tailgate.

Morgan let out a grunt as he hauled the Yeti to the dock, smashing his knee in the process. Slightly paranoid, he looked all around to see if anyone was paying attention to him as he rubbed the pain out of his knee. The coast was clear. He took a deep breath and rolled the cooler out toward the main entrance and the parking lot beyond. Easiest money he's ever made, he thought once more, sniffing in some lingering powder caught in his nostril. Easiest money ever.

******

Tony broke into a wide grin when he saw the view from the bow of *Doctor's Orders* turn left into Winyah Bay. An hour earlier, he told Leroy he would tail Morgan from land wherever he went. If he docked in Georgetown, he and Leroy would meet him at the marina, then intercept Morgan as he left the pier, presumably with whatever contraband he had received at sea. If Morgan docked elsewhere, Tony and Leroy would track the boat on land and still meet him wherever he landed. Tony put the odds of him returning to Georgetown Landing at about eighty percent. He simply didn't think the doctor was smart enough or savvy enough to dock elsewhere. Morgan would have no reason to think anyone would be on to him.

Tony parked his unmarked patrol car in the middle of a very crowded marina parking lot and watched the video on his phone of Morgan's yacht leisurely sailing back to the marina. Leroy would arrive any minute now. Tony's thoughts were not only expecting catching Morgan red-handed with his contraband, but what, if anything, this had to do with Jack Abromski's murder. And where was the *Fair Allowance* headed out this morning, with Emmy, and her dad, and Neil? Tony had a nagging suspicion that all these events were related somehow but couldn't pinpoint it. Perhaps after they put Morgan on ice for a bit, they'd get some answers.

In the side-view mirror, Tony saw Leroy pull his patrol car into the back end of the parking lot, out of sight from the marina docks. Tony exited his car and joined Leroy on the way to the pier leading to Dick Robbins's office. He had called ahead and told Dick to expect company while they waited on Morgan to leave his yacht.

"Good morning, Sheriff. And a fine one at that," Tony said with a wide smile.

Leroy was more down to business. "Good morning, Detective. Where is he now?"

Tony glanced down at this phone, then looked up towards the bay. "I believe that's our man coming in right now." He pointed to the yacht a quarter mile out, slowly sailing into the marina.

Now Leroy broke out into a big grin. "Good work on this, Tony. Let's go see Robbins while we wait for our prize to come out."

CHAPTER 20

Anxiety tempered Emmy's excitement. The closer she got to the start of her dive, the more nervous she became. From the moment she first saw the buoy and the sonar indications, her heart had soared with the discovery, but it also presented nagging questions. Why was a buoy there? Someone had to have put it there to designate the shipwreck site. But who? Instinctively, she knew who. Jack's killers. And if they had marked the site, they'd be back for the treasure — at any time.

On the other hand, she felt the thrill of what might lie below, coursing through her veins. She thought about the historical importance of the shipwreck, the enormous wealth it could yield, for whomever the rightful owners were. Most of all, she thought about Jack, and how the discovery of the treasure would serve as justice for him. It might all lie, just eighty-five feet below her. But with the ominous implications of the buoy, she wanted the task finished and to be on her way home with the evidence — safely.

Emmy had her suit and flippers on. Dad helped load the tank on her back, and she was ready to place her mask on her face and get started.

"Remember what we talked about, darling," Dad said, holding both of Emmy's shoulders in his hands.

Emmy saw him look directly into her eyes. He was serious, and she knew it. Emmy nodded.

"Go down, see what's there. If there's treasure, grab a couple coins and come back up. You don't need to map out the whole site. We're only here for the evidence. Got it?"

Emmy nodded again. She'd already heard the same thing three times. The buoy had freaked dad out as well. Neil was already beyond the pale, convinced whoever had placed it there would come back any moment to do who knows what.

"Got it, Dad. Now let me dive, ok?"

"All right. Be careful down there. Remember to decompress — twice. You haven't dived this deep in a long time."

Emmy rolled her eyes at the continuing lecture. True, she hadn't dived this deep in probably ten years. The sites she dove with Jack were all less than forty feet. Decompression protocols were negligent for that. This was a much more serious depth, pushing the limit of her equipment. Plus, the fact she'd never dived so far out at sea before, with no land in sight, was a bit nerve-wracking. Not that it mattered with diving, just one extra layer of stress added on.

"Again, Dad, got it." She placed her mask over her face, showing the discussion was over. Emmy backed up to the gunwale and checked her air flow one last time. This was it. It was time to dive for treasure. She flipped over the railing backwards and entered the sea.

******

Amelio hit the gas as soon as he finished filling his speed boat at the McClellanville marina, ignoring the no-wake rule. He knew the marina's owner wouldn't raise a stink, given the fact he was indebted to the organization. Amelio had good reason to hightail it out of the series of creeks leading out to the ocean. From the buoy's camera view, it appeared the intruders had anchored their boat, and the girl had put on diving equipment.

The speedboat split the winding creeks in two and when it hit the open ocean, Amelio let out its full power. Soon he and Enrico were cruising at seventy knots. Amelio set a course east-north-east directly for the wreck. *His* wreck, and it was damn sure going to stay that way. He pondered again who the trespassers were and felt certain they related back to Abromski. After Petrino had called and told him his body had been found, by his fiancée no less, Amelio did a little research. Emmy Sweeney was her name, a good-looking broad who worked at the Hobcaw Barony. It was hard to say from the buoy camera, but he bet that was her putting on the dive suit. He didn't have a clue who the two men were.

He also didn't have a clue how this boat found the wreck site, fifteen miles out to sea in the middle of nowhere. Thank goodness he had the foresight to install the anchored buoy and camera system. Constantine put the pressure on to salvage the treasure as soon as possible. Amelio's boss didn't comprehend how complicated an operation this was. He couldn't exactly walk into the local dive shop and hire the help he needed.

The salvage operation had been in motion since they discovered the first coin. Once he completed the historical research and Constantine released the needed funds, Amelio had been clandestinely securing the material and labor he would need for the operation.

An associate of one of his drug runners knew a sea captain who could manage an operation such as this — with the necessary secrecy, of course. His name was Diego Marcella, and he ran a sightseeing operation out of Charleston. He was also an avid diver and, for the right price (an extremely high one at that), he agreed to take on the project. Find the location of the wreck, he told Amelio, and I can have the vessel and crew needed with a week's notice. Once Abromski was eliminated and the buoy put in place, Amelio called Diego and gave the green light for the project.

Diego's plan was to anchor his boat and begin a nighttime recovery effort for as long as it took to clean the site of its treasure. Even though the bulk of the treasure by weight would be silver, the real value was gold. Plus, after over two hundred years in salt water, the silver would be highly oxidized and near impossible to clean. Gold and emeralds, however, would remain pristine. Diego insisted he operate only at night to reduce the possibility of being detected during the day. He had a crew of nine divers who would work in shifts of three, nonstop throughout each night.

Amelio's biggest fear from the beginning was being discovered. Even though they were outside the twelve-mile US territorial limit, they were conducting an illegal search and salvage operation and might still be under the Coast Guard's watchful eye. Any passing vessel could place a call to the USCG, hence the nighttime strategy. If caught, it would mean big trouble — for Constantine and especially Amelio, who would have to face his boss's notorious wrath — or jail, or both.

Now he had another complication. He would deal with it. The same way he dealt with that fish boat captain. Eliminate all signs they ever existed. The yacht of the intruders would soon join the fish captain's trawler alongside the remains of the *Concepcion*. And this time, he'd make sure there'd be no bodies washing ashore.

Amelio wondered how long it would be before the Coast Guard began a search and rescue operation when the three interlopers didn't return home. Did they tell anyone where they were going? Did they post an excursion plan with the Coast Guard? Although many vessels did this as a matter of marine protocol, Amelio doubted this boat did. If they were indeed conducting a clandestine operation, no one else probably knew about it. Probably. Amelio hated risks involving uncertainty. However, sometimes it couldn't be helped. At least he knew the Coast Guard shouldn't be conducting searches at night, so the original plan would still work.

For now, he had other unpleasant business to take care of. He knew he had the firepower needed for the task. Besides his and Enrico's handguns, he had an Uzi machine gun at the ready. He'd use the rocket-propelled grenade to sink the vessel, as it had Abromski's.

Amelio nodded his head with confidence as he raced into the wind toward the wreck site. Operations like this usually had setbacks of some sort. But he always overcame them — always. And he would complete this mission successfully as well.

******

David and Neil stood on the deck and watched Emmy flip over and enter the ocean. They remained silent for a minute, each lost in their own thoughts.

Finally, Neil asked, "So, how much air does she have?"

David continued to stare at the sea and answered, "About forty-five minutes. I expect her back to the surface in no more than thirty."

"Do you think that's enough time?"

"If she does what I told her, it should be."

"Does she though? Do what you tell her?"

David turned and gave Neil a sardonic stare. He chuckled nervously and said, "Sometimes."

"But she knows what she's doing, right? I mean, has she dived this deep before?"

David's face turned serious. "She has, but it's been a while."

Neil had trouble keeping still. He walked to the other side of the boat, then back to David, who hung his arms on the gunwale railing. "Is there anything we need to be doing?"

David shook his head. "Relax, she'll be fine."

"What about that buoy? What do you think it means?"

David rubbed his stubble and stayed silent as Neil waited impatiently for an answer. "We've already discussed this, Neil. It means someone else knows about this spot. That's why we need to do our thing and get out of here as soon as possible. Why don't you make yourself useful and go grab me a Diet Coke." David returned to gazing into the sea, wondering and worrying about what Emmy was doing, and how soon she'd surface, so they could get out of there. He looked at his watch again. Ten minutes; she should be at the bottom by now, hopefully finding some treasure.

Neil returned with the soda and handed it to David. "How soon before she surfaces?"

David didn't turn around. "Fifteen to twenty minutes — I hope."

Neil continued to pace the deck. Something caught his eye on the starboard side. He stared for a few seconds, then asked, "Do you have a pair of binoculars?"

David broke his gaze and turned to Neil. "Yes, in the cabin. Drawer on the left. You see something?"

"Yes, over there." Neil pointed to where he had seen a speck on the horizon.

David held his hand over his eyes to reduce the glare and stared out towards the southwest. "Shit," he muttered, then made a beeline to the cabin. He returned seconds later and focused the binoculars on the object they detected.

"What is it? What is it?" Neil's voice became increasingly alarmed.

David lowered the binoculars and said with grim certainty. "It's a boat, and it's headed this way. Looks to be a speedboat of some kind."

"Let me see," Neil demanded. David handed him the specs. Neil focused and saw the same uninviting sight. "Oh shit! Oh, shit!" He turned to David, his eyes full of panic. "What are we going to do?"

David grabbed the binoculars back and growled at Neil, "How about not panicking for starters." He mumbled something else and went inside the cabin and returned with his shotgun. "Whoever they are, if they're looking for trouble, they're going to find it."

Neil gasped. "You're going to shoot them? Out here? Are you crazy?"

David glared back. "Are you stupid? I don't know what they want, but I know how to defend myself. I suggest you go in the cabin when they get close."

Neil nodded silently, then asked, "What about Emmy?"

David shook his head and continued to watch the boat getting closer by the second. "Right now, she's safe. Let's just see what happens." But a pit had formed at the bottom of his stomach. Suddenly, everything was in jeopardy. Him, Emmy, Neil, and the *Fair Allowance*. Too late for second thoughts. David wondered if a single double-barrel shotgun would be enough to defend whatever was coming his way. And if it wasn't, there was no telling how bad things might get — and soon.

CHAPTER 21

Leroy watched *Doctor's Orders* from Dick Robbins's office window slowly make its way back to its dock. He had seen the video Tony showed him of Morgan's rendezvous and couldn't keep the smug look off his face. Robbins, however, didn't seem happy with the events unfolding. Leroy couldn't tell if it had to do with the fact that one of his customers was about to be arrested or that Morgan's mooring soon might stop paying rent. He didn't believe Robbins would have any trouble replacing Morgan's spot with a new renter. He wondered if the dockmaster's apparent anxiety might have something more to do with the contraband they were about to confiscate.

"When this gets out, Sheriff — whatever it is, it won't look good for my marina."

Leroy looked at Dick without an iota of empathy. "I'm sure the marina will survive." Then, after a pause, "Assuming it's not involved."

Dick bristled at the accusation. "I have nothing to do with Morgan. He pays his rent and goes by the rules. I've never had trouble with him."

Leroy glanced at Tony and smirked, but didn't answer. He turned his attention back to *Doctor's Orders*. The plan was simple. Morgan had to walk right past the office to exit the marina. He and Tony would simply step out of the office and intercept Morgan as he approached.

Leroy continued to watch as Morgan secured his yacht, then went below deck. When he came back up, he was lifting what looked like a very large cooler. From the struggle Morgan was having, it appeared the cooler had considerable weight. Leroy broke out into a wide grin.

"What do you suppose he has in that cooler?" Leroy asked Tony.

Tony replied with a deadpan face, "Maybe beer. Maybe not."

Leroy noticed Robbins didn't share Tony's humor.

Morgan continued to struggle with the cooler. He had exited the yacht through a door in the stern's gunwale and stood on the dock. He reached up a couple of feet and hauled the cooler from the boat onto the pier. From the office, Leroy could hear Morgan grunt and the cooler clunk onto the wooden dock.

Leroy turned to Robbins again. "So, have you seen our doctor haul heavy coolers from his boat before?"

Dick shook his head. "If I did, I wouldn't think anything of it. Lots of folks take coolers on and off their boats."

"Of course," Leroy answered softly. Morgan had begun his trek from the mooring to the main pier that led to the exit. Leroy and Tony took positions on opposite sides of the office door, out of sight of anyone looking in. "On my signal," he told Tony, then extracted his service pistol.

Tony nodded without a word and did the same.

Leroy peered out the corner of the window and watched Morgan turn onto the main pier, twenty feet from the office. He counted to five, then said, "Now."

******

Doctor Paul Morgan was high as a Carolina pine when he stumbled out of *Doctor's Orders*. Against his better judgement, he re-sampled some of his bonus stash and immediately wished he hadn't. Not only was he way too high to function properly, or even drive home, he was even more disgusted with himself for letting the coke control him. He knew there were rumblings at the hospital about his drug use. A malpractice suit was pending, alleging Morgan misdiagnosed a lung cancer patient, delaying treatment and causing her premature death. Morgan knew deep within his psyche the cocaine played a role in his poor judgment.

Now, after fumbling with the coke laden Yeti and smashing his knee on it as he strained to lift it out of the boat, all he wanted to do was get the shit delivered to Petrino and get home to watch the game. He rubbed his aching knee again, then ran his wrist across his upper lip, in case there was still any residual powder there. Couldn't afford to draw attention to his delicate task. The risk was almost all behind him now. Just get out of the parking lot and run down the street to Atlantic Seafood.

Morgan rolled the Yeti behind him, thankful for its long handle and wheels, and turned the corner to walk past Robbins's office. He glanced in the window and saw Dick sitting at his desk, paying him no notice. That's it, he thought, the last chance for anyone to discover him and his illicit cargo.

Just as he was about to pass the office door, it opened out, blocking his path. In the instant before his world crashed, Morgan wondered who would open the door if Robbins was at his desk. Visitors, he presumed. And he was right. But they weren't the kind of visitors Morgan wanted to see. All the blood drained from his face as soon as recognized the same sheriff and detective who had come to his home yesterday. What in God's name were they doing here, now, of all the times?

The two officers entered the pier and blocked Morgan from continuing.

"Good morning, Doctor," the sheriff said.

Morgan couldn't help but notice the sheriff's weapon drawn. Same with the detective. His mind tried in vain to compute the implication of what was happening. "Good morning to you, Sir," Morgan muttered. "If you would excuse me, please."

"What Cha got in the cooler there, Doctor Morgan?" the detective asked.

Morgan had forgotten both of their names. It wasn't important to him yesterday. Would have been nice now. He gulped, now beginning to realize they had somehow discovered what he was doing. "Just fish, Detective. Had a good morning fishing." Morgan's eyes darted back and forth between the two. It was obvious they weren't buying it.

"Oh yeah? What kind of fish did you catch?" The sheriff glanced sideways at the detective and chucked softly.

"You know, the usual — red snapper, whitefish, couple of groupers." Did he sound hesitant? Panicky? He sure felt it.

"Mind if we take a look?" the sheriff asked.

Morgan cleared his throat. "Actually, Sheriff, I do. Now, if you don't mind, I'm late for an appointment."

"Ha!" the sheriff chortled. "Hear that, Tony. Our doctor is late for an appointment. Probably needs to sell his *fish* before it goes bad."

Morgan's mind flashed at the irony. He did need to 'sell' his 'fish' at the fish market, and quickly. Now it didn't look like that was going to happen, and the implications of it not happening just scratched the surface of his addled brain.

The sheriff and detective moved closer together and took a step towards Morgan, looking at him straight in the eye. "I said," the sheriff stated in a tone that meant any kidding was over, "we'd like to see what's in the cooler. Open it, now!"

Morgan had arrived at peak panic and hyperventilated. A feeling in total contradiction to his coke fueled high. His jaw shook, and he blinked nonstop. Words failed him. After a few seconds, he made one last attempt. "I'm afraid I can't do that. You'd need a warrant, which I doubt you have."

But the sheriff had heard enough. Morgan saw him raise his weapon and point it right between his eyes. "Tony," he told the detective without taking his eyes off Morgan, "see what Dr. Morgan has in his cooler."

"Gladly," said the detective as he made a move toward the Yeti.

Morgan gave a brief thought about physically intervening, but at that point he realized the gig was up. He bent his head down to his chest and pinched the bridge of his nose. He said nothing more. The detective moved around him and opened the Yeti.

"Hmm, very interesting," said the detective.

Morgan watched with resignation as the detective lifted a bag of cocaine and showed it to the sheriff. Then he turned to Morgan.

"Looks like you caught some whitefish. Powdered whitefish."

"Very rare in these waters," the sheriff chimed in. Apparently, his sense of humor had returned. "And expensive. See what kind of quality it is, Tony."

Morgan continued to watch as the first stage of the end of his life as he knew it played out on the marina pier. The detective punched a hole in the bag with a small knife, then wet his finger and dipped it into the dense white powder. When he tasted it, he looked back at the sheriff and smiled even more broadly. Morgan groaned.

"Very good quality, Sheriff. I believe it's the cocaine subspecies of whitefish." The detective placed the bag of coke back in the Yeti and removed a set of handcuffs from his belt. He lost his sense of humor as quickly as he found it. "Paul Morgan, you are under arrest for possession and transport of a controlled substance. You have the right to remain silent."

Morgan turned his head and looked back at his yacht. He didn't hear the rest of his Miranda rights. He simply gazed out over the marina, the various yachts and fishing boats a blur to him; stoned from cocaine, stoned from the sudden turn of events, and stoned from the realization that the likelihood of him surviving this crisis after the Constantine organization found out what happened, were slim to none.

CHAPTER 22

When Emmy reached the ocean floor, she couldn't believe her eyes. Evidence of the shipwreck was everywhere. Corroded cannons, remnants of the ship's hull and masts, and various other debris littered the seabed for as far as she could see. Emmy thought of the massive task which lay ahead for whomever would undertake the job of mapping and salvaging the site, its enormous historical significance, and its incalculable treasure. Jack wanted it. The bad guys want it. Now she had found it.

As exhilarating as the old Spanish ship's finding was to her, Emmy's heart broke when she saw the opposite of a long-ago shipwreck. There, smack dab in the middle of the strewn wreckage, was the almost pristine *Sunny Daze*. She recognized it immediately and had to look to see how it had sunk before she began looking for treasure. A quick check of her dive watch showed she had plenty of time left.

The assessment of the *Sunny Daze* didn't take long at all. Most of the stern had been blown away, almost as if a bomb had gone off. The damage was worse on the starboard side. Otherwise, the trawler was completely intact. A good number of fish swam in and around the *Sunny Daze*, now acting as a life-enhancing reef. Emmy cringed at the cruel irony.

Now she had her primary task at hand. She swam back to the remains of the old shipwreck and poked around the debris. Anything wooden she touched crumbled in her hand, a testament to what three hundred years of saltwater could do. Anything that wasn't wood which remained was metal and appeared corroded almost beyond recognition. What exactly was she looking for? A chest of some kind? Loose coins? She didn't know, but the treasure, or whatever remained of it, had to be here somewhere. She checked her watch again. Fifteen minutes down, another ten minutes before she needed to begin her ascent. She knew she could extend it at least another five to ten minutes, even if dad would give her an earful for it. She really didn't want to surface empty-handed.

Emmy continued to search for anything which might catch the weak sunlight that made it to the sea floor, that might indicate gold. She swam over the debris field, poking her hand into anything that looked promising, but came up lacking each time. She began thinking this might all be a waste. That there wasn't any treasure here, and the wreck was simply an old fishing vessel that went down years ago. But that wouldn't explain the cannons she found, not to mention the coin she had and the background information she acquired. It had to be here — somewhere.

And then she saw it. At first, it was the slightest glint, catching just enough sunlight to snag her eye. Emmy swam to the mass of debris from where it had come, moved some boards which practically dissolved in her hand, and there it was; a pile of coins — gold coins, looking like they were minted yesterday.

Emmy's heart thundered in her chest, and she reminded herself to control her breathing. She picked up one coin and examined it. Just like the one she found on the beach, it had that Jerusalem cross on one side and the 713 imprint on the other. That settled it. She had found the missing ship of the lost 1715 Treasure Fleet. Emmy checked her watch. Right on time, she had another five minutes before heading back. She took two coins and placed them in the zipper pocket of her wetsuit, then explored a bit more of the wreckage.

That had to be just one chest, she thought. Theresa said there could be at least a hundred of them. How many were here at the site? How many others could have been scattered by dozens of hurricanes that had blown through in the past three-hundred years? No telling, but they were here, somewhere. What a find, was all she could think about.

With the coins secure in her hip pocket, Emmy browsed the site for a few more minutes. She wondered who would get the salvage rights, again thinking back to what Theresa had told her. That company in Florida, the Spanish government, the US government, the state of South Carolina — all could make claims to the prize. Surely, some kind of finder's fee would come her way in due course, but she wasn't focused on making herself rich. Her mind was on history and keeping the treasure from falling into the wrong hands.

And what about Jack? The secrecy he surrounded himself with was much more understandable now. But what was he after? Did he really think he was going to salvage the site himself and keep all the treasure? Did he have that much hubris in him? Was he that arrogant? She continued to ponder exactly how much she knew who Jack was.

Emmy scrubbed Jack from her mind and focused on finishing her task. The coins secure, she began her ascent to the surface. First, she needed to find the anchor line to the *Fair Allowance* so she could surface by the boat. She had swum at least fifty yards away while looking for the coins. The visibility was good, but not great. After a minute of searching, she found the anchor and its line running to the surface.

She breathed easier, even though she knew if worse came to worse she could have surfaced anywhere and found the yacht. Emmy began her ascent. Looking up, she couldn't yet make out the boat on the surface, and probably wouldn't until around thirty feet. She kicked her way up to where the depth meter on her watch showed sixty feet. Emmy paused and breathed steadily, letting the pressures release naturally in her body.

She maintained her depth level, thinking about the coins, how excited dad and Neil would be, then she thought again about Jack. She cast one last glance back to the seabed and the outline of the *Sunny Daze*. Her heart ached for her lost lover. The man she thought she knew so well, but perhaps she really didn't. The man she had committed to spend the rest of her life with, and now wouldn't.

The trawler's wreck proved once and for all that Jack was here last Monday and had undoubtedly found the treasure. Now, she had the proof she needed and could let the sheriff find out who killed Jack and bring justice for him, and to her and his family. Whoever they were, they were bound to come back to the site at some point, and now that she knew exactly where it was, she figured it would be an easy capture, and at no risk to herself.

Emmy checked her watch again — in another minute she could ascend to thirty feet. It was then she saw something so unexpected, so incomprehensible, that at first, she thought it was a hallucination, or some kind of mirage. The rope which secured the anchor to the ocean floor became slack and started descending to the bottom. Emmy looked up, then down, shaking her head, trying to make some kind of sense of what was going on. The rope was now was below her and would settle right next to the anchor.

Obviously, that meant only one thing. Someone cut the anchor line. But why? She peered up toward the surface, but still couldn't make out anything. Then she heard an enormous explosion coming from the surface. The shock of the sound wave flipped her over, momentarily causing her to lose her sense of direction. What the hell was that? If the cut anchor line was suspicious, the explosion confirmed something truly terrible had happened up there. Emmy looked to the surface again but still couldn't make anything out. Her breathing deepened as panic set in. What the fuck was going on up there?

It was time to ascend again. As much as Emmy wanted to go straight to the surface to see what was happening, she knew she couldn't. She swam upwards to thirty feet, looking toward the surface the whole time. As she neared the point of her second and final decompression stop, Emmy finally made out what was on the surface. And the sight shook her to the bone. The bottom of the hull which came into view was not the *Fair Allowance's*. Clearly not. The boat she saw was much smaller and thinner. She could see the outboard motors and they were not the same as her dad's yacht. Whose boat was that? Where was the *Fair Allowance*? And most critically, what was that explosion all about? Emmy had no answers for any of these questions, but the pit which formed in the bottom of her stomach told her she wouldn't like the answer to any of them.

CHAPTER 23

Neil froze with fear as he watched the speedboat close in on the *Fair Allowance*. David stood next to him, looking over the starboard side, hiding the shotgun behind his back.

"I don't think they're coming here to chat, David," Neil said, his voice trembling. The two stared at the approaching boat. It looked like there were two men on board, a tall one and a shorter fat one.

"If they want trouble, they're going to get trouble," David responded with determination.

To Neil, David seemed fearless. Neil, however, felt like he was about to soil himself. He gulped, then saw something even more terrifying. The taller man reached down and pulled out what looked like a submachine gun. Then he pointed it at the *Fair Allowance*. From Neil's point of view, there'd certainly be no chatting. Killing seemed to be more on the agenda. The speedboat came straight at them. Neil's last impression was the guy with the gun had a darker complexion and an even darker mood. Just before he heard the rat-tat-tat of the automatic weapon discharging, David grabbed Neil by his collar and dragged him to the deck.

"Get down, you fool," Neil heard David yell as they crashed to the floor. Bullets whizzed by just above them, a couple shattering the cabin windshield.

"Holy shit! They're going to kill us." Neil crouched below the railing, his hands covering his head. The machine gun stopped firing, but he was too scared to look above the railing. He thought he heard the speedboat coming around to the port side. David squatted next to him, shotgun in hand. "What are we going to do?" Neil whispered.

"We need to get out of here. Now you listen to me good."

Neil uncovered his hands from his head and stared at David. Fear gripped him and he couldn't respond verbally, just nodded his head.

"I'm going to have a shot at them. When I fire, you need to get to the bow and cut the anchor line. Then come back to the helm and hit the gas. I don't think they're going to follow us. With any luck, I'll disable them long enough to get out of here." He handed Neil the eight-inch hunting knife he kept under the console.

Neil partially found his voice. "W-What about Emmy?"

"She'll have to fend for herself until we can call the Coast Guard. Get ready, on my count. One —"

Neil couldn't believe how fast everything was happening. He tried to gulp again, but his throat was bone dry.

"Two —"

One last morbid thought crossed his mind. Yes, this is how he's going to die — shot to death out on the ocean. His body will be cast overboard and make a pleasant lunch for the sharks.

"Three, now."

Neil saw David stand and point the shotgun. Somehow, he snapped out of his panic. He rose to his feet, then scrambled around the cabin to the bow on the starboard side in a crouch. The sound of the shotgun rang out in his ears. Neil took a quick peek to his right. It appeared the shot did some damage as the short fat one had dropped. He focused back on his task and sliced through the anchor rope.

Still crouching, when he turned around and looked back, he saw David reloading the shotgun. That was good. What wasn't good was his next glance at the speedboat. Only the tall guy was still visible, and he had that machine gun in his hands again. In another split second, the rata-tat-tat came back, and more bullets covered the helm. Worse, he heard David scream out, "I'm hit," and then saw him crash to the deck.

Terrorized panic swept through Neil. He scampered back to where David laid. "Where are you hit?" he asked. Blood oozed out of David's shoulder and side.

"Never mind that," David moaned. "Get us out of here, now!"

Neil peeked above the railing again. This time he saw something even more frightening than the machine gun, as if that was possible. The tall guy had picked up an even more menacing gun. Neil wasn't exactly up to speed on his knowledge of military weaponry, but he recognized what the long barrel with a small football shaped object at the end meant. The man was holding a rocket-propelled grenade. It was time to get the hell out of there.

With one eye on the man who seemed determined to sink the *Fair Allowance*, Neil stood up at the helm and thrust the throttle to full speed. The acceleration slammed him back in the seat as the boat took off, now free of its anchor. But it pointed east, and he had to get back to land as soon as possible. First things first, though; he had to get as far away from the speedboat and the man with the RPG as fast as possible.

This also turned out to be a disappointment. He probably hadn't gone fifty yards out when he heard a brief high pitch whine, followed by an enormous explosion behind him. The grenade had hit the *Fair Allowance* on the back port side. Apparently, and fortunately, it missed the gas tank; otherwise, they'd have been blown to smithereens. The yacht continued on its own power but began to list to the left. Neil took a broad turn back toward the west and glanced again at the speedboat. The man peered out toward him, but now at least he wasn't holding a weapon.

Neil breathed a quick sigh of relief, but it was short-lived. As he completed his turn and headed back toward land, the *Fair Allowance* listed further to the port side. The boat was taking on water. It wouldn't make it back to the marina, or anywhere close. Neil looked down at David, who continued to lie on the deck, bleeding and moaning. He thought again about Emmy, underwater below the speedboat. There was nothing he could do for her. He shuddered to think what would happen if she surfaced and had to face that guy.

Looking straight ahead, the faintest outline of land appeared on the horizon, Neil forced some positive thoughts into his head. Maybe the guy would go back to where he came from and seek help for his buddy. They had recorded the GPS location of the wreck site — 33.3029 Latitude and 78.5824 Longitude. Once they got help, the authorities could go back there and look for Emmy. He prayed David would survive. If the boat held together, they'd be back in less than an hour. But it didn't look likely as the *Fair Allowance* continued to list.

The probability of the yacht sinking this far from land now seemed all but certain. Neil looked back. The speedboat hadn't moved from the wreck site. Good news for him, but bad news for Emmy. I bet he's just waiting for her to surface, he thought, nearly fainting at the possibility. But if the *Fair Allowance* sank, it would be curtains for him and David as well.

Why did he agree to come out here today? What was Emmy thinking? What was David thinking? Christ, what was Jack thinking, keeping this all a secret from everybody? Why didn't they all just let the authorities handle the situation from the beginning? He was sure the men in the speedboat, whoever they were, were the ones responsible for Jack's death. Now they may just have the blood of three others on their hands.

David moaned some more. Neil realized time was running out, both for David and his yacht. Then the motor cut off. Looking behind him, he saw the entire outboard submerged. They were going down. More panic hit. He grabbed the radio, turned it to the emergency Coast Guard channel, and hollered, "Mayday! Mayday! We're going down." Through the static, a reply came back asking for their position. Thank God for GPS, Neil thought and gave their current location. The *Fair Allowance* had stopped, and it wouldn't be long before it was under water. After giving them a brief description of what happened, they said they were on their way. Neil prayed they would find them in time. Then he knelt to check on David.

CHAPTER 24

Emmy couldn't believe what she was seeing. As she remained stationary at the thirty-foot depth, she racked her brain to make sense of what had just happened. The *Fair Allowance* was nowhere in sight. Could that explosion have been her dad's yacht? If so, wouldn't it have sunk right here? And what about the cut anchor? On the one hand, Emmy wanted to rush to the surface and find out what was going on. But she was also hesitant, her gut telling her there was trouble above.

She completed her decompression time and could now rise to the surface if she wanted. She had to do something. Staying at thirty feet wasn't an option. Emmy cast a wary eye to the surface again. No change. Then it hit her. Jack! A vision formed in her mind. This happened to Jack. He found the treasure, just like she did. Pocketed a couple of coins and when he went to the surface, they were waiting for him and killed him.

Now she bet the same criminals who had discovered the shipwreck and treasure were back, and they blew up the *Fair Allowance*. Who knows what happened to her dad and Neil, but the bad guys were still on the surface waiting for her. Emmy struggled to control her breathing and not let panic completely overwhelm her. Think, dammit think. Her breathing calmed a bit. She checked her air — twenty minutes before the tank was empty.

Emmy decided she wouldn't surface and face whatever had caused all the trouble. She would swim away, as far as she could, until her air ran out. Then she'd surface, hopefully far enough away from the wreck site and out of sight of the troublemakers. But first, she needed to know which way to swim. No sense swimming even further out in the ocean. If she headed back to the coast, at least she'd have a better chance of being rescued. It was fifteen miles to the shore. If she swam due east, she'd be slightly north of Georgetown, probably around Pawleys Island. That would be a daunting task, having never swum anywhere close to that distance. With any luck, it wouldn't come to that.

Emmy looked upwards, trying to determine which way was west. The sun would be in the eastern sky — high, but still slightly east. She examined the sunbeams at her depth. They refracted some, but she could still make a calculated guess which way was east, then swim in the opposite direction. It was an important decision, perhaps a decision of life or death. Whatever the case, she was wasting air and had to move. Emmy turned away from the sunlight's rays and began her journey towards the coast.

******

Amelio's anger boiled over. His face bled, having caught at least one piece of buckshot from that asshole's shotgun. But at least he was alive, which was more than he could say for Enrico, who caught the bulk of the shot in his head and torso. Amelio wasn't prepared for such a defensive action by the intruders. He cursed himself for the lapse in judgement which cost his friend and longtime colleague his life.

He could have chased down the yacht and finished it once and for all, but now he was more concerned about the girl diver. He knew the RPG did considerable damage to the yacht, although in his rush to get it off, the shot was less than ideal. It didn't hit the gas tank, which would have put an end to their brief excursion once and for all. The missile entered the water just before impact, softening the blow. Still, from what he could assess, the boat wouldn't get very far. It listed badly to the port side and, although it limped back towards the coast, Amelio could tell it would sink long before it reached land. Whether the Coast Guard could get there in time to rescue them was another question. If any of them were rescued and now knew the location of the shipwreck, there'd be even more trouble ahead. But he had his own immediate problems to deal with.

First was the girl. Amelio knew she was down there looking for the treasure, just like Abromski. He guessed her tank held forty-five minutes of air, and she'd been under for thirty minutes from when the cameras showed she went in. So, Miss Sweeney should surface at any time now, and he'd be waiting for her, just like he was for Abromski.

Amelio took a few seconds to wipe the blood from his cheek. It seared in pain. He knew he still had the piece of shot lodged in his flesh and he'd have to perform some self-surgery once home, something he wasn't exactly looking forward to. Then he'd have a scar on his left cheek to match the longer one on his right. What a day, what a morning. He still had to arrange pickup of the forty kilos at Petrino's place and then Diego's salvage crew were waiting on instructions to begin their operation. This morning's interruption would complicate that. He wasn't sure how much.

Amelio peered into the ocean for any sign of the girl. Still nothing. How long would he give her? She'd have to surface once her air ran out. What if she saw the speedboat's hull before she swam to the surface and saw her yacht wasn't there? Maybe she swam away below the surface until her air ran out. Amelio pinched the bridge of his nose and shook his head, thinking about the possibility the girl might slip away as well as the other two on the yacht. That would really cause problems.

He turned his attention to Enrico. There was no hope for him. His friend took the brunt of the shotgun blast. But for the grace of God, had Amelio been one step to the right of Enrico, instead of behind him, he'd be the one lying dead on the deck of his boat. And if things turned out as bad as they might, he'd wish he were in his friend's shoes, knowing the wrath Constantine was capable of.

Still, he needed to dispose of Enrico's body. But first he had to find the girl. Amelio peered into the water again and saw nothing. With his binoculars, he scanned the surface in all directions. The man's yacht was still faintly visible, now several miles away. But it didn't look like it was moving. That was heartening, at least. It should be underwater in a matter of minutes. He shook his head, disgusted by how the morning had turned out. The call to Constantine would not be pleasant. And if he couldn't report the three interlopers were dead, it could get damn ugly.

Amelio waited another ten minutes with still no sign of the girl. The thought of her swimming away underwater until her air ran out became more and more likely. And if she had put some distance between her and his boat, it was going to be very difficult to find her, even with binoculars. He couldn't wait much longer. He had to get back and arrange the pickup of the forty kilos.

He gazed again at Enrico and knew what had to be done. Amelio brought the anchor up and cut the rope. He tied the loose end around his friend's torso, making sure it was tight enough to secure him for a long time, like eternity. Without any hint of emotion, Amelio dragged Enrico's body to the speedboat's side and hauled it overboard, where it splashed into the ocean. He followed it with the anchor and as he watched Enrico's body disappear below the surface, he softly said, "Adios, amigo."

******

Emmy's air was getting low, and she knew she'd have to surface soon. The thought terrified her. The whole time she spent swimming as hard as she could, staying twenty feet below the surface, she dreaded the moment her air ran out and she'd have to stick her head above the water's edge. She feared the same man or men who killed Jack would be waiting for her. And even if there was no one tailing her, she'd still be miles from land with no hope of being rescued. Sure, she could continue to swim to shore, but she already felt exhausted and, with nothing to drink, would dehydrate before long. She wouldn't die violently. No, she'd simply drown.

The regulator showed her air on empty. Any second now she'd take a breath, and nothing would enter her lungs. From there, it would be a quick shot to the surface. Emmy was ready to face whatever lay in store for her. She thought again about how far she may have swum under water and how far she still had to go to get to land. There simply wasn't any way to figure out if — suddenly, as if someone turned a valve off, her air ran out. Emmy panicked, having almost no air in her lungs, but she kicked upwards and within ten seconds broke the surface.

She immediately looked all around and was relieved to see absolutely nothing. She spit the regulator out and breathed in the fresh salt air. Next, she needed to relieve herself of her tank and regulator. They were useless now. Emmy treaded water as she wrestled her way out of her scuba gear, something she never had to do while in the water. It proved tricky, but with some struggle, she wriggled out of it. The tank sank immediately. She kept her mask and, of course, her flippers.

Now she had a free moment to assess her location. Once she saw the direction of the sun overhead, she turned to the west and, in a moment of extreme relief, could see the Georgetown Light in the distance. But it was just a speck on the horizon, and she couldn't make out any other land. Emmy guessed she may have swum a mile, and it seemed to be in the correct direction. She remembered the lighthouse wasn't visible at all from the shipwreck site. Finally, she scanned the water's surface again for any sign of a vessel that might rescue her. Where was that boat she saw above her at the wreck site? Where was the *Fair Allowance*? All she could see was the ocean's blue surface.

Emmy floated on her back and rested for a couple of minutes. She tried to think of anything else she could do to be rescued, but nothing came to her. She was on her own, perhaps thirteen or fourteen miles from land, with nothing to drink. She could swim as far as she could but knew instinctively, she'd succumb to dehydration within a couple hours, if that, and still be far from land. But staying where she was, was no better. Maybe, as she swam to the west, she'd see a boat that would notice her. It might be her only chance at survival.

Putting all the negative thoughts to the side, Emmy flipped on to her stomach and swam to the west. Slow and steady, she used as little effort as she could. Her fins would provide the best propulsion. Whatever lay in store for her, she would accept her fate. But she wasn't going down without a fight. Just kick and stroke, kick and stroke. Somehow, she'd make it. She knew it. She just didn't know how.

CHAPTER 25

Neil knew he was going to die and was unprepared for it. It had been thirty minutes since he placed the Mayday call. There was no sign yet of any help. The *Fair Allowance* was almost all submerged. In a few more minutes it would be completely underwater and on its way to the ocean floor. He didn't know if David was still alive or not. He was alive shortly after the distress call when Neil placed a life jacket around him. But David had lost a lot of blood, and his face was white as a sheet. Better white than blue, Neil thought. David was also unconscious. Now, it hardly seemed to matter. They'd both be in the ocean soon. Neil didn't think he could keep David's head above water, as well as keeping himself afloat.

Where was the Coast Guard? He had given them their last position and thought they would send help right away. Presumably in a chopper. He felt certain they'd find them from the air with the boat still afloat. But he was far less sure they could find them with just a couple of heads bobbing on the surface and nothing but the ocean for miles around.

The *Fair Allowance* was toast. As soon as he moved the yacht out of range from the crazy guy with the bazooka, Neil went to the back and saw the damage was too much for the boat to handle. The explosion had ripped a hole in the port side, just a few feet from the stern and just at the water level. As the seawater poured in, it was only a matter of time before she sank. Neil pushed the engine full bore, trying to keep as much of the hole above sea level, but he knew it was a lost cause. After the Mayday call, Neil prayed the *Fair Allowance* would simply stay afloat until help arrived.

At least the gunman wasn't giving chase. Neil watched him on and off as he fled. It appeared the other boat had stayed at the wreck site. He felt nauseated, realizing the guy was probably waiting for Emmy to surface. The thought sickened him further; what began as a perfectly fine day at sea with Emmy and her dad would end with all three of them dead before noon. But nobody had died yet. There was still hope, even if slim, of being rescued.

The *Fair Allowance* slipped further into the sea. By now, the two of them were hanging on the railing at the bow, their legs dipping in the ocean. It reminded Neil of the last scene in Jaws; the *Orca* almost submerged, Chief Brody barely hanging on. Oh yeah, he now thought with remorse, we'll all end up as shark bait and they'll find none of us.

Neil checked on David again. He was still unconscious, draped over the railing. At least his life jacket was on. If they went in the water, he'd try to keep David's head up. But he wouldn't last long. Neil prayed again for some sign of rescue. His life began flashing before his eyes. All the things he'll never get to do. All the friends and family he'll never see again. He'd miss his parents so much. They were so good to him. And what happened after you die? Neil was never a religious type of person, and he never really thought about such things — the big unknowns he called them. Now what? Would he go to heaven? Would he go to hell? Maybe he'll be stuck in purgatory, wherever that was.

Neil cried. He wailed loudly at his misfortune. If David was conscious, he'd slap him and tell him to grow up, face it like a man. How does anyone face death with nothing but sheer terror? "Please, please," he looked to the sky and called out to no one, "Please rescue us. Please!" He buried his head in his arms. The boat sank some more. Now, only his upper body was above water.

Then he heard a soft rumble. Kind of like distant thunder, but the sky had only wisps of clouds. Neil tuned his ears to the noise. It was coming from the west. He squinted into the haze, looking for its source, but saw nothing. The rumble started getting louder. It wasn't thunder for sure. More like a thud-thud-thud sound. Kind of like a, oh please yes, like the sound a helicopter would make. Neil squinted toward the direction of the sound. It kept getting louder, unmistakable now. And then he saw it. It appeared out of the haze like a Godsend. A single helicopter, orange with a white stripe, flying low, coming straight at them.

Neil screamed and waved his arms. He cried again, but this time, they were tears of joy.

******

Amelio continued to curse his streak of bad luck. Foulness spewed from his mouth, heard only by a passing gull. The Sweeney girl had yet to surface, and he knew her air had to have run out by now. That could only mean she swam away after being tipped off because the other boat had left. He peered again through his binoculars for any sign of her swimming on the surface. But with the two-foot waves, it would be almost impossible to see a swimmer from any more than a few hundred meters. He tried to comfort himself that even the hardiest of swimmers couldn't make it fifteen miles back to the coast. Surely, she'd tire and drown long before then. But uncertainty would remain, and he'd have to report this to Constantine, a man who loathed uncertainty.

Then there was the other yacht. As Amelio waited on the girl, he kept an eye on the boat with the two men. He knew he had shot at least one of them, the older one. The younger man had cut the anchor and sped away. The RPG had done damage, but Amelio had missed the gas tank he wanted to strike. Had the grenade penetrated the tank, there would have been an enormous explosion, and the two men would be dead. But the yacht fled, albeit at less than full speed, with a gaping hole near its stern.

Once again, Amelio tried to take solace the boat wouldn't go far and would sink at sea. He tracked it as it limped its way toward land. About four miles out, he could tell the boat had stopped, guessing the motor had become submerged, and now he could barely make out what was left above the water. It looked like both men were hanging on to the tip of the bow. But they appeared to be alive. Another bad sign. Amelio weighed whether to head their way and finish them once and for all, but he was already behind schedule and needed to get back to McClellanville as soon as possible. He'd figure out what to tell Constantine later.

Then there was the problem with the wreckage site. If any of the three interlopers survived, they would know the GPS location of the site. Even if they didn't survive, they may have communicated it to someone else. Keeping the site location secret was paramount to the mission's success. Diego and his men were ready to begin the salvage operation. If the Coast Guard became aware of the site, there would be even bigger problems. Amelio knew there was more at stake than the riches the *Concepcion* would give up. The organization did not tolerate failed missions. You paid for them with your life.

Amelio started the engine and made his way back to McClellanville. He touched his swollen cheek again. The self-administered surgery he would need to remove the piece of shot wouldn't be pleasant. Far from it. He grinned when he thought about the matching scar he'd have on his left cheek, matching the one on his right. The other guy was less lucky then. Now it seemed luck played against him.

The speedboat powered through the waves on a direct course back home. He'd be there in another twenty minutes at top speed. He still had to contact the mules who were going to take their portion of the forty kilos from Petrino's shop to their respective locations in Raleigh,

Greenville, and Atlanta. Amelio placed a satellite call to Diego and told him to meet him in McClellanville in an hour. Things have changed and a new strategy needed to be developed. It was supposed to be a pleasant afternoon watching the football match. Now it would take on much more urgency.

Halfway back to McClellanville, Amelio heard a low rumble noise coming from the southwest. Within seconds, he recognized the sound — a helicopter. And that could only mean one thing. He cut the engine and grabbed the binoculars. Sure enough, it was the Coast Guard heading northeast out of their Charleston base. The direction where that goddamn yacht had floundered. "Shit, shit, shit," he muttered, heard only by a few passing seagulls. That probably meant at least one of them had survived. Now his problems multiplied further. If the guy gave away the location of the wreck site — well, Amelio had no answer for it.

Amelio approached the outskirts of Cape Romain and slowed the speedboat down just before he entered the series of winding creeks leading to his bungalow. His mind raced at the mounting setbacks to his operations. His cheek throbbed with pain. He was right in the middle of another string of profane swearing into the wind when his phone rang. It was Petrino's burner phone number.

"Now what," Amelio said out loud, rolling his eyes. He answered the call. "What is it?" he shouted curtly.

Petrino's voice was frantic. "Amelio. Morgan hasn't shown up with the goods. He's thirty minutes late."

Amelio shut his eyes as his mind fogged over. This couldn't be. How could this be? How much more bad luck was he going to endure on this God forsaken Saturday morning? He shook his head, trying to clear the cobwebs. "Let me get in touch with Morgan and find out what's going on. Go nowhere."

"Believe me, I won't," said Petrino and he ended the call.

Amelio immediately hit the speed dial for Morgan's burner. After ten rings with no answer, he ended the call, then looked to the sky and screamed as loud and long as he could.

CHAPTER 26

Morgan heard his burner phone go off. So did Leroy and Tony. They couldn't miss it, since it sat on the table in the station's interrogation room. Leroy kept looking back and forth between the phone and Morgan.

"Would you like to answer that?" Leroy finally asked after the fifth ring. He knew Morgan wouldn't. After all, who could it be, other than Morgan's contact, who by now had to be severely curious why the goods hadn't shown up.

Morgan simply shook his head. He's certainly exercising his right to remain silent, Leroy thought. The doctor hadn't issued one peep since his arrest at the marina. He made his one call to his attorney, Leonard Barry, a real blowhole, from Leroy's experience. Ever since, Morgan kept his arms folded and a scowl on his face. The phone finally stopped ringing.

Leroy looked from the phone at Morgan. "You know, Doctor, things might be easier on you in the long run if you cooperate with us a little."

Morgan kept his stone wall expression.

Leroy glanced sideways at Tony. "Detective, tell our good doctor how things might be better for him if he gives us some information."

Tony chuckled, then nodded. "Glad to, Sheriff. Let's start by keeping him alive."

Morgan looked up, showed some slight interest, but kept silent.

"Yes, good point. I imagine someone out there is less than pleased with you this morning. Perhaps that someone just called you. Maybe he has some not very kind words for you. Like if you don't deliver his goods, you might not be breathing much longer."

"But we could help with that," Tony contributed, smiling. "Keep you safe. Keep you hid. And when it comes time to go on trial, things could look much nicer for you if the people behind your little delivery mission that went south were also on trial. Do you see where I'm coming from?"

Again, no response from Morgan, but his eyes kept darting between the burner phone and the two law enforcement agents.

"Of course, we're going to find out who they are with or without your help," said Leroy, his voice taking a more serious tone. "And yes, you'll be safe as long as you're behind bars. But it's an unpleasant experience in the best of circumstances. You may not have ideal conditions, Doctor. You wouldn't know, since you've squirmed your way out of any real trouble your whole life. But that's about to change." Leroy leaned forward, getting within a foot of Morgan's face, staring straight into his eyes. "In a big way." Leroy sat back again but continued to glare at Morgan. "Now, while we're waiting for your attorney to show, we're going to give you a few more minutes to think things over. Meanwhile, we're going to see who was trying to call you just now." Leroy handed Morgan's phone to Tony and said, "Detective, do your magic with this thing."

Tony rose and took the phone. "My pleasure."

Just as Tony was about to turn to leave, Morgan said, "You're wasting your time."

Both Leroy and Tony raised their eyebrows and gave Morgan their full attention. "Please explain, Dr. Morgan," Leroy asked. "We're all ears."

Morgan maintained his steel-eyed glare. "The number is untraceable. You won't get any information from it."

Leroy rubbed his chin and nodded slowly. "So you say. Anything else you'd care to share with us?"

Morgan squinted, paused, then retorted, "Yeah, you guys can go fuck yourself."

Leroy continued to nod. "I see, then." His voice deepened in disgust. "Tony, why don't you escort the doctor to one of our holding cells until his attorney shows. You know, the one at the end. Then find out what you can from his phone. I'm thinking Dr. Morgan here is blowing smoke up our asses." He turned his attention back to Morgan. "That will give you time to think things over a bit. Maybe next time we talk you'll have wiped that smug look off your face. Jail time can have that effect. And try to get comfortable. You're going to be here a while."

Morgan said nothing and continued to sneer at Leroy and Tony.

******

Amelio stood in front of the mirror in the luxurious master bath of his McClellanville home and prepared to self-administer first aid to his face. The piece of buckshot which had lodged in his cheek had already caused his face to swell and he knew he risked infection if not properly treated. It would be painful, but that was the least of his concerns. He had plenty of powerful painkilling drugs to help with that. The real pain was his current predicament.

Amelio could feel the walls closing in on him. The impending rescue of the intruders, the possibility that the Sweeney girl found the wreck, and its treasure, and may yet survive. Now the realization that Morgan failed to deliver the forty kilos of cocaine put him in a severely compromised position like never before. He had to draw on his extensive experience to formulate a plan.

It wasn't the first time operational plans had run awry. Deliveries have failed before. Previous treasure hunts had been compromised. There were shootouts with both their competition and law enforcement. And he survived each one of them. He would survive this crisis as well. He just needed to keep his head on straight and make a new plan. Then he'd call Constantine with the bad news, but with confidence a new plan would succeed as well.

His mind pondered what could have happened to Morgan. It boiled down to two possibilities. First, Morgan split with the cocaine hoping to sell it himself. This would be an extremely poor choice for him. There was no way anyone in the US, or even in all the Americas, where that much cocaine would show on the open market without Constantine finding out. The boss would send out the word to lookout for the purloined goods and as soon as it surfaced anywhere, he'd know about it. Then it would be easy pickings to find Morgan and eliminate him in a most painful method.

The second prospect, equally unsavory for Dr. Morgan, was he'd been picked up by law enforcement. This would create additional problems for Amelio and Constantine in that the forty kilos would disappear forever. If Morgan had tried to keep the cocaine and sell it, the goods would eventually be recovered. But if it fell into the hands of the Coast Guard, or the FBI, or the DEA, or maybe just the local police, the cocaine would never again see the light of day and Constantine would be out of his sizable investment. This would be bad news indeed.

Amelio couldn't understand how someone could have caught Morgan. Obviously, he'd been careless. Was he speeding or driving his boat recklessly? Or perhaps his loose lips somehow tipped off the authorities. Amelio would have to make some discreet inquiries to see if this was indeed the case. If it were, and Morgan was behind bars right now, then he might give the cops information about the organization. That would only lead to more trouble.

But as much a problem as Morgan and the cocaine presented, it paled to the predicament Amelio faced with the shipwreck site discovered. The whole venture depended on secrecy. How was he supposed to mount a salvage operation on the scale he needed if the Coast Guard knew not only about the wreck, but exactly where it was located? This was his biggest concern. Didn't matter. Diego was due soon. They'd develop a Plan B and then report it to Constantine. He just wished he knew what had happened to the three intruders.

Amelio gritted his teeth in pain as he dug the sterilized tweezers into his swollen cheek and fished around for the piece of shot. The longer this took, the worse the fresh scar would be. At last, he found the piece and grabbed hold of it. As he pulled it out, Amelio let out a grunted scream. He held the piece up and glared at it with spite, then tossed it in the trash. His cheek throbbed, but the worst was over. Soon a couple of Percocets would ease the physical suffering. He still needed to disinfect. Once more, Amelio clenched his teeth together and swabbed alcohol in the wound. The operation completed, he bandaged his cheek, then swallowed his painkillers. The physical pain would soon be over, but the mental anguish would linger. He dreaded the call to Constantine. It would cut deeper than any piece of shot. And if he didn't get his shit together, it would be more than painful. It would be fatal.

CHAPTER 27

"I'm scared," Emmy said to herself. "I'm really, really scared."

She'd been swimming for over an hour and felt her energy slipping away. The exertion of her escape underwater, followed by the surface swimming, had drained her. Severe dehydration gripped her, forcing her to stop several times to ease cramps. So many scattered thoughts went through her mind as she trudged on westward to whatever fate held in store for her. But cutting through all her thoughts and feelings was overwhelming fear.

Emmy thought about her dad and Neil, and what may have become of them. She thought about the Barony and the job she loved so much. She thought about the treasure, her two coins secure in her hip pocket. What would become of it? And through it all, she thought about Jack and the cruel end that fate had destined for him. Would she be reunited with him after death if she didn't survive? Emmy was never one to be too philosophical about anything. Funny how that had a way of changing once you're in a life-threatening situation.

Above it all was an overwhelming sadness. So much had changed in the past week. She realized she would miss so much, and knew others would miss her too. How could life turn sour so abruptly? In the depth of her despair, Emmy forced herself not to give up. It ain't over till it's over, she told herself. Who said that? She wasn't sure. Her mind couldn't be sure of anything except for the fact she wasn't dead yet.

How would it happen? Would she suffer? She imagined at some point she'd simply lose all strength and sink, never to surface again. She'd swallow seawater and would drown quickly. At least she hoped so. Maybe a shark would come along and bite her in two. Wouldn't that be a fit ending? Emmy cramped again, the pain shooting from her toes up her leg. She floated on her back, praying the cramp would ease. Each one came on stronger and lasted longer. She cried, then whimpered at her suffering.

When the cramp eased, she looked again to the west. The coast was visible, but still so far away. She knew she'd never reach land swimming. Her only hope was to be rescued. But how was that going to happen? If her dad and Neil didn't make it, no one would even suspect they were missing for a while. She guessed mom would eventually be concerned later in the day and call for help. But that would still be hours away and she'd be long gone by then.

Once more, Emmy summoned what strength she had left and began slow strokes, but it didn't last. She cramped again, this time in both legs. She turned on her back and tried to stretch out her dehydrated muscles. The pain was intolerable. She tried to reach her flippers with her hands to help stretch, but in doing so, she dipped below the surface and swallowed a bit of water. Not enough to choke, but the salt taste in her throat slapped her mind into focus. Emmy coughed it out and floated again on her back. Once more, the cramps eased.

At this point, she gave up trying to swim. She knew her only hope was a rescue. Swimming would only bring on more cramps more quickly. So, she floated and let her mind ease. It would be all right — her death, in the ocean she so loved. What a nice place to die. Alone, nothing but the warm sea embracing her and the blue sky above. A feeling of peace came over her. A resignation, a letting go. How long would it be? Minutes? Maybe an hour or two. If the cramps stayed away, she could float all day. But then what? What if she was still floating after the sun set? That terrified her.

What about the current? If she was just floating and not swimming, she would move with the current. But which way was it going? If the current moved west, she might float to shore. But if it moved any other way, she'd only move further away. Emmy tried to determine where she was. The Georgetown lighthouse, still far away, looked to be about twenty degrees south of due west. If she was still floating for an hour, she'd look again and try to see if it perceptively changed. If, that is, she was still alive.

Emmy continued to float. It was so much easier than swimming. The cramps had let up for now. Peace, she thought over and over. Peace in the ocean, peace in my soul, peace in the world. The world that's left for me. Here, now, if only — if only.

******

Emmy had no way of knowing how long she floated. It seemed like she had fallen asleep. She thought she had dreamed. A dream of being with Jack. It was their last trip together on the *Sunny Daze,* earlier in the month. They were diving in their usual haunt. They were underwater. Jack pointed something out. She couldn't tell what it was. But she wasn't swimming, she was just floating, watching Jack — admiring him. Her heart beat loudly. She could hear it thump, thump, thump. Jack pointed up to the surface. Emmy looked at him quizzically. Why was he pointing up? He appeared to be quite emphatic about it. Something important was up there.

The thumping sound seemed to get louder. Now it was more like a thumpa thumpa thumpa sound.

A wave splashed over Emmy's face, waking her from her dream. She looked all around — still nothing. But the strange sound was still there — and it wasn't her heart. It came from above. Emmy looked to the sky

— still nothing but sunshine and a few clouds. She listened more intently to where the sound came from. From the southwest, yes, from land. She broke out of her float and tread water. Then she saw a sight that melted her heart. It was a helicopter — that was the sound. And it headed in her direction.

Adrenaline shot through Emmy's body like a lightning bolt. It had to be a Coast Guard helicopter on a rescue mission. And it was her they were trying to rescue. Suddenly, Emmy was wide awake and began waving her arms frantically. She told herself repeatedly, I'm going to survive, I'm going to survive. But only if that helicopter sees her. At first, she screamed at it, but soon realized no one would be able to hear her. Save your energy, girl. Focus on treading water and waving.

The helicopter approached closer, maybe a couple miles out, but it seemed to be headed off to the south. Would they miss her? The thought of a rescue so close and then not happening was too much to bear. She couldn't continue to tread water and wave both hands at the same time much longer. But if she went back to floating, they would miss her for sure. Emmy kept a close eye on the helicopter while she continued to wave her arms. It passed her to the south. Her heart dropped. "Please come back," she begged. "Please, please come back."

The helicopter was past her now, heading further out to sea. Emmy stopped waving but kept treading water. She kept pleading and begging for it to turn back. She prayed as hard as she had ever prayed in her life. That wasn't a lot. She had sort of an ambivalent relationship with God. But she promised that would change if she could just get rescued. Oh, would it ever change.

Then her prayer was answered. The helicopter took a wide turn back to the north. In another minute it headed back west — back to land, and back toward her. Now it was heading straight at her. Emmy started waving both hands again, this time screaming for help as well. It was only a mile away, still coming at her. This was it, this had to be it. At only a half mile away, she saw the greatest sight she had ever seen in her life. The helicopter slowed down and descended. She saw somebody wave to her out the window. They had seen her. Tears of joy streamed down Emmy's face as she shouted out loud, "Thank you, God! Thank you, God!"

******

Fifteen minutes later, Emmy was in the arms of a stranger. A very good-looking muscular stranger who had just placed Emmy in a harness securely fastened to her torso. The man, Aviation Survival Technician, Rick Goddard of the USCG gave the men on the MH 65 helicopter, now stationary above the spot where Emmy had floated for over an hour, a thumbs up. Emmy was so overwhelmed with joy, she kissed the handsome deliverer smack on the mouth. Why not? she thought. He's my knight in shining armor, my Prince Charming, and my savior, all rolled into one. They lifted Emmy and her Godsend above the water and, moments later, they boarded the helicopter.

Her first surprise was seeing Neil. She was thrilled to see him, but her immediate reaction was, where's dad? She needed answers, but before she could receive any, the crew on the chopper surrounded her and gave her their full attention. Emmy allowed them to remove her fins and wrap a blanket around her, then give her a drink, which sort of tasted like Gatorade, but was told was a special rehydration formula. She devoured it.

As the helicopter began its way back to Georgetown, Emmy emerged from the surrealness of her rescue and took stock of the situation.

"I'm fine, really," she told the crowd of men around her. She found Neil, who came to her side. "Neil, what happened to you? Where's Dad? Is he all right?"

"He's at Georgetown Memorial Hospital right now, Emmy. They shot him twice. He's lucky to be alive."

"What! Shot? By who? What the hell happened when I was down below? I heard an explosion underwater, then saw another boat on the surface but not the *Fair Allowance*."

"Oh, Emmy, it's been such a horrible day. I can't believe what we got ourselves into. I just, I just, oh I can't believe we found you." Neil started crying. "We thought you were gone, but I told them they had to go back to look for you."

Emmy smiled. It was so good to see Neil in his usual highly emotional state. "Neil," she said sternly, grabbing both his arms. "I'm alive. You're alive. Now tell me what happened."

Neil gulped, then sniffed in his tears. "All right, I'll start when the trouble first showed up. I guess you were down about twenty minutes. We were expecting to see you surface soon when this speedboat approached." Neil recounted the episode the best he could remember, while Emmy stared at him in disbelief. She gasped when Neil told her how they were hit with machine gun fire, then gasped again when he told her about her dad firing his shotgun back at them.

"Did he kill them?" she interrupted him. Every sentence seemed more incredible than the last.

"Can't say for sure. I think he hit one of them pretty good." Neil continued with the explosion that disabled the *Fair Allowance*.

"An RPG! Are you *kidding* me?"

"I think so. I mean, I've only seen them in movies. They said that if it hadn't hit the water first, we'd have been blown to pieces."

Emmy sat with her mouth gaped open. "Unbelievable," she muttered. "Go on then."

Neil finished the story with the *Fair Allowance* sinking, and the amazing helicopter rescue of him and her dad.

"They flew us straight to Georgetown Hospital. The last thing the medic told us was David was stable and should survive. Then I begged them to go back out and look for you. And we found you, Emmy. It's a miracle. It's a freaking miracle."

Neil stopped and waited for Emmy to digest the complete story. "So, tell me. What happened to you?"

Emmy nodded some more, trying to determine where to begin. "Well, when I came up to the last decompression stop, at thirty feet, I saw a hull, but I could tell it wasn't the *Fair Allowance*. I panicked, then had a vision the same thing happened to Jack. So, I didn't surface. I swam underwater, hoping to head back to land, until my air ran out. When I came up, there was nothing around, so I swam on the surface towards land."

Neil's eyes popped. "You thought you could swim to land? That's over fourteen miles."

"No shit, Neil." Emmy could tell her nerves were still raw. She didn't need to get upset with him. From what he just told her, he rescued her as much as the Coast Guard did. She continued in a softer voice. "So, after an hour or so, I started cramping. I thought I was going to drown. All I could do was float. Waiting to die." The realization of just how close she came to dying washed over her. Tears formed again when she grasped how much gratitude she owed Neil. "I thought for sure I was going to die out there in the ocean." Emmy's tears flowed freely. "Thank you so much for coming back to look for me, Neil. I owe you my life. Thank you, thank —" Before she could finish, Neil embraced her in a great bear hug. Both bawled like babies.

After a minute, Neil broke the embrace and dried his eyes. "What about your dive, Emmy? What did you find? Did you find the wreck?"

Emmy gave Neil a wry smile. "I did. It was amazing. But the first thing I found was the *Sunny Daze*. It looked like it had just sailed, except the whole stern was blown apart. Then all around it lay the remnants of this Spanish ship. Just pieces of it everywhere. I saw a few cannons covered with barnacles. That was the only thing I could make out."

"What about the treasure?" Neil asked anxiously. "Did you find anything there?"

Emmy's smile broke into a wide grin as she reached behind her and unzipped her wetsuit pocket. "I did indeed." She removed the two gold coins, then shielded herself so that only Neil could see them. "Check this out."

Neil looked at them and immediately screamed bloody hell.

CHAPTER 28

Leroy sat with Tony in the sheriff's office, fuming over Morgan. "What have you been able to determine from the video on Morgan's boat?" he asked his detective.

After booking Morgan and placing him in his cell, Tony took fifteen minutes to review the footage and make some calls. The DEA was the most likely source of helpful information. Tony had seen enough drug runners in his time to know the speedboat, commonly referred to as a Cigarette boat for its long sleek outline, was used by the cartels to move drugs from South America to the east and the west coast. He edited the video feed and pasted the portion showing the speedboat to his contact in the Charleston DEA office. Five minutes later, he received a very excited call back, wanting to know more.

"DEA is hot on it, Sheriff. They have it pinned down to one of three cartels. One guy was so excited he was already on his way out the door to drive up here. He'd like to get to know our doctor some more and take a sample of the contraband back with him."

"And what have we determined about the drugs? Do you have the test results?"

"Just got it back from the lab." Tony showed the attachment he opened on his phone. "99% pure cocaine. It's only that pure straight from the source."

"Which would be?"

"My guess is Colombia, but we won't know for sure until the DEA does more extensive testing."

Leroy pursed his lips and exhaled through his nose. "No telling how long that doctor's been running drugs through the marina. You think Robbins had any inkling about it?"

Tony shook his head. "Nah, not by the surprise look he had on his face when we showed up. But my guess is this will be a major interruption in the flow of cocaine to the Carolinas. I'd expect more bodies might show up soon."

"Great. Terrific. All we need." Leroy rolled his eyes.

Leroy's desk phone rang. His eyes popped when he saw who was calling. "It's the Georgetown Coast Guard. Wonder what they want. I'll put it on speaker." Leroy pressed the speaker button and answered the call. "Sheriff Keating speaking. What's up?"

"Sheriff, this is Officer in Charge Alex Duval, USCG Georgetown. I wanted to alert you to a Mayday call that came in a few minutes ago."

Leroy raised his eyes to Tony's. Both men had their interest piqued. "Go ahead, Officer. What can you tell us?"

"A call came from a man who said his yacht had been under attack. He was sinking. Looks to be about twelve miles offshore of Georgetown east northeast. Charleston has a chopper heading out there now, as well as our own response boat.

Leroy's interest shifted to a major concern. The Coast Guard would have jurisdiction for any violence at sea, but his team would need to be involved in tracking any perpetrators on land. "Under attack, you say? Any other details?"

"Yes, sir. The vessel in distress is the *Fair Allowance*, registered out of —"

Leroy's eyes bulged, and he slammed his hand down on his desk. "The what! Holy Christ!" he shouted into the phone. Tony's look of astonishment matched his own.

"Yes, sir. You're familiar with the vessel?"

Leroy pinched the bridge of his nose and shook his head. He heard Tony moan. "Yes, I'm afraid so. The boat has been on our radar for the past few days. Please keep me informed about any updates you can provide."

"Yes, Sir. We will."

"Thank you, Officer." Leroy ended the call and stared at Tony. "Now what the fuck do you think that's all about? Something to do with Morgan? With the drug runners?"

Tony was rubbing his forehead and shaking his head. "I don't know, Leroy. The *Fair Allowance* wasn't going in the same direction this morning as Morgan. And the distress call came from northeast of here. Morgan came back from the southeast."

"Who did you say was on the *Fair Allowance* this morning? Sweeney and who else?"

"It looked like Emmy, the daughter, and Goodsen, Abromski's mate."

"Great," Leroy said with as much sarcasm as possible. "And how would someone attack them enough to sink a yacht that size?"

"It would have to take a lot of firepower to do that. Like something a —"

"A drug runner would have." Leroy finished Tony's sentence for him.

"Yeah. Like that."

"Well, fuck me sideways. We don't even know who's still alive out there."

"No, Sir. We don't."

More silence. Leroy's brain raced with different scenarios. The connection between Sweeney and Morgan could not have been a coincidence. But what's the link? First drugs, now treasure. It seemed to be a volatile combination. "Where do you think Sweeney was headed this morning?" he finally asked

"I think you're thinking what I'm thinking. Am I right, Sheriff?"

"That they were going after that *goddamn* shipwreck out there, weren't they?" Leroy yelled across his desk.

"I believe you're on the right track."

"Against my *explicit* orders for her to stay out of the investigation." Leroy's voice rose in full disgust.

"It would appear that way."

"And now its bit them all in the butt."

"Sounds like it may have got them all killed."

"That's all I need. First Morgan, and the DEA, and now the Coast Guard. What a way to spend a holiday weekend." Leroy thought he could feel steam shooting out of his ears. "I hope they survive, if for no other reason, so I can chew their asses out."

"I hear you, Sheriff. I hear you. But if they survived an attack from the drug runner, they could provide some valuable information for us and the others."

"Let's hope so, Tony. For their sake, as well as ours. Let's hope so."
******

Leroy sat on pins and needles for the next twenty minutes, waiting to hear from the Coast Guard. There wasn't anything to deploy until he knew what was going on. He called the DEA contact, Special Agent Doug Glasier, and told them what was going on. Glasier replied he was on Highway 17 in McClellanville and would be in Georgetown in twenty minutes. He'd meet Leroy wherever he was.

When the phone rang, Leroy picked it up before the first ring ended. A quick glance told him it was the Coast Guard.

"Hello, Officer."

"Sheriff. I have an update on the Mayday call for you."

Leroy could sense his heart quicken, along with his breathing. "Go ahead."

"Our rescue chopper picked up two males in distress. One had been shot twice, the other uninjured."

Leroy grimaced. Shot. More complications.

Alex continued. "Chopper will be at Georgetown Memorial any minute now."

"Good, good, I'll meet it there. What about the woman? There was a female on the vessel as well." A pause on the phone. It sounded to Leroy like Alex was asking someone a question.

"Yes, Sir. Confirmed female passenger is missing. I'm told she was diving and didn't surface. I'm sorry I don't have more information for you at this point."

"That's fine, Alex. Thank you for the update. Please let me know of any further developments. Can I meet you at the hospital?"

"Yes, Sir. I'll do that. Goodbye."

Leroy hung up, grabbed his keys, and bolted out the door. He met Tony, who was waiting for Glasier at the front door.

"Just heard from the Coast Guard. Rescued two males, one shot. The girl is still missing. They're dropping the victim off at Georgetown Memorial. I'm heading that way. Why don't you take Glasier to the hospital when he gets here. I have a hunch these two cases must be linked somehow."

"Gotcha. Should be close behind you."

Leroy hustled to his patrol SUV and fired the engine. With lights blazing and sirens wailing he tore out of the parking lot. He arrived at the emergency entrance not three minutes later, right when they were bringing David in. He saw just enough to know it was David Sweeney on the gurney, heading straight to the operating room. Leroy looked around the lobby and realized there wasn't anyone there to give him information.

"Where's that other kid?" he said out loud to no one. He expected to see Neil accompany David into the hospital, but he was nowhere to be found. Leroy rushed outside just as the Coast Guard chopper lifted off again. "I'll be damned." The helicopter headed back toward the coast. Leroy radioed Alex, who had yet to arrive.

"Yes, Sheriff. I'm heading to the hospital now."

"I'm there now. The rescue chopper dropped off the gunshot victim, then took off again. What's going on?"

"Yes, Sir. They're going back out to search for the missing female."

Leroy stood in the lobby and stewed. That meant he had no witnesses to talk to and would have to wait until the chopper returned, with or without Emmy. His mind raced at the flood of events playing out this morning. "Understood," he replied. "We can regroup at the hospital."

"Will do, Sheriff. I'll be there in five minutes."

"Thanks." Leroy ended the call. He saw Tony's car pull into the parking lot. One thing at a time, he reminded himself. Keep your head on straight and tackle one problem at a time. It would require every ounce of patience he could muster.

CHAPTER 29

The call to Constantine went even worse than Amelio feared. The boss wasn't just irate about learning the wreck site had been compromised. When told his cocaine shipment had gone missing, Amelio had to hold the phone away from his ear to keep from being blasted out. Heads would roll soon and Amelio wasn't sure his might not be first in line. He reassured Constantine repeatedly, the situation, even with the complications, was under control. Diego would arrive in McClellanville within the hour, and they would come up with an expedited new game plan. As far as the cocaine went, Amelio admitted it might be a lost cause if Morgan was pinched. But he hadn't yet received confirmation this had happened. If Morgan was on the run, his sources would track him down like a wounded gazelle on the open prairie.

Constantine was yet to be satisfied. He insisted he be on the phone when Diego arrived. That compounded Amelio's headache. He hated being micromanaged, especially when the plans had to be changed on the fly. But there was nothing he could do about it. Keep your head on straight, he reminded himself, or it might not stay on at all.

Amelio tried to relax as he waited for Diego to arrive. Everything he had worked for all these years might crash down on him soon if luck continued to turn against him. He wouldn't let that happen. Luck, he reminded himself, is just a state of mind. And it never stays the same. Luck always changes. It was about time it changed for him.

The security system alerted him to a visitor at the entrance gate. Amelio looked at the monitor and recognized Diego's black Cadillac SUV. He remotely opened the gate and, a minute later, greeted his guest at the front door.

"Welcome, welcome, Diego, my friend. Come in. My apologies for the urgency needed today. Things this morning have been a bit, let's say, unsettled. May I get you a tequila before we begin?"

"Of course," Diego said, the concern clear on his face.

Amelio went to the bar and poured two shots of his best tequila.

When he delivered the drinks, Amelio raised his shot glass and said, "Salud. To the successful retrieval of the lost gold of the *Concepcion*."

"Salud," Diego replied as they downed their drinks.

"Please have a seat. We have much to discuss," Amelio told him. "There is one minor complication, I'm sorry to say. Mr. Constantine has insisted he be in on the discussion this morning." He saw Diego's eyes widen, not surprisingly. Nobody wished to have any more direct discussions with the boss than necessary.

"I see. This is not good news."

"Unfortunately, not. There has been another complication on another front. It's been a difficult morning."

Diego chuckled. "Of that I can see, my friend. A little too close with the razor this morning? Yes?"

Amelio touched the bandage on his cheek. "You might say that."

"So, tell me. What happened out there? Why this sudden change of plans?"

Amelio gave his guest a brief rundown of the encounter at the wreck site. Diego listened without interrupting, but the surprise and uncertainty on his face was obvious to Amelio. When he finished, Amelio felt he had earned Diego's understanding and empathy.

"My apologies for the razor joke, my friend. This indeed puts us in a tough spot."

"Yes, you see my point. But I have some ideas I wish to go over with you. Let's get our heads together first. I told the boss we'll call him at two o'clock with our plan. That gives us not quite an hour."

"Sounds good to me," Diego replied. "What do you have?"

Just then, Amelio's burner phone rang. When he saw the number, he told Diego, "Excuse me for just a minute. I need to take this call." Amelio walked out of the living room and went into his office down the hall, then closed the door.

"What have you found out?"

"I think he's been caught." Sonny Petrino's voice sounded rattled.

"And why do you think that?" Amelio demanded. His patience was already worn thin.

"Morgan's yacht is in its usual dock. Plus, his truck is still in the parking lot. I don't think he took off on foot."

"That doesn't mean he's been caught." Amelio rubbed his temples, trying to force down the blossoming headache. It wasn't proof, but Petrino was probably right. But how? That's what he really wanted to know. Still, losing the cocaine was yet more bad news that he'd have to convey to Constantine on the upcoming call.

"Do you think someone else may have picked him up?"

"Like who?" Amelio shot back.

"How the fuck would I know?"

Amelio shook his head. This conversation was going nowhere. "Keep digging. Talk to the guy at the marina. Maybe he saw something. I have to go."

"Wait." Petrino's voice sounded even more urgent. "I need to know about that other thing. The sale."

Amelio couldn't believe his ears. This guy had the audacity to bring that up now. "What about it?" he asked with disgust. He heard Petrino gulp on the other end.

"If the cocaine job falls through, I won't get paid for the delivery. I need the money. I've waited patiently for a price. When am I going to get it?"

Amelio's temper blew. He screamed into the phone, "You got one hell of a fucking nerve asking me that! With all the other shit going on today, you want to know about your sale. Find out what happened to Morgan, and I'll think about it. But not today. I'm busy. Now earn your fucking keep before you end up like your friend Abromski." Amelio ended the call and closed his eyes, forcing himself to remain calm.

What a shitstorm. What a nightmare. When he felt his breathing back under control, Amelio went back to his guest in the living room. "Ok, sorry about that. So, here are my thoughts about the salvage operation."
******

Amelio dialed Constantine's number on the speaker phone set up on the coffee table. He and Diego sat on the sectional surrounding the phone. Amelio held his breath waiting for Constantine to answer. He hoped and prayed the boss would support this new plan. He also hoped the plan would work. Amelio had doubts about both.

"Hello, Amelio," Constantine's voice boomed through the speaker. "I'm anxious to hear what you have to present."

"Yes, Sir. I feel we have an excellent strategy considering the recent developments. First, I apologize for not having any further updates on the intruders, but we're assuming at least one of them has been rescued and have notified the authorities."

Constantine grumbled at the other end. "Yes. It is wise to make this assumption."

"So, we feel we must act soon. The sooner we can make a salvage attempt, the less chance of being detected. But this will also mean scaling back the scope of the operation." Amelio held his breath. In this circumstance, both greed and time were the enemy. "We have abandoned a multi-day nighttime operation, as that would still be several days away, and time is of the essence here. Diego will have one ship ready by the morning with a crew of nine. We want to collect as much as we can in one day. I will accompany him in the speedboat as an armed escort." Amelio held his breath and hoped this would be sufficient.

"Understood. And how much treasure can you expect to recover in one day?"

Amelio rolled his eyes. Always with the impossible questions. "That, Sir, will depend on what the divers find at the wreck. But we'll have three sets of three divers searching nonstop for the entire time we're there. We're focusing on just the gold. With any luck, it will be a descent haul."

"And if there's a Coast Guard presence stationed there. Are you prepared to eliminate it?"

Now Amelio shook his head. The boss had no respect for any form of government authority. He probably thought Amelio could take on the entire US Navy if needed. "With all due respect, Mr. Constantine, that wouldn't be a wise decision." Amelio glanced up at Diego, who violently shook his head.

"Amelio," Constantine's tone of voice changed from amenable to commanding. "Need I remind you of the imperative nature of your mission. Failure is not an option. You are to take all necessary steps to ensure its success. That includes eliminating any governmental interference." Now his voice rose to shouting. "Am I making myself clear on this?"

Amelio glanced at his guest, who appeared ready to shit himself. He felt the same.

Constantine continued before Amelio could reply. "You already fucked up my cocaine shipment, you fool. You screw this up and you'll lose more than just your commission. Now do your job! I don't want to hear from you again until the end of tomorrow when you tell me how much gold you've recovered. And it better be more than a few coins."

The call abruptly ended. Amelio envisioned his boss slamming the phone down. Now what? His guest remained silent, digesting the implications of the call.

Finally, Diego said, "You hired me to run a salvage operation, Amelio. Not fight a war. What's going to happen if the fucking Navy shows up when my divers are a hundred feet down?"

Amelio rubbed his chin, thinking of a response. His cheek flamed. His mind raced. He stared Diego down and replied. "Then I'll take care of them. You heard Constantine — do your job. I'll do mine. You do yours."

CHAPTER 30

Emmy held her breath as the helicopter set down on the landing pad at Georgetown Memorial Hospital. Dry land never felt so good. During the ten-minute flight from her rescue spot to the hospital, she received the full story of what happened on the surface during her dive. All she could think about was her dad. Would he make it? How bad were his injuries? No one on the chopper could say for sure, but they all gave her hope that David would pull through.

She didn't wait a second after the door opened. Emmy jumped out, now barefoot, wearing only her swimsuit, and raced to the ER entrance. And who was the first person to greet her? That damn sheriff. With all the turmoil of the morning, Emmy hadn't given a moment's thought to how she'd explain herself to the police. She hoped he wouldn't start laying into her. Fortunately, the look on his face was one of empathy and not anger.

"Miss Sweeney, I'm so glad to see you. Are you all right?"

Emmy stared at the sheriff, still trying to determine if he was upset with her. "I'm fine. What about my dad? What have you heard?"

"He's in surgery now. We're told it may be another hour before he's out."

It appeared the sheriff wanted to talk with her some more, but Emmy heard her name called out from behind. Emmy turned and saw her mom running toward her with her arms wide open.

"Emmy, Emmy darling. You're alive! Thank God you're alive."

Emmy opened her arms and allowed the full embrace of her mother, whose words turned into sobs.

"Oh Emmy, oh Emmy," Mom continued to cry.

"I'm sorry, Mom. I'm so sorry. This is all my fault. I messed up," she said, now also crying. The two continued to sob until Emmy broke her embrace and dried her eyes. "The sheriff just told me Dad's in surgery. What have they told you?"

Mom nodded her head as she tried to form words. "They, they said he was shot twice." This led to another bout of sobbing.

Emmy waited patiently for information she didn't already know.

"One in the shoulder, the other in the chest. But I heard from a nurse that he'd survive."

Now Emmy joined her mom in shedding tears of joy. Her dad would survive. They would all live through this day from hell. She didn't know how, but she drew her strength from a newfound faith forged not an hour before, in the ocean, when all seemed lost. She was a survivor. So was dad.

Neil and the Coast Guard crew entered the lobby and joined Emmy and her mom.

"Miss Emmy," said AST Goddard; the Savior, as Emmy would always know him by. "You need to get checked out first before you do anything else. Please follow me."

Emmy appeared helpless and didn't want to leave her mother. Her look told Goddard what she wanted.

"Of course, your mother can come with you."

"I'll stay out here, Emmy," Neil told her. "And wait for you."

"Thanks, Neil. I shouldn't be long." Emmy followed Goddard and a nurse into the main hospital corridor, mom close behind. When she turned back one last time before the door closed, she saw Neil standing there, and right behind him was the sheriff, who was now flanked by several other law enforcement officers. They all watched her enter the corridor. Emmy knew before long they would want answers.

******

After Leroy watched Emmy disappear through the doors, he turned his attention to Neil. He couldn't wait to get to the bottom of what happened out at sea, and this would be his first chance to get the kid's story.

Now, Tony and Special Agent Glasier joined him. Tony had shown Glasier the video of the cocaine pickup and they were all very eager to get Neil's story. Leroy now believed the two events at sea were connected and he wanted answers.

Leroy caught Neil's eye as he stood in the middle of the lobby and went over to him.

"Neil, we're all glad you made it out of your predicament." He could see the unease in Neil's eyes. "You remember Detective Meachem from the other day. This is Special Agent Glasier from the Charleston DEA and Officer in Charge Duval from the Georgetown Coast Guard station. We'd like to get your story of what happened out there. Can you give us a few minutes of your time?"

Neil slowly nodded his head. "Sure, Sheriff." The reluctance was clear in his voice.

"Let's go over here where it's quiet." Leroy pointed to the far end of the lobby. He would have preferred a private meeting room, but didn't have the luxury. Once there, he rearranged some chairs in a circle. Neil and the four officers took seats facing each other.

"Before we begin, Neil, Detective Meacham is going to show you a brief video clip. I want to know if this is the same boat and men that attacked you and Mr. Sweeney."

Tony had the clip called up and showed it to Neil. Leroy watched his expression closely. As soon as Neil saw the speedboat approach Morgan's, his eyes lit up.

"That's them. Oh shit, that's them all right. Where was this taken?"

Leroy took a deep breath. Why do people being questioned always want to ask questions? He ignored it. "Ok, Neil. Take us through what happened. Let's start with why you went out there in the first place."

Leroy saw Neil bite his lip. If he doesn't fess up and admit they were off on some treasure hunt, things would get unpleasant. Neil hesitated some more.

"I'll tell you," he said. "Emmy said she was going to tell you anyway, so I'll tell you now. There's a shipwreck at the site where we were attacked. A Spanish galleon that went down in 1715 in a hurricane. The rest of the fleet sank in Florida, but this one apparently made to South Carolina. The coins there are worth a fortune."

"And how did you find this wreck?" Leroy interrupted. He wanted to keep Neil focused on the information he wanted.

Again, Neil paused. "Emmy and I could determine it was the last place Jack and I fished, a week ago Friday. We suspected Jack was on to it and was searching for it, even though he told me they were just fishing. We were sure Jack had found the wreck and was diving for its treasure on Monday. We, she —," Neil stated emphatically, making sure the cops knew it wasn't his idea, "wanted to find the site first and confirm it. So, we got her dad involved and went out there this morning."

"And you found it."

With tight lips, Neil nodded. "We did. Strange though, there was a buoy at the site of the wreck. We didn't think it through at the time, but the guys who attacked us must have placed it there to mark the location."

"And more than likely, placed a camera on it," Tony broke in. "And when they saw you as an intruder, they went there to intercept you."

Neil pursed his lips and exhaled through his nose. "Hmm. Didn't think of that."

"Ok," said Leroy, holding up a hand, "back up a minute. How did you, or Emmy, suspect Jack had found a shipwreck site that contained treasure? We know Emmy found Jack in his diving suit. What am I missing?"

Again, Neil paused and bit his lip even harder. "I wasn't supposed to say anything. But with what happened, and Emmy told me she'd come to you after this anyway, and um —"

"Spit it out, Neil — and what?" Leroy was reaching the end of his patience.

"It's because of the coin she found."

Leroy's eyes popped wide open. "What? What coin, Neil? This is the first I've heard about any coin being found."

Neil rubbed the back of his neck. His nervousness was palpable. "She found one of the gold coins from the wreck. I mean, when she found it, she didn't know it was from the wreck."

This was news to Leroy and the others. He leaned in towards him. "And when did she find this coin?"

"The day she found Jack. It was on the beach, close to his body."

Leroy slapped his forehead. "Son of a bitch. And she kept that from us. And you did too?" His voice rose with his anger.

Neil buried his head in his hands. Leroy thought he might start crying. "I'm sorry, I'm sorry. I knew we should have told you sooner. But, but —"

Leroy realized his gruff questioning was counterproductive. "It's all right, Neil. We're just glad you all are safe now. So, Emmy has this coin in her possession?"

Neil looked up again. His eyes were red, but he cracked a wry smile. "She does, and now she has two more to add to it."

Leroy couldn't contain his surprise. "Then, I take it she found the wreck on her ill-fated dive? And the treasure as well."

"Yes, Sir. Yes, she did."

"Well," Leroy chuckled. "I can't wait to see what these coins look like."

A voice from behind the men startled Leroy. He turned around and saw Emmy walking toward them.

"You can see them right now, Sheriff." Emmy reached into her pocket and pulled out one of the coins. She was wearing shorts and a T-shirt, the summer clothes that Maureen had brought to the hospital. She also wore a sheepish grin.

Leroy couldn't mask his surprise at the quick change in Emmy's appearance from just minutes earlier. "Miss Sweeney, you look a hundred percent better. Show us what you found."

Emmy handed Leroy the coin. The others crowded around to look at it. After a few seconds, Leroy said, "I believe we have a few things to discuss, Miss Sweeney."

This time Emmy smiled back and replied, "I'm ready."

CHAPTER 31

Sonny Petrino couldn't wait any longer. The events of the past week kept raising his stress level and now he felt maxed out. He cursed his ties to the Constantine organization, regretting ever taking part in it. It had brought him nothing but trouble.

It all started with Dr. Morgan. A simple conversation about fish two years back led to Sonny becoming a cog in the organization's contraband trafficking. Usually drugs, but he never knew what illegal material they were moving. The job was simple. After an alert from Amelio, Morgan would drop off the smuggled goods in a Yeti cooler. Sonny would keep them safe until a series of other traffickers arrived and took their prescribed portions with them. From there, Sonny neither knew nor cared what happened.

The money was good, but not that good. Sonny was in debt from his gambling addiction and was fifty-thousand dollars in the hole when the operation began. Two years later, he was still that much in debt, despite joining Gamblers Anonymous a year ago. His vice was online Blackjack. That, and a lot of football bets.

The fish business was tough. He barely made enough to sustain himself. Between the ever-dwindling supply of quality fish, the competition from the big grocery chains, and the constant haggling with the suppliers over price, Sonny battled his anxiety with gambling, which only led to more depression. If the smuggling operation was uncovered, his exposure to Constantine would lead to much bigger trouble.

Sonny paced back and forth behind the counter of Atlantic Seafood. It was a holiday Saturday and there should have been more customers. But the store was empty, and all Sonny could think about was the financial hole he couldn't seem to dig his way out of. He seethed at Morgan for setting him up, then allowing Amelio to lowball him on the payments for his services. Morgan, a man who couldn't keep from beating himself on the chest, had told him what Amelio paid him for his high-risk rendezvouses. It was ten times what Amelio paid Sonny. And now that his gambling was caught up within the tentacles of the Constantine organization — again by circumstances outside of his control — the meager three grand he made for each delivery went straight to paying Amelio the shark loan level interest rates on his debt.

All that changed six weeks ago, when a Godsend literally fell in his lap. The gold coin from the lost fleet. He told Amelio about it, feeling he'd receive a rich reward. Surely, Sonny felt, if the organization found a hoard of treasure at sea because of his discovery, he'd receive a very generous reward indeed, perhaps even a percentage of the take.

Amelio didn't exactly tell him no, but neither did he make Sonny any promises. Sonny wanted to at least sell the coin after researching its historical value. But he was told by the organization not to put it on the open market. These things were extremely delicate. The cartel always sold their looted shipwrecked treasure on the black market, away from the prying eyes of various legal entities who may have a legitimate claim to them.

So, Sonny waited. When the coin was ready to sell on the black market, he would be compensated. They wouldn't tell him how much he'd earn. That depended on how much other treasure they could extract, among other market variables. But the ballpark estimate Amelio gave him fell far short of what he knew he could make on the open market.

He'd done his homework. Other similar coins from the 1715 Treasure Fleet fetched upwards of fifty thousand dollars each. Sonny salivated how much more a new coin from a previously undiscovered ship might fetch. He guessed twice that much. But listing it on eBay, or some other open marketplace, risked the ire of Amelio, which also meant risking his own life. So, Sonny hesitated. But his patience ran thin.

Now, he had to run this errand for Amelio. Go talk to the dockmaster at Georgetown Landing. See if he could find out what happened to Morgan. Sonny grimaced to himself. Without a payout for holding the cocaine, he wouldn't have the cash needed for his gambling debt payment, due in a week. He became desperate and desperate times called for desperate measures. Sonny put the thought out of his mind the best he could and prepared to head to the marina. He'd have to close the shop for a little while, but he'd be back within the hour.

He also made a mental note to call on Emmy Sweeney. Jack's death hit him hard. Not only was he short on the supply of fish now and for the foreseeable future, but he had a nagging feeling he had somehow played a role in his death. An indirect role, to be sure, but that coin started the ball rolling in a direction he was helpless to stop. Now Jack was dead, and he was still in dire straits. Yes, he needed to make it up to Emmy somehow. He wasn't sure how yet, but he had some ideas that were brewing just below the surface. It would be a way of killing two birds with one stone. Maybe even three or four birds.

******

Sonny cautiously made his way down the Georgetown Landing Marina's main pier. It was his second visit of the day, a couple of hours after the first. Earlier, he hadn't left the parking lot but stayed just long enough to spot Morgan's yacht and his truck. Now he had to venture into the marina and ask questions. Both carried risk.

First, he casually walked past the office and made his way to Morgan's moor. He spent a couple of minutes looking around, then climbed onto the boat and perused inside. Who knew? Maybe somehow the cocaine was still on board, although that was remote. He found nothing out of place, except the Yeti cooler he used for his contraband was nowhere in sight. This wasn't a good sign.

Sonny took a deep breath and did what he had to do. He walked back to the main pier and knocked on the dockmaster's door.

"Come in, it's open."

Sonny opened the door and looked in. A man sat behind a desk with cluttered material all around. Sonny assumed he was the dockmaster in charge of the marina.

"How may I help you?" the man asked.

"Hello. Um, I was supposed to meet with Dr. Morgan this afternoon. He invited me to go sailing with him today."

The man gave him a suspicious look. "And you are?"

Sonny resisted a gulp and stared straight back at the guy. "I'm just a friend."

"A friend, you say?" The man's voice carried suspicion in it far more than it should have. Sonny stood his ground.

"That's right. Do you know where he is?"

The man stood up and walked over to Sonny. The look of suspicion in his eyes told Sonny something was up. "I'd expect by now he's in the Georgetown County jail."

Sonny blinked. He knew he needed to role play and make it sound convincing. "That fucking bastard, he didn't!"

The man's interest piqued. "He didn't what?"

"He got pinched. I told him a thousand times if he kept screwing around with that shit, he'd get caught."

"So, you knew what he was into?"

"Well, I mean, I didn't know for sure. He just talked about it. The man was so full of himself."

Now it appeared the dockmaster was more sympathetic. "That's Morgan all right. So, how do you know him? I haven't seen you around here before."

"We're just friends." Sonny now needed to make a smooth but hasty exit. "We go back to USC Med School. I've been out here a couple times, but it's been a while. Anyway, I got to run. Thanks for the info."

Sonny was about to turn for the door when the dockmaster asked, "And what was your name? The police might be interested in asking you some questions."

Sonny bit his lip as a suitable pseudonym popped in his mind. "Danny Ardovino. I'd be glad to offer whatever help I can. Thanks again." This time, Sonny didn't wait around for more discussion. He opened the door and hurried to the pier, then out to the parking lot. He didn't look back.

******

Once back at the shop, Sonny collapsed in his office chair. He'd put himself in a risky situation and had to lie his way out of it. He was sure the marina's security footage had recorded him. All because of Morgan's hubris and carelessness. Now Morgan stewed in a jail cell. The organization's entire drug running operation on the Southeast coast was in jeopardy, and his own fate hung in the balance. What a fucking day.

He had to call Amelio — one more distasteful task to do. The news would not be good. Morgan's arrest meant the cocaine had been confiscated and the organization was out who knew how many millions. Plus, if Morgan talked, the repercussions could be devastating. If Morgan was smart, he'd stay in jail. The doctor probably wouldn't last two hours on the street.

More important was what would happen to him. Sonny unlocked his desk drawer and pulled out the gold coin. Examining it again, he knew it was his only hope for salvation out of the mess he made for himself. But the risks were enormous, and he wasn't ready to take them quite yet.

Sonny retrieved his burner phone, used only to call Amelio, and made the call.

"What did you find out?" Amelio demanded. So much for pleasantries.

"Morgan is in jail. The cocaine is gone."

"And you know this because?"

"The dockmaster said as much. There were no drugs on the yacht. I had to lie to cover myself."

"And you better have been convincing. I'll call back when I have new instructions for you."

"Amelio, what about the —". Too late. The man who held all the strings had hung up.

CHAPTER 32

Sonny decided not to reopen. His mind tormented over his current dilemma. Guilt and shame tore through his body and corroded his thinking. Amelio would expect another payment in a few days and without the credit from the cocaine operation, he wouldn't be able to come up with the cash. Then there'd be hell to pay. The cartel had very specific ways of dealing with creditors who couldn't come up with payments due. They all involved a great deal of physical pain.

Sonny had reached the end of his rope. The coin was his only salvation, even if it might also end up being his doom. The question was how soon before a sale on the open market would catch the attention of the cartel. Sonny thought through the consequences of such an action. It wasn't only the cartel he had to be concerned about. The listing of such an inimitable item would cause shockwaves throughout the world of rare coin collectors, shipwreck memorabilia, and historians. He'd be an instant celebrity but wouldn't want any of that kind of fame or attention. Maybe he could use a pseudonym and remain anonymous. But sooner or later, he'd be on the cartel's radar. More likely sooner.

So, his plan had to be broader and more permanent. It would mean ending his business and leaving town. And not just Georgetown; he'd have to leave the country, for good. He still had relatives in Italy, around Salerno, where he thought he could disappear forever and avoid being found. The difficulty was hanging around long enough to collect the funds from the auction and then leave the country before the cartel found out. It would have to happen fast — days, not weeks — maybe even hours.

Sonny worked on the auction. He took pics of both sides of the coin and refreshed himself on the history of the lost fleet. It had to be convincing, but not overdone. He thought about hiring someone to do a more polished auction but couldn't think of anyone he knew or trusted. In the end, he thought he had done a pretty nice job. He chose eBay, simply because it had the largest reach, and he knew there were several other coins from the 1715 Treasure Fleet on the website. Then he had to decide on a price. He settled on a starting bid of $75,000. If there were no early bidders, he'd lower it a bit but didn't want to go much lower. He set the auction for forty-eight hours, hoping it wouldn't be too short, but concerned it might still be too long.

He reviewed it again and again, tweaked the description a couple more times. Now it was ready. All he had to do was click to start the auction. But he couldn't do it. It was all so risky. Sonny took a deep breath and went over all his plans again. After the auction ended, he would get paid and ship the coin. Then he'd pack the bare necessities and catch the next flight to Rome. He had a friend who would gladly take over the business, no questions asked. Anybody else who asked what happened would come up without answers.

Then there was Amelio and the cartel. They would, of course, discover what he did and would come after him. But Sonny would leave no trace behind. And his relatives in Italy had connections which would keep him safe. Not exactly like Michael Corleone in The Godfather, but not too dissimilar. But look what happened to him. Sonny shook his head and told himself to snap out of it. That was only a movie.

Something else gnawed at him. He danced around it as he put his plans together, but couldn't confront it — Jack Abromski. Ever since Emmy told him what happened, Sonny felt consumed with guilt. It all began with Jack, and now he was dead. Sure, Jack took it upon himself and put himself in the situation he did. But it wouldn't have happened without Sonny's involvement and that coin. It all came back to that blasted coin.

He had to clear the air with Emmy before he disappeared. He had to tell her the truth. She deserved that much. He knew he could trust her, and he certainly wouldn't tell her where he was going. But it would give him peace of mind to get the whole story off his chest. So, he would contact Emmy and arrange a meeting. Then he'd start the auction. It was the least he could do.

Sonny dialed Emmy's number. Jack had given it to him in case of an emergency. There was no answer, and it went to voice mail. "Emmy, this is Sonny Petrino. I hope everything is well with you. Well, I mean as well as can be expected. Listen, it's very important I see you as soon as possible. There are some things you need to know. About Jack. Please call me when you get this. Thank You."

Not the smoothest message he's ever left, but it got the message across. Sonny looked at his computer screen again and reread the auction listing. It was almost time.

******

Emmy sat in a chair beside her dad's hospital bed, holding his hand, when she heard her phone ring. She didn't recognize the number and let it go to voice mail.

Mom asked, "You're not going to answer that?"

"Shhh," Emmy hissed and listened to the voice message. A concerned look broke out on her face.

"Who's Sonny Petrino?" mom asked.

"He's Jack's primary customer. Owns Atlantic Seafood."

Mom nodded silently. "What do think that's all about?"

"I don't know. I'll call him back in a bit."

Emmy turned her attention to her dad. Two hours had passed since his surgery, and he was still heavily sedated. Emmy had been there for the past hour, ever since that band of law enforcement finished grilling her repeatedly about the morning's escapades. She knew they were being polite and professional, but could tell, just beneath the surface, they were seething at her. Especially that big Black sheriff. But she couldn't blame them. After all, she not only withheld evidence from them, but disregarded his direct order not to go snooping around by herself.

Plus, she agreed to turn the two coins she had found over to them. Lent them, they assured her. However, the final disposition of whether they were hers to keep would probably have to be settled in court. Once word of the shipwreck and its treasure trove got out, there would be an enormous interest in it. But for now, the wreck site and the events of the morning were a crime scene and investigation. Emmy found herself smack dab in the middle of a shitstorm, the likes of which she'd never been a part of.

However, she still had the first coin she found on the beach, safely tucked away in her bedroom drawer. Emmy promised the sheriff she'd turn that coin in as well. Don't worry, he told her. No rush. Just don't go putting it on auction anywhere. Emmy had laughed about that. It never even crossed her mind. On auction, she had asked; you mean like eBay or something? Exactly, she was told. If any of these coins appeared on an open market, it would create an enormous buzz in the rare coin world, not to mention any number of historical societies. And that would be just the beginning. Emmy assured them she'd do no such thing.

Right now, all she wanted to do was go to sleep. But she was determined to wait until her dad woke up. She hadn't seen him since she went in the water. It seemed like ages ago, even though it was only a few hours. Since he and Neil escaped before she surfaced, dad wouldn't even know she was still alive.

Emmy kept holding his hand but felt her eyes getting heavy. Just rest, she told herself. You'll be right here when he wakes up. She must have dosed off. She dreamt about being in the water, helpless, nothing else in sight. Out of nowhere, someone reached out and grabbed her hand. Pulled her to safety. The hand wouldn't let go; it kept squeezing her. Emmy, Emmy, she heard her name in a haze. "Emmy, you're alive."

"Huh?" Emmy woke with a shock. She was still in the hospital, in her chair at her dad's side. When she opened her eyes, she saw dad awake and squeezing her hand. His eyes were full of tears.

"You're alive, Emmy. Thank God, you're alive."

Tears spontaneously burst out of Emmy's eyes. She bent over and gently hugged her dad's face. "Yes, Dad. I am. And so are you." Those were all the words she could muster. Emmy let her tears fall free and continued to press her face to his.

CHAPTER 33

Back at the station, Leonard Barry, the newly minted attorney for Dr. Morgan, waited for Leroy to return from the hospital. Leroy greeted him in the lobby with barely an obligatory handshake. Barry wanted answers, to which he received none. He demanded to see the evidence against his client, which was denied. Then he insisted bail be posted, to which Leroy told him not a freaking chance on a holiday Saturday. The lawyer left the station after a brief visit with his despondent client, finally telling Leroy he'd be back in the morning with an emergency request to the court to post bail. Good luck with that, were Leroy's last words to him.

With Barry disposed of, Leroy turned his attention to the quickly escalating crisis at hand. He reconvened the task force, joining Tony, Special Agent Glasier, and the USCG Georgetown's Officer in Charge, Alex Duval in his office. The four men sat around the rectangular table normally used for interrogations, but also for brainstorming sessions like this. In the hour since finishing the interviews with Neil and Emmy, SA Glasier did some research on their suspects.

"All right," Leroy began, "let's get our heads together and decide what to do about this mess. Doug, bring us up to speed on what you've found out about these guys."

"Gladly, Sheriff. We believe the two men on the speedboat are from the Constantine crime family, out of Colombia. We got a match on the boat from our office in Miami, where they now have their main base. We don't know who the two guys are, but we're betting they're the cartel's Carolina connection. We've been on the lookout for these guys for a while now, suspecting them of running drugs and other contraband from Miami into the Carolinas. This is the first time we've had visual contact with any of them. Congratulations, Sheriff, on the capture of the cocaine shipment. It's quite a haul."

"Thanks. Credit goes to Detective Meacham here. He put the GPS camera on the boat's bow. But what about their ties to this apparent shipwreck off our coast?"

"Your guess is as good as ours, Sheriff. Apparently, they got wind of the wreck and the treasure it holds. Miss Sweeney mentioned something about another coin besides the one she found and kept hidden. I suspect that coin somehow made its way to the cartel. She mentioned Captain Abromski knew about it, as well as this guy at the local restaurant who did the financing for his sonar. Could he have connections to Constantine?"

"I doubt it," answered Leroy. "But we can't rule it out. I know Tom Boswell. He's well respected in the community. Tony, put him on the list to feel out."

"Will do," Tony answered.

"So," Glasier continued, "we can assume the Constantine connection had intel on the coin. And with Morgan's connection to the cartel, that makes the security video from the marina last Monday a probable tipoff to the cartel. And that buoy out there leads me to believe they attached a camera to it as well. They wouldn't need a buoy just to mark the location. Their GPS works as good as ours. But surveillance video would have tipped them off to Sweeney's untimely visit."

"Do we think they think we know about this yet?" Duval asked. "The element of surprise could benefit us here if they don't."

"No," Tony chimed in. "We can't be sure. From what Goodsen told us, the speedboat stayed at the site, presumably waiting on Emmy to surface. They may assume there were no survivors, but they wouldn't be sure, which means they'll have to presume they're alive and told authorities."

"Which would mean what?" asked Duval. "We know they want the treasure badly and are most likely prepared to launch a salvage operation. Most likely sooner rather than later."

"How soon?" asked Leroy. "Are we talking days, weeks?"

"I'd say more like hours," answered Duval. "Certainly not more than a day or two."

"And they'll bring firepower to defend it," said Glasier. "We already know they have automatic weapons and RPG's. We better bring at least as much if we're going to face them off at sea. Do we need to bring the Navy in?"

Leroy glanced over to Duval, who winced. Leroy understood. Nothing irked the Coast Guard more than having the Navy upend their jurisdiction.

"No," Duval stated emphatically. "We can handle whatever they bring. Charleston has two eighty-seven-foot Cutters with 50-caliper cannons on the bow. It can handle any armed speedboat."

The four men sat silent and nodded for a few seconds. Glasier stated, "We need eyes on them, just like they have eyes on us. I say we go out there this afternoon and place our own camera on that buoy."

"That will tell them for sure we know about the site," said Duval. "I thought we wanted the element of surprise."

"We do," countered Glasier. "But it's crucial we know when they're there. We're going on the assumption they know we know."

Leroy could sense this was becoming a war of nerves between the Coast Guard and the DEA. He stayed out of it as much as possible.

"I have a better idea," Duval stated. "We can deploy a surveillance drone from our Charleston Command Center. That way, we'll have eyes on them, but they won't know we're looking."

They all looked at each other. Leroy sensed everyone liked it.

"That would be fantastic." Glasier said. "How soon before you can get it deployed?"

"I'll need clearance from Charleston, and we'll need to let Washington know what's going on. But I don't see an issue considering what we're dealing with here. I'd say we could have a bird in the sky by this evening."

Leroy noted the smiles across the table. This was the good news he had hoped would come out of the meeting. Tony's smile disappeared, replaced by concern.

"I don't know much about these types of drones. Wouldn't you risk detection if they were at the site and saw this thing hanging out over them? What about the noise?"

Duval focused his attention on Tony. "No, Detective, we'll fly the drone to at least fifteen-hundred feet. It would only be a speck in the sky to anyone on the surface. The drone itself is less than two feet in diameter. And they wouldn't hear a thing from the sea surface."

Everyone at the table nodded their approval. Duval continued, "Better yet, the drone has a magnification of 1000X with a two-billion-pixel resolution. At deployment height, you'd see a gnat land on a guy's face. Plus, it's equipped with real time GPS, as well as infrared capacity. Nothing on God's earth could escape its view."

"And once you see them begin their salvage operation," Glasier broke in, "you'll know what assets you'll need to take them down."

"Exactly," stated Duval, smiling. "They won't know what hit them."

Leroy brimmed with confidence at the prospect of this scenario coming to fruition. He couldn't wait to see it happen.

CHAPTER 34

By late Saturday afternoon, Emmy simply wanted to crash, just like she did on Thursday. Was it only two days ago? Seemed like an eternity. After dad woke, she spent another hour with him in the hospital room. Mom would spend the night but encouraged Emmy to go home and rest.

Emmy didn't fight it. There was so much to do tomorrow. She had to make plans at the funeral home. That was supposed to happen today, but obviously didn't. Then, Jack's family was scheduled to arrive by Sunday evening. She certainly wasn't prepared for that to happen. The events of the day had cast a new light on Emmy. Well beyond a feeling of gratitude, it was more spiritual, almost ethereal. She knew it would leave a lasting impression on her. Each day, every day forward would feel like a blessing, a gift, and she was determined to make the most of every day she had left on this earth.

Just before she crashed in the comfort of her bed, a cheerful Sandy by her side, (what would have happened to her precious retriever if she never came home?), Emmy remembered the urgent message from Sonny Petrino. What was that all about? He didn't know what had happened today, and she certainly wasn't in any condition to tell him. But she felt obliged to return his call, and through her fatigue, dialed his number.

Sonny answered on the first ring. "Emmy. Oh, I'm so glad you called back. Is everything all right?"

Emmy closed her eyes and shook her head. All right? How was she supposed to answer that? "Let's just say it's been a long day, Sonny. What is it that's so important?"

"I must see you as soon as possible. It's extremely imperative."

The urgency in his voice was unmistakable. In fact, she'd never heard Sonny so on edge. He was always an easy-going guy in her experience.

"Um, Sonny, I'm afraid I can't today. I'm exhausted after what I've been through. Can you maybe tell me on the phone? Just give me the highlights. Maybe I can see you tomorrow after I get some sleep."

Silence on the other end, then, "Emmy." This came out soft and serious. "Did something happen to you today?"

Alarm bells went off. What is he talking about? What does he know about what happened? Emmy felt a wave of anxiety wash over her. "I'd rather not discuss it now, Sonny. How about I come to see you in the morning? Will your shop be open?"

"Yes," his voice sounded resigned. "Yes, I'll be here. How early can you come?"

Emmy pinched the bridge of her nose. Something was definitely up with this guy. She moved her other tasks from her mind and gave him priority. "I'll be there at nine. Will that work?"

"Yes, thank you, Emmy. I'll look forward to it. I think you will be well served with what I must tell you. Goodbye."

Emmy saw the call end and stared at her phone. Well served? What in blazes could that mean? She looked at a concerned Sandy and told her, "What in the world do you think that's all about, girl?" Didn't matter now. She turned her phone off and was asleep as soon as her head hit the pillow.

******

Amelio continued to stew throughout the afternoon. He knew he was on the hook for both the lost cocaine and the bungled encounter at the wreck site. The cocaine, now in the hands of the authorities, was a lost cause. Now he had to worry about what Morgan may have spilled to them. Amelio knew Morgan would say anything to save his own skin. If that meant selling out the organization, it would be terrible news indeed. Of course, whatever happens, things will end badly for the doctor.

The recent call to Constantine confirmed this. He could almost hear the boss's temper sizzle on the other end of the line. I'll take care of that doctor, he told Amelio. You concentrate on the treasure. Fine with him. Too bad for Morgan.

What Amelio didn't know, which was eating at him, was whether the authorities had discovered the wreck site, which would mean at least some of the intruders survived. There was still a chance they didn't, which would make his task much easier and safer. But even if they had, he still felt his plan would succeed. It would just be more treacherous.

So far, at least, there had been no other vessels at the wreck site. If any of the intruders had survived and told the authorities where it was, Amelio presumed they would have sent a ship of some kind out to investigate. But here it was, now Saturday evening, and no boats had come anywhere close to the site. Could that mean that the authorities haven't been alerted and the intruders all died?

He couldn't stand the uncertainty. Amelio paced his living room, debating his predicament. So much was at stake. The thought of another disappointing call to Constantine didn't sit well with him. Stick with the plan, he finally decided. It's still a good plan. If there weren't any more interruptions, Amelio would have a decent haul of gold in his hands by the end of tomorrow. Then his next call to Constantine will be with brighter news.

Amelio poured himself a double shot of tequila. Once drained, he relaxed some. It had been a horrible day; one of the worst days of his life. But he survived and would live to see tomorrow. And tomorrow would be a better day, a much better day. Of this, he could be certain.

CHAPTER 35

Emmy spent a restless night tossing and turning. Even taking an Ambien, the nightmares came on one after the other. There were episodes of her drowning, being held captive by ruthless pirates, a treasure chest full of gold that seemed always just out of reach. And Jack — she dreamt of Jack again, but this time he seemed angry at her. Why? she asked him. He replied in a ghostlike manner. She shouldn't have come after him.

She woke drenched in sweat at 2:15 AM, feeling drugged and confused. Sandy was there, her soft moans somehow reassuring that her dreams were not in fact reality. Emmy tried to reassure herself it was just a form of post-traumatic stress manifesting itself through her subconscious. Whatever it was, it made her a nervous wreck. She stumbled to the bathroom and drank a glass of water. Then fell right back to sleep.

She woke to the morning sunlight through her curtains at 7:30 AM. A little late for her, but at least her remaining dreams were more normal. Emmy staggered out of bed to make coffee. Then she remembered the cryptic meeting she was supposed to have with Sonny Petrino. Whatever it was all about, she'd soon find out.

At exactly nine o'clock, Emmy knocked on Atlantic Seafood's front door. The sign still said closed, but Sonny was there and opened it immediately.

"Good morning, Emmy. Thank you so much for coming out this early. Come in. Can I get you some coffee?"

"That would be great, Sonny." Emmy entered the vacant shop and looked all around. The counters were empty. She wondered if he was even open on Sundays. "Are you going to be open today?"

"No, no. Not today. Have many things to do," Sonny told her, waving his hands with his back turned. "Here, come back to my office. I have coffee already made."

"Ok, sure." Emmy's curiosity rose further. What many things? she wondered. And what is this news that concerned Jack? She followed Sonny to the back of the shop and glanced around his small, cluttered office. She watched him fumble with the coffee. He certainly appeared to be nervous.

"Cream and sugar?" he asked.

"No, just black. So, Sonny, what's going on? You have me concerned."

Sonny handed Emmy a Styrofoam cup with steaming black coffee. It smelled wonderful. She saw on the counter a bag of some Italian blend coffee. She sat down beside his desk and waited for him to begin. This was not the man she talked with two days before, nor the man she had known for the past three years.

Sonny took a ragged breath. "Emmy, what I must tell you has to remain confidential. Will you promise me this?"

Emmy looked Sonny dead in the eye. She could keep a secret, sure. Now she absolutely needed to find out what this gentle fishmonger had to say. "Of course, Sonny. I'll keep this between you and me. Absolutely."

"Ok, good." Sonny looked around as if someone was outside the door.

Emmy thought, now he's acting paranoid.

He turned his attention back to her. "I am going to admit some things to you. Things that I am ashamed of. Things that are illegal." Sonny paused again.

Emmy stared at him, her eyes burrowing into his. The mention of something illegal put her on edge. He had her undivided attention.

Sonny reached into the top drawer of his desk and removed a small box. "I'm going to show you something nobody has ever seen before. At least, I believe not until this past week." He opened the box and showed Emmy a gold coin. The coin with the Jerusalem Cross on it.

She gasped, her hand shooting to her open mouth. "You have it! You have the second coin!"

He gave her a queer look. Puzzled, he asked, "Second coin? What do you mean?"

Emmy's brain raced at the implication of the second coin. "I'll tell you; I promise. But first, tell me how you have this coin."

Sonny continued to shake his head, showing his confusion. "Are you telling me you have another coin just like this?"

She realized they were talking past each other. Both had important information that the other didn't. And they both wanted answers. She stared at Sonny, still wanting him to go first.

"Emmy, we need to level with each other. Yes, I have important information regarding this coin. If you also know about it, then you must also know about where it came from. Is this true?"

Emmy's heart raced. This meeting would yield far more than she expected. "Yes. Yes, I do. The missing ship of the lost Spanish Treasure Fleet of 1715. It's out there, east of Georgetown, about fifteen miles. I was there yesterday. I dove and found the ship and its treasure. Now, there's much more to talk about what happened yesterday, but I want to know how you have that coin and what did it have to do with Jack?"

She saw the astonishment on his face. She was ready for answers.

"Emmy, I can't believe this. This is — amazing. All right. I'll tell you everything if you promise to tell me the rest of your story as well. We may have a common goal, and a common enemy."

Enemy — the word flashed through Emmy's mind like a knife. She knew exactly who the enemy was — Jack's killer. The same men who attacked the *Fair Allowance* yesterday. "Thank you. I will. I believe you're correct. Go ahead, I'm listening."

He took a deep breath and another sip of coffee. Then rubbed his brow, collecting his thoughts, and began. "It all started with the enormous grouper Jack caught back in July. Remember, the big fish I told you about that Jack and I got in an argument over?"

"I do," but she couldn't imagine what that had to do with the coin.

"Yes, well, we agreed on the price and the fish sold very well. But it wasn't the fish that was so valuable. It was what I found *inside* the fish. You see, when I cleaned this monster, after Jack had left, I removed a huge amount of inner organs. They get tossed into a chum barrel, which I usually sell back to the fishermen for chum bait. I remember thinking this amount of guts would fill the entire chum barrel by itself. I grabbed one fistful. It must have been its stomach and felt something hard. Very unusual, although occasionally a large fish will eat something it shouldn't, something hard, like a shell or piece of garbage. But this felt different. It was smooth and round. So, I dug it out of its guts, and low and behold, it was a gold coin. This coin here."

Emmy's mouth gaped open, and her eyes popped straight out upon hearing this. So that's how this whole thing started. But she knew there was much more to the story. She nodded silently and let him continue.

"I was quite shocked, as you could imagine. I went online and did some research. That's when I made the connection to the 1715 Treasure

Fleet. The fleet went down off the coast of Florida, but three of the ships were never accounted for. Did you know this much?"

"Yes, I did." She sat on the edge of her seat, waiting to hear how this connected to Jack.

"So," he bit his lip and paused. "This is where I am going to level with you. And tell you about my connection with the drug runners. You see, it started with my gambling addiction. I got in over my head and was deep in debt to these people. So, to avoid some very unpleasant consequences, I agreed to act as a front to their smuggling operations. They would bring drugs up the east coast, then a contact would rendezvous at sea and bring the drugs in, then I would store them until their other distributors picked it up. It was a very low risk for me, and it kept me afloat. But I couldn't get ahead and eventually realized I was nothing but a ploy for them.

Then, when I found this coin and saw how valuable it was, my first instinct was to list it and sell it. I confided in my contacts with this organization. I knew they also ran ill-gotten treasure on the black market. If they could somehow find this shipwreck, I thought I might get a slice of the profits. They promised me this. Of course, they promised me many things that didn't come to pass. But somehow the wreck had to be located.

You must understand, Emmy, I was desperate to get out from under them. The connection was Jack. Jack caught the fish that had swallowed the coin. If he could search the area he fished in that day, he might find the wreck. So, I showed him the coin and the story behind it. He was hooked, as we say, the coin being quite tempting bait. But I didn't tell him about the organization.

After a couple days, Jack told me he would need more sophisticated sonar to do that kind of search. If he found something, he could dive for it. So, I lent him the coin so he could get financing for this sonar. When he got the loan, he returned the coin to me and promised to let me know if he found anything.

Then, a week ago, Friday, he came in all excited. Said he found the wreck and was planning to dive for it on Monday. So, so —"

Emmy couldn't believe what she was hearing. The pieces were coming together — and she knew they'd lead to an ending that would make her sick. "So, you told them, didn't you? These drug running criminals. You told them about what Jack had found."

"Yes, I did."

Emmy sat still, trying to fathom the implications of what Sonny had just told her. It was devastating. Her eyes narrowed. Her feelings were ambivalent. She despised Sonny for his involvement in what led to Jack's murder. But she was thankful for his forthcoming and honesty. There was still more to find out. "Now, let me ask you this. Does a certain Dr. Paul Morgan have anything to do with this?"

This time, Sonny gasped. "You know him? What do you know about him?"

"Yes, I know about him. I know he followed the *Sunny Daze* out from the marina last Monday. How is he connected to you?"

Sonny paused.

She saw his reluctance, but it was way too late to be withholding information. "Come on, Sonny. We're being honest with each other here. I want the whole story. Then I'll tell you the rest of mine."

Sonny hung his head. "Yes, he's connected. He was the middleman with the cartel. He would take the drugs at the rendezvous point and bring them to me. I didn't know he had tailed Jack. But it makes sense. The cartel knew about the wreck. They must have put Morgan up to tail Jack out of the bay. I'm so sorry all of this happened."

She continued to put the pieces together. "He was following us out of the bay yesterday morning as well, but went southeast instead. I wonder what he was doing then?"

"Humph," he grunted. "He picked up a load of cocaine. That's what he was doing. But he didn't show up here. He got caught. The dockmaster at the marina confirmed this to me. The bastard's behind bars now. I tell you, Emmy. I am done with all this. I'm selling my coin on auction and then I intend to disappear. Now you know the complete story. Please tell me yours. Let's start with how you found your coin."

Emmy stood up and dumped her cup in the trash. This was all so incredible. Sonny knew who had killed Jack. Undoubtably, they were the same people who had attacked the *Fair Allowance*. They want anyone with knowledge about the wreck and the treasure dead. That's why they tried to kill her dad and Neil; and would have certainly killed her as well. It was her turn now. She promised Sonny she would tell her story after he told hers. She owed him that much.

"Yes, so, let's start with the hurricane." Emmy sat back down and told him everything. The post hurricane inspection, finding the coin on the beach, then finding Jack. She told him about her visit to the Rice Museum, then Tim at Coastal Catch where she learned about this second coin. Then the ill-fated plan to find the wreck with her dad's and Neil's help.

Sonny sat and listened, nodding his understanding. But when she mentioned sailing to the wreck site, she noticed his heightened agitation.

"And you found it? You found the shipwreck!"

"Yes, we did. There was a buoy at the site, which we found odd. I dove and found the wreck and took a couple of these same gold coins. But when I about to surface, I noticed the hull on the surface was not the *Fair Allowance*, but some kind of speedboat." Emmy continued the story of her ordeal, and what had happened to her dad and Neil.

Sonny sat, mesmerized by the account. Emmy could also tell his anger grew when it became clear the criminal organization he was a part of was responsible for not only Jack's death, but the attempted murder of herself, Neil, and dad.

When she finished, she told him, "So, you can help the police bring these murderers to justice. Right?"

He froze, the fear clear in his eyes. "No! No, I can't."

"What do you mean you can't'? You have to."

He stood and paced the office, shaking his head. "Emmy, don't you see? I'm complicit. If I tell them about Constantine, they will put me away. I'll never be free. I'll either be in jail, or if I'm on the street, I'd be as good as dead."

Emmy's tempered flared. "Well, we can't just keep this to ourselves! The police must know who's behind all this. If you don't tell them, I will."

"You'll do no such thing," he declared, the anger exploding out of him. "You promised this information would stay confidential. You promised me, Emmy."

She swallowed and tried to find some way out of this dilemma. She did promise her silence, but she had to find a way to bring justice for what was done. "Then," she finally said, her voice calmed down, "what do you intend to do?"

"I have an idea. But I'll need your help."

Emmy pursed her lips, but she listened to him. She listened to a man with as much intent for revenge as she had. His plan had plenty of risk, for both of them, but in the end, she felt it would work. Sonny would get his revenge and disappear to wherever he wanted. Emmy would receive justice as well. The only question was whether she would live through it. After what she went through yesterday, she felt she was, in some way, living on borrowed time. How much time she had to borrow was anyone's guess.

CHAPTER 36

After bidding Emmy goodbye, Sonny went back on his computer and called up the eBay auction. Emmy's revelation of the despicable actions of Amelio and his gang was his last straw. With the new plans, he couldn't wait two more days for an auction to play out. Even if he took out Amelio today, he knew Constantine would soon find out and be after him with another one of his thugs.

So, as part of his revised action plan, he'd change the auction to a twenty-four-time limit. He may not get the full value of the coin, but it was a risk / reward situation. And his life was worth more than the few thousand extra dollars he might have received from a longer auction. Plus, a longer auction may draw the attention of other less desirable elements — like law enforcement. They were to be avoided at all costs.

Sonny edited the auction to reflect the shortened time frame. He also lowered the starting bid to $50,000. Verified payment would need to be received within six hours and the coin would ship via FedEx immediately thereafter. If all went according to plan, he'd have his funds transferred to a safe clandestine account his uncle had set up in Salerno by Monday night. Once he shipped the coin, he'd drive to Atlanta and catch a direct flight to Rome on Monday morning. The only person he planned to see between now and then was Emmy, and of course Amelio. But his time with Amelio would only last a few seconds — the time it would take to shoot him dead.

Sonny had his edits finished and reviewed the draft one last time. He stared at the screen, the arrow of his mouse hovering over the start auction button. Everything would change once he clicked. There was no turning back. News of the treasure from the missing ship of the lost fleet would soon flood the rare coin world. It was an act of defiance to the organization. But it was an act of survival for Sonny. He took one last deep breath and clicked to begin the auction.

******

Tony spent some time on Saturday afternoon with Glasier and learned more background on the DEA's struggle to stop the flow of cocaine into the Carolinas. Back in June, they pinched a dude hauling a batch of coke driving north on Highway 521 just outside of Georgetown. The following day, after the guy somehow made an obscenely high bail, they found him with his throat cut in the woods outside of McClellanville. This convinced the DEA that a major cartel was operating somewhere in the Georgetown area.

DEA had been working with the Coast Guard, who had been on alert for suspicious marine vessels since that event, but without success. They figured there was a rendezvous system in place outside of the twelve-mile territorial limit. Any recreational boat could have brought drugs into port without raising suspicion. Now, with Morgan in custody and a whole shitload of cocaine chilling under the sheriff's lock and key, their suspicion was confirmed. But shipwrecked treasure? Now that's a different story

Back at home that evening, Tony set about researching rare coin auction sites. He knew eBay was the largest general auction website by far. His search found one main site for rare coins — The Heritage Foundation. He figured if anyone from the other side wanted to sell any of the coins they may have encountered, and didn't go straight to a black-market site, it would be one of these two websites. After learning the history of this ship, there was no telling how high a price one of those coins might fetch. He knew it was a long shot. Crime organizations of this magnitude as a norm don't expose themselves on public auction sites. Tony didn't want any stone left unturned.

He searched on the two websites for anything related to the 1715 Treasure Fleet. Each site had several auctions of coins and other relics which came from the fleet, all of them found off the coast of Florida. The prices were pretty eye-popping, with the best-preserved gold coins topping $50,000. Should one of the coins from the new wreck site show up, Tony was sure there'd be a huge interest, coming from a previously unknown shipwreck. The auction would also display the 713 date, confirming the uniqueness of the coin.

He retired for the night. It had been an eventful day. For now, he had the rest of the holiday weekend off, but Tony had a feeling it wouldn't stay that way. He had a hunch somebody from the cartel would make a move soon. Then the sparks will really fly.

******

It didn't take long. Tony enjoyed sleeping in on Sunday morning. When he finally got out of bed, it was almost ten. He checked the two auction sites, and low and behold, he hit pay dirt. A new auction on eBay. Two pics, the front and back of the new coin, 713 clearly visible, with a proud declaration of the first find of a new wreck site, presumably the *Concepcion* ship from the 1715 Treasure Fleet. The auction started at $50,000 and would only list for twenty-four hours. It was just posted twenty minutes ago. Tony's hair bristled on the back of his neck. Here was the chance to nail these goons right out of the gate.

Excitement surged through him as he thought about what needed to be done. It was straightforward. He needed the IP address of the auction. From there, he'd know what computer the listing came from, and he'd pay the unsuspecting auctioneer a visit, assuming it was local. Tony felt sure it would be — but one step at a time.

He called Calvin Nash, the department's IT guy, and gave him the information from the auction. Calvin said he'd get right on it and call Tony back when he had the address. Tony ended the call and placed a call to Leroy. So much for a relaxing Sunday off. This would be so much better.

******

The IP address came back local all right. Right under their noses, in fact. Twenty minutes after calling the sheriff, Calvin called back and told Tony the computer used for the auction was located at 37 Meeting Street in Georgetown. Tony did a quick check and found it to be Atlantic Seafood. He thought, now why would a fish market be placing such a valuable and suspicious auction? He called Leroy back.

"Sheriff, got the lowdown on the IP address. Right here in Georgetown — Atlantic Seafood, on Meeting Street. You familiar with the place?"

"Really? No, well, let me think. Yes, I've been there a time or two. Some burly Italian guy runs it."

"All right. Let me track down the name. I'll meet you there in, say, twenty minutes."

"Works for me," answered Leroy. "Good work, Tony. Something here sure smells fishy."

Tony rolled his eyes at the lame pun. That was something he would have come up with. Touche for the sheriff. "Gotcha."

******

Tony pulled into the small parking lot and found Leroy waiting on him.

"What'd you find out?" Leroy asked.

"Owner's name is Sonny Petrino. Sole owner. Been in business five years."

The two walked up to the front door and saw the sign saying closed. Not surprising for a Sunday. Except when they saw the normal business hours sign showing Atlantic Seafood was open seven days a week, starting at 9:00 AM each day. It was 10:45 AM.

"Our guy sleeping in this morning?" Tony asked, not expecting an answer.

"Maybe. But I'm sure he's watching his auctions from somewhere."

"Got a home address?"

"I do. It's on Merriman Road, on the north side of town."

"Well, let's see if our fishmonger is at home."

As the two walked back to their vehicles, Tony said, "Have you made the connection yet?"

Leroy squinted and frowned. "No, what connection?"

"A fresh seafood market. Where do you think he gets his fish from?"

Tony saw the light come on in the sheriff's head.

"I'd say from the local commercial fishermen. And he just recently lost a supplier, didn't he?"

"He did." Tony now sported a wide grin. "A supplier who also presumably had his hands on a rare gold coin."

"Bingo!" said Leroy, pointing to his detective. "Let's find this guy and get to the bottom of it."

CHAPTER 37

Constantine's patience, never a deep reservoir to begin with, had run down to a trickle. His two Carolina projects; the long running successful drug running operation, which Amelio had managed for years, and now the enormous potential treasure of the *Concepcion*, were both in jeopardy. Yesterday was a bad day. One of the worst the cartel's leader had had in a very long time. First, the news of the missing cocaine shipment. Then, he's informed by Amelio of the intruders at the shipwreck site.

Amelio had all day to find out what happened and fix it. Instead, Constantine learned that the drug running middleman, Morgan, had been caught, making the cocaine a lost cause. On top of that, the intruders could not be confirmed dead, and it could not be determined if they had found the treasure. But Amelio had confidence that none of the intruders survived. What about law enforcement? What would they know at this point? Amelio felt sure they were out searching for the intruders yesterday afternoon and had come up empty. Had they found the intruders, then they'd be aware of the location of the wreck site and would have gone out there and found the buoy. But no one had. To Amelio, that meant no survivors and no one else knew about the wreck site.

Constantine felt less certain and demanded the salvage operation continue without delay. He had ended his call with Amelio with yet one more threat. Recover the treasure or else. Amelio understood what 'or else' meant.

There was another task that needed to be done. One of which only he could do. It involved a contact Constantine used only when absolutely necessary. Morgan's carelessness presented such a situation. And the undertaking needed to be done as soon as possible. Constantine wasn't sure how long Morgan would stay behind bars. It was a holiday weekend, and that probably meant Morgan couldn't get out on bail before Tuesday. But Constantine knew Morgan was a very wealthy man, and money talked, regardless of the situation. Lawyers could be had, and judges could be bought.

One thing he knew for certain; as soon as Morgan got out on bail, he'd hop in his yacht and head straight out to sea. Didn't matter if he had a restraining order, an ankle monitoring bracelet, or whatever. Fleeing the law was nothing compared to escaping what Morgan surely knew would come from the organization. That was why Constantine had to act first. He dialed the secure line he used for only these matters. The man was known by very few and went by the pseudonym Estallido — Spanish for big bang.

"What is it?" Estallido answered. Pleasantries were unnecessary.

"I have an urgent need. I need this taken care of today."

"Where is it?"

"Georgetown Landing Marina, Georgetown, South Carolina. A yacht named *Doctors Orders*."

"Hmm, a yacht, yes. How big?"

"Good size. Maybe fifty feet."

A pause on the other end of the line. "You will provide transport, yes?"

Constantine rolled his eyes and thought, no, you idiot, I expect you to walk. "Of course. A plane and a pilot will be waiting at my airstrip. There's an airport just outside of Georgetown. It's only a few miles from the marina. A car will be waiting."

Another pause. "A moving target, yes? You wish to have this done with him on board?"

"Of course. But make sure he's out of the bay first."

"Sunk or total destruction?"

Constantine grinned widely. "For this asshole, total destruction. Nothing but little pieces on the bottom of the ocean."

More pausing. "You know my fee for this kind of job."

More eye rolling. "Of course. Cash. Half before you leave, half when the boat is gone."

"Very well then. I will handle it."

"How soon can you get here?" Constantine's breathing heaved. He hated waiting for anything.

"It's ten o'clock now. I'll be there by noon."

Sooner would have been better, but he'd live with it. "Everything will be ready. Goodbye."

After ending the call, Constantine sat back on his deep cushioned leather sofa. With the Morgan problem put to bed, he focused on the other hot button issue, the status of the salvage operation. He hoped it was already underway. Just as he was about to call Amelio, Roberto, one of his in-house servants, and an otherwise useful gopher, burst into the living room.

"Excuse me for the interruption, Mr. Constantine, but I think you need to see this."

Roberto rushed over and handed Constantine his phone. It had a picture of a gold coin with a Jerusalem cross. Scrolling upwards, he could see it was an auction for the coin — on eBay. A quick read confirmed his worst fear. Someone had put a coin from the *Concepcion* wreckage on a public auction. Constantine seethed as the implication of such an action set in.

He had given Amelio explicit instructions that none of the treasure from the *Concepcion* was to be put on a public auction. It would ruin the entire plan, exposing the discovery to the public, even catching the attention of law enforcement. He had already set up channels with his black-market connections to sell the coins from the salvage operation. Now it was all in jeopardy. His patience with Amelio had run out.

"How long has this auction been out?" he demanded.

"Just an hour, Sir. I've been checking the public auction sites each morning, as you instructed."

"Then who posted this?"

"I don't know, Sir. I'd have to run a trace on it."

Constantine glared at Roberto. He could feel his temper about to explode. "Well, don't just stand there, you idiot. Find out who posted this!"

"Yes, Sir. I'll let you know as soon as I find out." Roberto turned and made a hasty retreat.

Constantine stood and made his way over to the bar. A little early to start the tequila, but he needed something to calm his nerves. There were very few possibilities as to who may have posted the coin. Amelio had the coins from Abromski, and Petrino, the fishmonger, had the initial coin found. The only other option was if somebody else had found the coins; like one of yesterday's intruders. But Amelio assured him there were no survivors. What he needed was answers; answers, followed by retribution.

He dialed Amelio's burner phone number. It was answered on the second ring.

"Yes, Mr. Constantine. What is it?"

"What are you doing now?"

"I'm about to head out to the wreckage site and begin the salvage operation."

Constantine sensed the irritability in Amelio's voice. "That's good. But I have another problem that just came up. Somebody posted a coin from the *Concepcion* on eBay." The tone of his voice left no doubt regarding his irritation. He could hear Amelio gulp.

"That's impossible, Sir. There's no way —"

"I'm looking at the *fucking* auction right now, you imbecile. I want to know who posted it!"

"I can assure you, Mr. Constantine, I did not post the coins in my possession. It must have been Petrino. But he gave me his assurances, and he knew the consequence of such an action."

"What about the intruders from yesterday? At least one may have survived with a coin."

"I highly doubt that, Sir."

"Amelio!" Constantine screamed into the phone. "I've had it with your assurances. You have fucked up every part of this operation as well as our drug running operation. I'm out three million dollars of cocaine. Now the whole marketing of the *Concepcion's* treasure is in danger. All because of your incompetency."

"Sir, it must be Petrino. He called yesterday asking about his coin. He needs cash bad. I'll take care of him, Mr. Constantine, I promise."

"This is your last chance, Amelio. I expect by the end of the day you will have recovered at least some of the treasure. And I want Petrino found and eliminated, and his auction shut down. Don't disappoint me again, Amelio. Don't!"

Constantine hung up on Amelio and downed his shot of tequila. He went to the bay windows overlooking the eastern edge of the Everglades. Dark clouds were building over the swamp, with thunderstorms sure to follow. It fit his mood perfectly. If Amelio failed again, there'd be a storm the likes he'd never seen before. In some respects, it was already raining.

CHAPTER 38

Amelio finished gathering the things he needed for the salvage operation and headed out to the boat garage, cursing the entire way. Immediately after the latest disastrous call from Constantine had ended, he called Petrino's number. No one answered. That, in and of itself, convinced him of Petrino's complicity and guilt. He'd been told many times to keep the burner phone provided to him on and available 24/7. Amelio, like his boss, did not leave voice mails.

So then, he concluded that Sonny Petrino had violated a cardinal rule of the organization. Two rules, in fact. Amelio could only presume the man's gambling debts had gotten the better of him. Still, he couldn't believe Petrino would be so brazen as to put the coin, his only leverage, out there in the open and expect to get away with it. He wouldn't, of course. As soon as the salvage operation was under control, he'd track Sonny down and that would be the end of him.

Amelio packed a cooler of refreshments; soft drinks, sandwiches, and some beer for Diego's crew once the mission completed. Diego had left Charleston an hour earlier by boat and should soon be at the wreck site. He had a crew of nine divers and a mate. The plan was to get as much of the gold treasure as possible that day by tag-teaming his divers into three sets of three. Diego figured with these resources, there'd be nonstop exploration throughout the day and night. He also carried enough arms and ammunition to ward off any other nosy treasure seekers. He had his own machine gun, his FN-57, and another RPG — if worse came to worse. The only genuine concern was whether the Coast Guard got involved. That could make matters quite delicate.

In just over forty-five minutes, Amelio arrived at the wreck site. Diego's boat was already there, and the first three divers were almost ready. He anchored and hopped on to Diego's deck.

"Any trouble this morning?" Amelio asked.

"None," answered Diego. "Are you expecting any?"

Amelio gazed out to sea. Ever since he first came to this place not quite a week ago, it had brought nothing but trouble. Five people killed, including his friend and loyal assistant. His own cheek still throbbed from the pellet he removed. "With God's grace, there will be no more."

Amelio watched as the three divers prepared to go under. Each carried a bag with them. With any luck, in less than an hour, the first real treasure haul will come to the surface. Yes, there were other problems he had to contend with, but for the first time since this all began, Amelio expected to soon see some tangible results.

What he didn't see, nearly undetectable fifteen-hundred feet above them, was a Coast Guard drone capturing everything they were doing.

******

On the viewing end of the drone, Lieutenant Liz Coleman, on duty since seven that morning, jumped with excitement when Diego's rig came into view. She called over to Captain Russell Donovan, the commanding officer at the USCG Command Center in Charleston, who was on the lookout, anticipating just such an encounter. The two watched with interest.

"Do you recognize them, Sir?"

"No, it's definitely not the speedboat they described yesterday. My guess is it's the boat they're going to use for their salvage operation. Let's see who else may show up."

Ten minutes later, Amelio's speedboat came into view.

"Is that the speedboat you mentioned, Sir?"

Donovan glared at the monitor and grinned. "I believe it is." He turned his two-way radio on. "Lieutenant Stark. Are you there?"

"Roger," came the immediate reply. Lieutenant John Stark piloted one of two cutters the Coast Guard kept at the Charleston base. After the alert went out yesterday afternoon and the drone was deployed, all Coast Guard personnel in Georgetown and Charleston were ready to respond at a moment's notice.

"We have two bogies at the shipwreck site. I want two manned and armed response boats ready to leave ASAP."

"Roger that, Sir," came the reply. "I'll let you know as soon as we hit the water."

Donovan ended the radio call and focused back on the drone monitor. "Let's get a closer look Lieutenant,"

"Yes, Sir." Coleman ramped up the magnification and zoomed in on the two boats. It appeared the guy on the speedboat had tied off to the larger vessel. In another couple minutes, he was onboard and gathering the other men together.

"A lot of activity on deck, Sir. Looks like they're getting together for some kind of meeting."

Donovan counted ten men, plus the one from the speedboat. Sitting ducks, he smiled at the picture on the monitor. They're just like sitting ducks.

******

Amelio felt confident enough to share a beer with Diego. The first set of three divers were now at the bottom, hopefully stuffing their bags full of gold coins and bars. The anticipation of seeing large quantities of gold made him giddy with excitement. Just as he took his first swig, the cold brew washing down his throat, his satellite phone rang. Amelio pulled it out and saw the call came from Petrino. He chuckled and wondered why the idiot would call him. Would he really be dumb enough to call and tell him about the auction?

"Sonny, I was just thinking about you this morning. Why are you calling me?"

"We have a situation," came the answer. Petrino's voice sounded dead serious.

"That we do, my friend. That we do. But perhaps you should enlighten me as to your particular situation."

"We need to meet. In McClellanville. I have the girl. The one who went diving yesterday."

When he heard this, Amelio choked, then spit the beer out of his mouth. The girl? Just that information alone sent a chill down his spine. Petrino had his attention now. Amelio had a sinking feeling there would be more unappetizing news as well. "What are you talking about?"

"You know very well what I'm talking about. But she's safe, with me. I'm at your McClellanville home. At the gate. Where are you?"

Amelio tried without success to put together in his mind what was happening. Let him talk, he thought. Find out what's going on. "I'm indisposed now. I'm not at home. But you have my attention, my friend. Tell me what you have to say. Tell me what you want." Amelio pulled out his iPhone and connected it to the security camera app at his home. There was Petrino, at the front gate. And he had a woman with him — gagged, with her arms tied behind her back. This was quite interesting.

"I want you home as soon as you can," Petrino continued. "The girl is the only one who knows what happened at the wreck site yesterday."

"Then they rescued her. What about the two men?"

"No, Amelio, she wasn't rescued. The two men are dead. Their boat you blew up sank and they were not rescued. Miss Sweeney came up from her dive and swam to shore. She barely made it."

Amelio shook his head. This made no sense. "You're lying. She was fifteen miles out at sea. Someone had to have rescued her and informed the authorities. What are you up to?"

"No, Amelio, I'm telling you, she swam. She had flippers, and the current helped her. This is what she told me. But she made the mistake of coming straight to me. Because of the coin, Amelio. She found the wreckage and brought two coins back with her. She knew about the first coin, the one I found. Abromski was her fiancée, Amelio. He must have told her. That's why she was out yesterday looking for it. But she was a fool to trust me. Now I have her as hostage."

Amelio listened but had a hard time believing it. "You're feeding me bullshit, Petrino. Now, tell me what you want from me."

"A fair trade. That is all I'm asking. I know you have thirty thousand dollars in cash, the money you were going to give to Morgan. But Morgan's in jail and your drug running operation is busted. I want that thirty K and you can have the girl. No one else alive knows about the treasure, Amelio. Except Miss Sweeney. You can have her. Give me the money and I will disappear. All your secrets are safe. But if you don't agree with this, I will turn the girl loose and she will go to the police."

Amelio found it difficult to swallow the story. If this woman had somehow made it to shore, then perhaps the tale was plausible. Abromski's fiancée; that much he knew. And could she have gone to Petrino before the cops? If the authorities knew about the wreck site, they would have searched the area thoroughly. But the buoy cameras showed no visitors, and the site was clear this morning. But here was this woman, apparently held hostage by Petrino, at his front gate. He couldn't deny that. Amelio continued to stare at the security footage at the gate in one hand while he held his Sat phone with the other. For a minute, he was lost for words.

"Amelio, are you still there?" asked Petrino.

"Yes, yes." Amelio snapped out of his trance. "Ok, then. I'll agree to your terms. The cash that was meant for Morgan in exchange for this woman. I can be there within the hour."

"Very well, my friend. It is a wise choice. Can you let us in your home? We will wait for you to return."

"Yes, certainly." Amelio played along. He made several selections in his home security app and saw the front gate open. After the two entered, he closed the gate and locked it behind them. Now they wouldn't be going anywhere. Anywhere alive that is.

"Thank you, Amelio. We shall wait for you in your living room."

Amelio took a deep breath. "Have a snack, my friend. Help yourself. Anything you wish. I'll be there as soon as I can." He ended the call. Yes, eat well, you asshole. For it will be your last meal.

CHAPTER 39

Once inside Amelio's home, Sonny untied Emmy and removed her gag. He moved around, inspecting the place for hidden cameras

"Are you sure this is going to work?" Emmy asked. "He didn't sound too convinced."

"It will work. Trust me."

Once untied, Emmy walked around the spacious living area. "So, this is how drug dealers live. How is it no one ever found out about him here?"

"Amelio spends most of his time in Miami working for the organization. It's only when there are shipments coming into the Carolinas that he spends time here. The discovery of the *Concepcion* played right into his hand."

"Do you think he's out there now? Diving for the treasure?"

"I would suspect so. I don't know where else he would be."

"Then he'll be caught out there, won't he. I mean, I don't know what the Coast Guard or the police are doing, but they know the location. Then they'll catch him out there, won't they? Then there's nothing else to do here. Right?"

"If they do, then we will move on. Our separate ways."

Emmy thought about her situation some more. Was it a mistake coming out here with Sonny, a confessed associate with this crime organization? It seemed to be against her better judgment, something she certainly lacked the past few days. It kept coming back to justice for Jack, as well as Neil and her dad. No one else knew about this Amelio character. She didn't know if the Coast Guard or anyone else would catch him. If this plan didn't work, then justice may never be served. But, she had to admit, as gruesome as it was, she'd love nothing better than to see Jack's murderer shot dead in his own home.

"What about getting out of here?" Emmy asked, thinking the entire process through. "Assuming he doesn't shoot you first. I'm sure he locked that gate again, and only he can open it."

Sonny shook off her concern. "Once he's dead, I can open the gate from his phone. But even if I can't, I know a secret way out."

Emmy rolled her eyes. Of course you do. "You're kidding, right?"

"Oh no. The time Amelio invited me to a party last year, he showed it to us. Over here." Emmy followed Sonny from the living room into the master bedroom. In the corner, he lifted a throw rug, and there was a trapdoor underneath.

"Where does it lead?" she asked.

"Not sure. Somewhere outside the property. That's what he told us. He said they'd never capture him here, even if they found him."

Emmy watched Sonny open the trapdoor. There was a steep staircase that appeared to lead down into an underground tunnel of some kind. She looked at Sonny, grinning back at her. She had to give him credit. He knew far more than she would have imagined. Then she pondered this guy, Amelio, the source of all her troubles. Jack's presumed killer. He would have killed her had she not trusted her instincts and stayed below the surface at his boat yesterday. He'd never be captured here, according to Sonny. But will he be killed here? Or would this turn out to be a set up that will get Sonny killed? And her as well.

******

Amelio debated how long he should keep Petrino waiting. There really wasn't any rush. His uninvited guests weren't going anywhere. The story he fed him gnawed at his mind. How much of it was true, or not? Who exactly is this girl, Emmy Sweeney, Abromski's fiancée, who had caused much of the trouble he currently faced? He had no reason to believe she *wasn't* the girl who went diving yesterday. But to have actually swum to shore? He simply couldn't buy into that.

Still, if she was indeed rescued, and told the authorities, why would Petrino be holding her hostage? And why wasn't the Coast Guard out here patrolling the area? Amelio shook off the unknown and focused on what he knew. The treasure — now within his grasp.

"How soon before the divers surface?" he asked Diego. Amelio's patience, as usual, wore thin. But this time there was an added layer to his annoyance. A sinking feeling that all was not as it seemed.

"Perhaps ten to fifteen more minutes," Diego answered.

Amelio looked at the sky. Wouldn't it just be something if there were a drone up there spying on them? He saw nothing, but didn't look long, for his attention was diverted by a sound coming out of the southwest.

When he looked in that direction, he couldn't believe his eyes. Off in the distance, perhaps five miles out, were two vessels heading his way. For an instant, he froze, but quickly regained his senses and reached for his set of binoculars. What he saw confirmed his worst fears. Two unmistakable Coast Guard cutters were moving in his direction. They would be here in minutes. Amelio panicked.

"Get those divers up here now," he demanded of Diego. "We're going to have company. Bad company." He pointed to the two ships.

"Oh, shit!" screamed Diego. He turned and faced Amelio. "I can't communicate with my divers. You know that. You told me we were clear of suspicion. Why did you say that?" Diego paced the deck, consumed by panic.

Amelio wasn't interested in answering any why questions. He had plenty of his own. For an instant, he faced a monumental decision to fight or flee. Fleeing meant a certain forfeit of the entire treasure. As unpalatable as that seemed, fighting would mean either death or capture. Even with the firepower he had on board, he knew it would be no match against two armed Coast Guard vessels. And even if he could disable the vessels, there was no way to escape. Hell, he'd probably face a Navy helicopter gunship before he made it halfway back. The answer was simple. Get the hell out; Diego and the treasure be damned.

He had one advantage: that of speed. Amelio figured he could out flank, then easily out run either vessel headed his way. Sure, they'd follow him. But a new plan quickly blossomed in his mind. Get back to McClellanville, dispose of Petrino, then take the Sweeney girl hostage. He'd escape either by boat or car, depending on circumstances.

"You're on your own, Diego. My apologies." Amelio jumped from Diego's boat to his own and quickly untied the line securing the two boats. Then he fired up the engine. "Adios!" he called back as the engine drowned out Diego's cursing. The last thing Amelio saw of his bungled salvage operation was Diego shaking his fist at him.

Amelio headed to the east, ninety degrees away from the approaching Coast Guard vessels. Right away, he saw one ship break away and begin a path towards him. He gunned the speedboat to full speed, reaching seventy knots within seconds. He'd have no trouble outflanking the vessel following him. The question was how much time he'd gain before arriving home. Certainly, he'd be far enough ahead by the time he entered the winding creeks of Cape Romain. They'd never be able to find him. Unless they had another way to track him.

******

Lt. Coleman watched the whole scenario unfold in front of her. Captain Donovan watched as well and stayed in communication with Stark on board the lead cutter, now headed to the wreck site. They saw the speedboat arrive, and its driver go to the other boat and talk with the men on it. Then, three divers went into the water. They could even see the overconfidence on the men's faces when they opened bottles of beer.

"What are they drinking?" Donovan asked Coleman.

Coleman zoomed the camera. The resolution didn't blur one bit. "Looks like Corona, Sir."

Donovan chuckled. "Hope they enjoy it. It'll be the last beer they'll relish for a long time, if ever."

"Ok, now it looks like they've spotted out boats. They're pointing their way. The speedboat guy is looking at us through binoculars."

Donovan got on the radio. "Lieutenant Stark, we have visual that you've been spotted. Looks like some panic occurring on our target."

"Roger that," answered Stark. "We see them as well. Keep us posted."

Donovan watched the two guys argue for a bit, then the speedboat guy returned to his boat, untie the lash, and start his engine. "Speedboat is leaving the scene. Headed coarse due east."

"Got it," said Spark. "I'm going after him. Lieutenant Wilson will handle the dive ship."

"He's looking to outflank you," said Coleman. "No problem, we'll keep an eye from above."

The two continued to watch the speedboat head away from the coast. "It's time to get our land help on board," said Donovan. "Wherever this guy wants to dock, we'll be waiting for him."

CHAPTER 40

Pablo Santara had spent twenty of his allotted thirty minutes swimming around the wreck, looking for the gold coins they had promised were there. He and the two other divers recruited in such a rush by Diego had poked in and out of many pockets of rotting wood and debris. They found plenty of tarnished and oxidized silver, quite a bit of it, in fact; bars and coins, but were explicitly told to recover only gold. To this point, they had found none.

He started thinking there wasn't any gold at all, contrary to what he was told. They showed him a picture of the gold coin they would find. And as an incentive, there was some vague promise of maybe keeping a coin or two, depending on how much they found. Specifics were short, but enough to lure the three out of their normal day jobs for such an adventure.

Now, with only ten minutes of air left, plus the fifteen minutes it would take for two decompression stops, Pablo began losing hope. He reached into another hole in the wood and broke it apart. The three-hundred-year-old planks dissolved like sugar in water. Each time he reached into one of these crevices, he winced at the thought of a Moray Eel waiting to bite through his glove. But this time, he found something other than crumbled wood. It was hard metal, a box of some kind. Pablo wiped away the rest of the rotted wood and tried to lift the box. It seemed to be stuck in the mud.

He alerted the other two divers to come and help. In another minute, all three tried to lift the box, but it was either stuck in something or simply too heavy. Pablo took his flashlight and flooded the box with light. When he wiped away some barnacles and crud off the box, he saw it had a lid on top. More wiping and then they were able to open it. What they saw inside stunned all three divers. It was full of gold coins. Pablo's heart raced so fast he thought it would burst right out of his chest. Gold, lots of it. The mother lode.

Realizing they had only minutes left before heading to the surface, Pablo handed each of the other two divers a cloth bag and began filling his with the coins. Two minutes later, they had three bags with enough gold coins to make a small fortune, or maybe an enormous fortune. They were vague when he asked how much each coin was worth.

But time was short, and they had to get to the surface. The problem revealed itself immediately. They couldn't swim upwards due to the weight of the bag. Pablo knew gold was heavy, but didn't expect it to be so heavy it would impair swimming upwards. He looked at his watch again. They were past the time to begin their ascent. He had only five minutes of emergency spare air. Now, they'd have to use some of it.

Pablo signaled the other two to remove weight from their bags. A minute later, with the jettisoned gold coins strewn on the ocean floor, they began their ascent, now with their bags half full. Still a good haul, and they would be certain to return with new tanks later that day. Pablo made a mental note where they were in relation to the anchor line of Diego's vessel. Now they could swim upwards.

It was difficult. They had to kick continuously to keep from sinking. The time spent at the decompression levels was agonizing, but they all knew not to be tempted to cut their time short. Air was also in short supply. But they were close now. Pablo focused on his prize. The congratulations from Diego when he saw the bags of gold would make this all worth it. He fantasized about how many of the coins he'd be allowed to keep. Whatever reward awaited them by the higher ups, Pablo felt certain it would be generous. Plus, there would be plenty more to haul up now that he knew where the chest laid.

Another problem presented itself at the last decompression stop at thirty feet. Looking up, Pablo recognized Diego's vessel's hull and the anchor line from it they had used as a guide. But now, there was a second hull visible. They were told before the dive that Amelio would join them in his speedboat. Pablo knew what that looked like — from above the surface and below. This second vessel was no speedboat. It was much longer and wider. Perplexed, Pablo had no choice but to surface. Probably another one of Diego's crew coming to assist with the dive.

This turned out to be a bad assumption. When Pablo broke the surface, instead of seeing Diego reaching out with a helping hand, he stared down the business end of a gun. Too shocked to say or do anything, he heard the man shout at him to get out of the water. As Pablo dragged himself on to the ship, he realized the second boat was not another of Diego's crew, but was a Coast Guard ship, and the man pointing a gun in his face was an officer of the USCG. The day which held so much promise had officially gone to shit.

CHAPTER 41

Leroy and Tony came up empty in their search for Sonny Petrino. After finding no one at the Atlantic Seafood shop and nobody at his home in North Georgetown, the two officers tried in vain to find somewhere else he might have gone. The neighbors all said he kept to himself and had rarely seen him anywhere besides his shop. He didn't appear to have any relatives in the area, and nobody seemed to know of any close friends.

They next went to Sonny's two remaining suppliers. Calls to both men came up with nothing. Neither had any idea where the illusive fishmonger might be.

Frustrated, Leroy was about to call it a day. All they had was the auction, and if it sold before it ended tomorrow at 10:00 AM, they could track the shipment. The eBay site stated that FedEx would ship the coin as soon as payment was confirmed. It would be a simple task to stake out the local FedEx offices and wait on Petrino.

However, Leroy didn't want to wait. With so much going on with this shipwreck / treasure hunt, he wanted to be in the game. He had already put out an APB for Petrino's Ford SUV. Now, it seemed to be a waiting game.

"Let's go to the hospital and see how David Sweeney's doing," Leroy told Tony.

Tony smiled back. "Can't let it rest, can you?"

"No. And you can't either."

"Have you checked in with the Coast Guard this morning?" Tony asked.

"I did. Earlier, before this came up. All's quiet out at sea."

"There's trouble brewing, Sheriff. I can smell it."

Leroy didn't doubt it. Sometimes his detective amazed him with what could only be described as a sixth sense. "Well, Tony, you just keep on smelling. Come on, let's go to the hospital."

******

Leroy quietly knocked on the door of David's private room.

"Come in," he heard Maureen say. Leroy entered the room, followed by Tony.

"Good morning, Mrs. Sweeney. How's our patient doing?"

"Ornery as usual. Wants his boat back."

Leroy chuckled. "I'm afraid the *Fair Allowance* is a fish reef now, David. You're lucky you're not swimming with them yourself."

David grumbled in his bed. "You catch those bastards yet?"

"Not yet. But we have some good leads this morning."

Leroy received the information David could provide the previous evening when he visited him after recovery. There wasn't much to add that Neil hadn't already provided.

"And what does that mean?"

"Well, David. We have eyes in the air right now and we're waiting on them to make a move on the wreck site. Once they do, the Coast Guard should have the situation well in hand."

"Yeah? And what about Morgan? Did he have a hand in this?"

Leroy noted earlier the distrust between the two men and how David suspected Morgan following him out of the bay yesterday morning. "Well now, we're not at liberty to discuss that with you, but again, the information you provided to us has been very helpful. I'll have to leave it at that." He turned to Maureen. "What are the doctors saying, Mrs. Sweeney? Have they said how much longer he'll be in here?"

"At least a couple more days, Sheriff. Hopefully not longer, for both of our sakes."

"Well, we wish you a speedy recovery, David. I'll keep you posted if anything else breaks on the case."

"Thank you, Sheriff. I appreciate it. Can't wait to see the bastard who did this behind bars."

"We all do. By the way, have you seen Emmy yet this morning? I thought she might have been here."

David shook his head. "Haven't seen her. You know where she is, dear?"

"Yes, as a matter of fact. She returned her call from that fish store owner. What was his name again?"

Leroy snapped to attention. He saw Tony do the same.

"Petrino," answered David. "Sonny Petrino."

"What kind of business did Emmy have with him?" Leroy asked, trying not to come across as overly excited. Tony grabbed his pad and pen.

Maureen saw the look of concern come across the two men. "Well, I'm not sure. He called Emmy when we were here yesterday. Said he had something important to tell her. I know she went home and slept after the day she had yesterday. But she called me this morning and said she'd be here after she met with Mr. Petrino. I haven't heard from her since."

Leroy saw Tony frantically writing.

"What time did she call you, Mrs. Sweeney?"

Marueen's face broke into concern. "I, I'm not sure. Wait, let me check my phone."

Leroy watched with keen interest as Maureen fumbled in her purse and searched for her iPhone.

"Is he involved in this?" David asked, noting the lawmen's reaction.

Leroy didn't answer but stayed focused on Maureen.

"Let's see. Yes, she called me at eight-forty-five this morning. Told me she was meeting Mr. Petrino at his fish market at nine o'clock."

Leroy glanced at his watch. 11:05 AM. "And you haven't heard from her since?" he asked, the urgency clear in his voice.

"I have not. What is it, Sheriff? Is he involved? Dear God, is Emmy in danger again?"

"Mrs. Sweeney, David, I'm sorry I can't give you any specifics, but Sonny Petrino is a person of interest in this case. Not a suspect, ok. But we wish to talk with him. Go ahead and try Emmy again. See if you can reach her."

Everyone in the room stared at Maureen and held their breath as she speed-dialed Emmy's number. Maureen sighed when it went to voice mail. "Emmy darling, it's your mom. Please call me as soon as you get this. It's very important. Please be safe." Maureen ended the call after leaving the voice mail. "I'll text her as well," she said.

Leroy scratched his head, looking for answers. Everyone in the room looked at him with the same perplexity. After everything that girl had gotten herself into, now this! Leroy just couldn't believe it.

"David, Mrs. Sweeney, we need to go. You have my number. If you hear from Emmy or Mr. Petrino, call me immediately."

"Of course, Sheriff. Of course we will."

"Come on Tony, let's go." Visiting hours were over. This was shaping up to be another crazy day.

******

Leroy raced down the stairs while Tony struggled to keep up. Once in the parking lot, he stopped outside his car and paused to catch his breath.

"You don't think —" started Tony.

"I don't think what? That Sonny Petrino is involved with the Constantine organization and that Emmy Sweeney has just gotten herself into a heap load of trouble — again!" Leroy tried to control his temper without success. "Yes, Detective, that's exactly what I think."

"We can track her phone, by GPS," offered Tony. "But that will take some time, especially on a holiday Sunday."

"I don't think we have that much time. Wait, there's one person who may help us."

"Yeah, and who's that?"

"Dr. Morgan."

"You've got to be kidding me." Tony laughed at the suggestion.

"It's worth a shot. Morgan's tied to Constantine. If Petrino is as well, he may offer us information on him."

"At what price, Leroy? He's not giving anything away for free."

"He wants to make bail. We know that. Perhaps we can give him a little encouragement on that end if he plays the game with us."

Tony snorted. "At this point, Sheriff, what do we have to lose?"

******

Ten minutes later, the two stood outside the jail cell holding Paul Morgan. He looked like crap. Leroy marveled at how just twenty-four hours behind bars could make a man look like he aged a decade. Morgan's hair was a mess. The days' worth of growth on his face came in all gray, and his eyes had some faraway lost look about them.

Still, when he saw Leroy and Tony approach, his interest perked.

"Gooood morning, Doctor," Leroy boomed. "And how are you feeling this morning?"

"Like shit," Morgan moaned. "The food in here sucks."

Tony cracked a wry smile. "Perhaps you'd like to place a Door Dash order for lunch," he said.

"Hmm," replied Leroy. "Maybe we could arrange that."

Morgan's eyes darted back and forth between the two lawmen, sensing something was up. "What do you want? I already told you I'm not ratting anyone out."

"Indeed, indeed," answered Leroy, rubbing his chin and nodding his head. He stayed quiet, watching Morgan closely.

"I want to know when I'm going to get a bail hearing."

Leroy continued to nod. "Hear that, Detective. The doctor wants to know when he can get out on bail."

"I don't know, Sheriff. I understand Judge Waterson's docket is pretty full. Could be awhile."

Both men continued to stare at Morgan.

Finally, Morgan asked, "But I'm sensing you might help move it up. For something. What do you want?"

Leroy nodded at Tony, then glared at Morgan. "Sonny Petrino. Know him?"

Morgan continued to look skittish. "I know of him."

"We're looking for him. Any idea where he'd be?"

"I'd imagine he'd be at his fish shop."

"Not there. Not at his home, either. Give us a clue and we'll see about moving your bail hearing up."

Leroy swore he could hear the wheels spinning in Morgan's head. It was time for some answers.

"McClellanville," Morgan said in barely a whisper.

"What about it? Where in McClellanville?" Leroy felt like grabbing his neck and forcing it out.

"You'll move my bail hearing up. To Tuesday? Morning?"

"You tell us where in McClellanville, and I'll see you get a hearing Tuesday morning."

"Fine. There's a house on the creek. It's isolated. I don't know the address. Lots of security. Go down Pinkney Street to the end. It's off to the left. You may find more than you bargained for."

Leroy nodded his approval. "We'll see what we can do."

His phone buzzed. It was Donovan's number at the Coast Guard. "Yes, Captain, what do you have?"

"Sheriff, I need everything you got and head to McClellanville. I'll have the address in a minute. The noose is tightening."

Leroy and Tony smiled at each other. This is what they've been waiting for.

CHAPTER 42

Amelio had his speedboat at full throttle as he approached Muddy Bay on the outer edge of Cape Romain. His panic was in full bore ever since he ditched Diego and, for all intents and purposes, the entire salvage operation of the *Concepcion*. At this point, he couldn't think about the consequences he'd have to face with Constantine. His only concern was to save his own skin.

He took the first turn leading into the main creek that went past the Cape Romain lighthouse too fast. Amelio jerked the wheel to the left and almost flipped the boat. He whistled past the marsh grass protecting Lighthouse Island, and in doing so, scraped the bottom of the boat on an oyster bed just below the surface. Amelio eased back on the throttle to prevent a capsized catastrophe. Still, he pushed the boat as fast as he could negotiate the winding turns.

He kept looking behind him every few seconds. For the last ten minutes, he'd lost sight of the Coast Guard vessel. Could that mean he'd lost them? Could he be that lucky? Amelio refused to take false hope in the event he didn't.

They knew the location of the wreck. The story Petrino fed him was now obviously bullshit. The Coast Guard had rescued the girl, and she'd given them the GPS location of the shipwreck. But how did the authorities know he was out there this morning? The only answer he could come up with was that they had a drone high above and were watching the whole time. If that was the case, he was truly fucked.

If it were true, they'd follow him all the way into the cape and its miles of winding creeks. A place where, in any other circumstance, he'd lose any pursuer. Now he had to think of even more dire possibilities. But he had one chance. Get to the house. Even if the Coast Guard followed him all the way in. Even if the cops had surrounded his house by the time he got there. There was still a way out. Plus, having a female hostage would add to his leverage.

Petrino had no intentions of making whatever deal he blabbered on about. He was there to kill him, pure and simple, then steal his cash and go who knew where. The girl was just a ploy to him. It got him inside the house, Amelio gave him credit for that. But that would be as far as it got. He wasn't worried about Petrino. It was his house, and he knew every secret entrance, every hidden passageway, and the way out to safety. And he'd take it, once he got rid of Petrino.

Assuming he could make it out of McClellanville undetected, he could then dispose of the girl. She'd only be of use to him in a jam. But he didn't want to get too far ahead of himself. First things first.

Amelio rounded the last bend of the creek leading into his hideaway bungalow. No other houses or nosy neighbors were anywhere to be seen. He idled the speedboat and eased into the boat garage, then remotely closed the door behind him. He powered down the speedboat, but didn't bother to tie it off in case he needed a speedy getaway. Amelio hopped out of the boat, but instead of exiting the side door to the dock and the back entrance to the house, he opened a trap door on the floor in the far corner of the boat shed. The door led to a tunnel under the creek and below his house. From there, it led to a hidden staircase which opened into his master bedroom. Then he'd pay a surprise visit to his guests. A visit they'll never see coming.

******

Lt. Coleman maneuvered the drone, tracking the speedboat all the way into Cape Romain. Captain Donovan kept a close eye on the drone's view over her shoulder, while staying in contact with Lieutenant Stark in the patrol boat following the speedboat. Stark was now several miles back and about to enter the series of creeks that buffered the coast inland to McClellanville.

"Where do you think he's headed?" Coleman asked Donovan.

"I don't know. There's a whole lot of nothing in Cape Romain. McClellanville is the only town with access there. He may just be looking for a little inlet as a place to hide."

"Do you think he knows about our drone, Sir?"

"Not sure, but I'll bet he suspects something like that. If he wants a place to hide, Stark will be on his ass in minutes. I've got a feeling he has something else in mind."

As if on cue, Coleman saw the speedboat slow down as it approached a home on the creek.

"You're right, Sir. He's in McClellanville township. Looks like he's pulling into that boat shed by that home there."

The two officers watched as the speedboat disappeared into the shed.

"I expect him to come out and go into the house from the back," stated Donovan. "It's time to get the ground forces in. Check the address of that place." He grabbed the phone on the desk and dialed the sheriff's number.

Leroy answered on the first ring. "Sheriff Keating here. What do you got?"

Donovan updated the situation.

Coleman interrupted him. "Captain, here's the address." She handed Donovan a piece of paper.

"Sheriff, it's 1745 Pinkney Street in McClellanville. We'll pinch it off from the creek side. What other resources can we muster immediately?"

"Call Glasier at DEA. He'll love to jump in. I'll have three cars there in ten minutes. McClellanville PD should have a couple available as well. We'll set up a perimeter, but we'll need a plan and someone to take point."

"Agreed. If he holes up in his house, we'll need to bring the FBI in from Charleston. I'll contact them as well. He's not going anywhere by sea. If he makes a run for it on land shortly, it'll be up to you guys."

"Understood. You have eyes on him now?"

"We saw him enter his boat shed. Waiting on visual of him exiting. Right now, no."

"OK, we'll stay in touch. It's time to nail this guy once and for all."

******

"Here he comes," Sonny told Emmy, peering out the backside window, watching the speedboat come down the creek. "I knew he was probably at the wreck site. Won't be long now. Here, I'm sorry, Emmy, but I'm going to have to tie you up again."

Emmy nodded. She understood the plan. Amelio would need to see her tied up, just as Sonny described it. Once Sonny shot Amelio and he was out of the picture, they could get out of this place and be done with each other. Emmy didn't exactly relish the thought of being used as bait, nor did she care to escape in some tunnel she knew nothing about. But she desperately wanted justice for what happened to her, and dad, and especially Jack.

Sonny quickly retied the rope around her wrists behind her back and replaced the gag. Now all she could do was watch — and pray.

The plan was simple. Amelio would come up from the boat shed and walk across the dock, then up the stairs to the deck and enter the house from the back. He'd see Emmy tied up on the couch, but Sonny would be out of sight on the other side of the bay window. The instant Amelio stepped through the door, he'd be shot dead.

They waited. Nothing happened. No one came out from the boat shed.

Emmy grunted and shrugged her shoulders.

Sonny put his finger to his lips. "He senses something isn't right. Be patient, he'll come up."

Emmy wasn't patient or confident. She was, in fact, scared to death. How and why did she get sucked into this cockamamie plan? She continued to stare out of the window at the boat shed. Why would Amelio stay in that shed? Maybe he wasn't coming into the house at all. If he suspected a trap, he may just leave. Then what?

With all her attention focused outside on the boat shed, she didn't hear anything coming down the hallway from the master bedroom. By the time she heard something click and looked around, it was too late.

CHAPTER 43

"Where the hell is he?" Donovan demanded. For the last ten minutes, the drone footage hadn't changed. "Is he holed up in that boat shed?"

"I would say so, Sir. Unless he has direct access to the house without going outside."

Donovan fumed as he stared at the monitor. He wouldn't put it past that son-of-a-bitch to have something like that built into his house. He'd seen, and heard from previous captures, the elaborate extent these drug dealers go to securing their hideouts. This guy was probably no different.

The drone footage showed a modest compound, nothing like some of the other mansions he'd seen. But from what he saw just from the overhead view, the security in place was extensive. Walls enclosed the entire property. He could tell there were multiple cameras placed around the perimeter. Probably nothing moved in or around that home without the owner knowing about it. Plus, he guessed it would take a lot more than a wink and a smile to get through the front gate. They may have to deal with just that possibility before this shit show is over.

The drone picked up vehicles coming in from the main road that led to the long, private driveway. Flashing red lights were clearly visible on all of them.

"Looks like the calvary has shown up. And here comes Stark." Donavan saw the Coast Guard cutter easing into the creek area outside the boat shed. "We got him surrounded. But the FBI and DEA are going to have to do the heavy lifting." He switched to walkie and radioed DEA. "SA Glasier, we have our cutter and the local assets in place. Suspect is on the property, but we do not have a visual. What's your ETA?"

"Fifteen minutes out," crackled the response. "How many targets are there?"

"As far as we can tell, just the one. But I can't confirm there isn't anyone else in the house."

"Copy. Let me know if anything else changes."

"Roger. Will do. Over."

Donovan turned his attention back to the drone monitor. "What about that car at the front entrance?" When he first noticed it, he assumed it belonged to the owner. But the more he thought about it, the more unsure he became. It was a standard Ford SUV. Hardly the kind of vehicle a rich cartel member would own. He asked Coleman, "Can you zoom in and get a tag #?"

"Sure thing. I'll lose coverage of the boat shed for just a few seconds, Sir."

"Just make it quick"

The view from the drone shifted to the right as the camera zoomed to the back of the SUV. "SC plate ZHN348"

"Got it," Donovan wrote the tag number down. "Go ahead and zoom out." He got back on the radio. "Sheriff Keating, are you there?"

"Right here, Captain."

"There's a Ford SUV outside the front door. I need you to run the plate number ASAP."

"No problem."

"It's SC ZHN348."

"Got it. I'll have an owner in a couple minutes."

"Roger, thank you, Sheriff."

Donovan went back to the drone monitor. Still nothing. Eventually, something had to break. Something.

******

As soon as he got off the radio, Leroy called in the license plate number. Then he asked Tony, "What do you think? Think that's Petrino's car?"

"That would be my guess. Why he's there is more of a mystery."

"As is the Sweeney girl. If she's with him."

"But is she with him voluntarily, or is she a hostage?"

"Tony," Leroy said with exasperation, "at this point, I don't know what the fuck to think."

"Piece it together, Sheriff. Petrino posts an auction for this coin on an open market. Forget for a minute how or why he has this coin. Guys in that kind of organization don't put valuable items on a public market. They deal only in the black market. So, either Petrino is not involved with Constantine, or he's gone rogue. But don't ask me why."

"He's got to be with the cartel. Why else would Morgan pin him?"

"Agreed. So, maybe he's gone rogue. He's had some kind of fallout with them and wants out but needs the cash first."

Leroy chuckled at that. "Well, good luck to him, if that's the case." He glanced down as his cell began it ring. "It's Derek at the station." Leroy answered, "Yes, Derek, what do you have?"

"Sheriff, the tag number you gave me is registered to a Sonny Petrino. Georgetown address."

"Bingo," shouted Leroy. "Thanks Derek. I owe you one." Leroy ended the call.

"Well, that answers that," said Tony, "Now what?"

"I'm calling the FBI back to bring them up to speed. They better get here soon."

Leroy was about to place his call when he heard two gunshots coming from inside the house. He and Tony looked at each other in shock. "Oh Fuck!" Leroy cried out. "Now what?"

*****

From inside the house, Sonny continued to peer out the bay window, searching for Amelio. He stayed hidden behind the drape on the left side of the window so he wouldn't be visible to anyone who walked up the deck to the back door. Emmy sat on the couch, in plain view from the back deck, watching intently as well. They'd been there for ten minutes since the speedboat pulled into the boat shed.

Emmy mumbled something behind her gag and pointed her head at the window.

Sonny caught her drift. "He must be hiding from the Coast Guard. Don't worry, he'll be here."

The two then saw a sight neither expected. A large Coast Guard patrol boat came into view and stopped in the creek just outside the boat shed, blocking the entrance.

Sonny smiled at Emmy. "I was right. Amelio was tailed back here from the wreck site."

Emmy glared at him. This whole setup stunk. She couldn't believe she let herself get talked into it. Sonny was a criminal, just like this guy Amelio and the rest of their crooked organization, or cartel, or whatever it was. Once again, two days in a row, she had let her sense of adventure, tainted by her desire for justice get the best of her.

She continued to stare outside at the Coast Guard vessel in the creek, as several armed Coast Guard personnel paced the open deck, guarding the entrance to the shed. But still no sight of anyone coming out of it.

Emmy felt a shiver go down her spine. A sinking feeling that something terrible was about to happen. Then it did.

From out of nowhere, she heard a gunshot, then another. Emmy felt warm blood splatter on her face. She turned and saw Sonny collapse to the floor, blood pouring from his head. He never made a sound, just crumbled into a heap — motionless and bleeding — dead.

Emmy tried to scream as she looked up and saw a man with a gun pointed at her head walking straight toward her. For a split second, she believed she was about to die.

"Shut up," she heard him say, with a Spanish accent. But he didn't shoot.

So, this must be Amelio. The one responsible for the whole mess. The one who shot her dad and sank his boat. The guy who would have killed her if she had surfaced yesterday. The man who killed Jack. Emmy sat there, doe-eyed, in shock, shaking uncontrollably.

Amelio stepped over Sonny and peered out the window. "Shit," he spat out, apparently seeing the Coast Guard vessel out back for the first time.

Emmy wondered how he got into the house without being seen outside the boat shed. She figured it was another one of his secret passageways. But what was he going to do next? If he was going to kill her like he did Sonny, he'd have done it by now.

"Get up," he ordered, turning away from the window and once again pointing his gun at her.

Emmy struggled to her feet. The rope still bound her hands behind her back and the gag tied tight in her mouth, preventing her from speaking.

Amelio roughly grabbed her by the shoulder and turned her around, then checked the rope securing her wrists.

She tried to speak, but it came out as an unintelligible series of ooo's and ahhh's. He wasn't in the mood for conversation, anyway. He spun her around again, stuck the gun in her back and ordered, "Move. Down the hall."

Emmy knew exactly where she was going. To the bedroom, and the trapdoor, and from there who knew where, or what, or how in the world she was ever going to survive one more ordeal.

CHAPTER 44

Amelio couldn't believe how his string of incredibly bad luck just wouldn't let up. Right after he had taken care of Petrino, he looked out his back window and saw a Coast Guard cutter parked outside the boat shed. That confirmed his worst fears. He'd been tracked to his home by a drone. It meant his planned escape by boat was now dead in the water. Even if he could get past the boat, unlikely given the menacing looking automatic weapon on its bow, and outrun it, they'd continue to track him out to the ocean. Eventually, he'd run out of gas and that would be the end.

He had two advantages yet to play. The first was a hostage. The Sweeney girl, conveniently already tied and gagged, would serve as a last resort if things closed in on him even more. And if he could escape, he could do away with her easily enough. God only knew what amount of trouble she'd already caused him.

The second edge was his escape tunnel. He had it installed when he built the house for just such an emergency. Like the connecting tunnel that got him out of the boathouse, the escape route he would take now led from the corner of his bedroom, below ground and then to a spot well outside the security gate. It came back up to the ground level in a wooded, uninhabited area two hundred yards beyond the gate.

Tucked away, at least a half mile away from the nearest dwelling, at the end of an overgrown dirt road, sat a Jeep 4x4 — his getaway vehicle. Once there, he'd continue down a rugged, barely visible dirt path away from McClellanville, where it eventually came out to a road below Highway 17, just south of the Santee River.

Once outside whatever dragnet the cops had set up, he could drive down to Miami and rejoin Constantine. Amelio shuddered when he thought of the consequences of facing his boss again after everything that had gone to shit. Of course, he'd be blamed for everything. But he had nowhere else to turn.

One other disturbing issue, as he contemplated his escape. The authorities would eventually enter his home and find their own treasure trove of incriminating information. Everything from his list of criminal contacts, the salvage operation details, and all the records of the drug hauls were on his computer. Sure, it was passcode protected, but probably not enough to keep the IT experts at the FBI from breaking in. Now, however, time was of the essence, and he had to get out of the house before it was too late.

He grabbed the girl and forced her down the hall and into the bedroom. Then he opened the trapdoor and the two of them went down the steep steps leading into the tunnel. Amelio closed the trapdoor behind him, being careful that the rug still covered the door, before he and the girl began their journey into the escape tunnel. After a few feet, they passed the intersection that led out to the boat shed. This time they took a left and headed down the narrow, dimly lit passage which instead went to the spot outside his property. There, he would taste freedom again — God willing. Amelio shoved Emmy in the back and hollered, "Move!"

******

Leroy panicked after hearing the two gunshots. He immediately radioed Donovan.

"Shots fired. Shots fired! Any visuals?"

"Negative, Sheriff. The guy must have a secret tunnel into the house from the boathouse. We've seen nothing entering or exiting the house. We're monitoring both visual and infrared. Nobody's going to leave without us knowing it."

"Unless they have some other secret passageway to get out," Leroy corrected him. "Listen, we need someone to get inside. We're locked out here. I have nothing to get through or over that wall. When is the help from Charleston getting here?"

"ETA should be less than ten minutes."

"What about your patrol out back? Can't somebody get in the house from the back?"

"At this point, I'm afraid not. We can't risk a water escape."

Leroy fumed. He feared who might be shot inside. He didn't have a clue why Petrino and Emmy were inside that house, but felt certain one or both had been shot. He didn't like the idea of a mission without a lead in command. This was out of the league of the Coast Guard. The real help was still minutes away and someone in that house needed help now.

Tony saw Leroy's frustration. "I feel the same way, Sheriff, but there's nothing we can do now except wait for the calvary."

"I know, I know. That doesn't mean I have to like it." He continued to glare out the windshield at the tall wall in front of him. Helpless, he thought, just fucking helpless.

******

Emmy continued to fear for her life. Another horrible situation she found herself in, again, she thought — again. Sonny was dead. That was an image she'd never get out of her mind. And now she was a hostage to this guy, Amelio, the supposed brains of their operation. But he didn't look too smart right now. He looked freaking scared.

She staggered forward through the tunnel. It had just enough LED lights strung on the ceiling to see where she was going. Still, she stumbled several times, nearly falling on her face once, since she couldn't use her arms to balance. Each time she tripped, Amelio would stick the gun in her back and demand she keep moving.

And where exactly were they headed? She imagined the tunnel would exit somewhere outside the property. That would be his escape mode. The authorities would stay focused on the house, and they'd be outside all of it. Then what? It wasn't like they'd simply walk into the town of McClellanville and catch an Uber. She was sure he had another plan, and whatever it was, didn't foretell well for her.

This went on for a good five minutes. Then they came to what looked like the end of the tunnel. There was a steep set of stairs, maybe ten of them, that led up and some sort of hatch at the top. Amelio pushed Emmy aside, then climbed the stairs and opened the hatch. Bright sunlight poured into the tunnel.

He stared back down at Emmy, then climbed back down. Emmy looked at the opening. There was no way she'd be able to climb out of this hole without using her hands. Amelio didn't seem to be concerned.

"Go ahead," he commanded, "get up there. I'll push you through the hole. You run and I'll shoot you in the back. Understood?"

Emmy nodded vigorously. He's going to push me through. Ain't that just great, she thought, rolling her eyes. She climbed, trying to maintain her balance with her arms tied behind her back. When she reached the top step and poked her head out the hatch, she got her first glimpse of where she was. Before she could make any kind of assessment, she felt two hands grab her ass and shove her upward, rough and tumble like.

Emmy gasped in pain as her ribs slammed against the side of the hatch. One more shove and she was outside the hole, laying on the ground, moaning. In an instant, Amelio was outside the hatch. Before Emmy could get a handle on where they were, Amelio shouted for her to get up. Another not so simple task to do without arm support. Amelio saw her struggle and grabbed her under her armpit, then hauled her to her feet.

Now she could see where they were. It looked like the middle of a jungle. Thick brush dotted with palmetto trees was evident in every direction. She could see the remnants of a dirt path off to her right. And a short way away, hidden around some oleander bushes, was a jeep. One of those open top 4x4s with a roll bar people loved to take to the beach. Except they weren't going to the beach. This was his getaway vehicle. God only knew where they were headed now.

Amelio closed the hatch behind him and pointed the gun at the jeep. "Get in," he demanded. Like she had a choice in the matter. He opened the passenger door and forced her inside, then high tailed it around to the driver's side, reached under the seat for a set of keys and fired the jeep up.

Emmy shook her head in despair. Where is he taking me now? she asked herself. Will anyone be able to follow us? And what is he going to do to me? She had no answers — only fear. And she had fear in spades.

CHAPTER 45

Lt. Coleman continued to monitor the drone footage like a hawk. Ten minutes had passed since they received word two gunshots were heard inside the home. But still, no activity outside the house was visible. Coleman had her drone feed set up as a split screen, half actual video and half infrared. If anyone tried to sneak out under the cover of the thick brush around the home, the visible may not detect them, but the infrared would.

Right now, the scene hadn't changed since the Georgetown County Sheriff and local McClellanville PD had arrived. They had moved out around the perimeter of the security wall which surrounded the house on all sides except for the creek access. The Coast Guard cutter kept watch on any activity at the water's edge. But until the FBI and SWAT units arrived from Charleston, they couldn't breach the perimeter.

Meanwhile, one or two people were inside, presumably shot and possibly dead. But according to the Georgetown Sheriff, there were at least three people inside, two of whom arrived in the SUV parked out front. Trying to figure out how that fit into the picture was anyone's guess — and above her paygrade.

What they paid her and relied upon her for was to detect anything or anybody who went outside that house. Other than the cops on the perimeter, nothing warm-blooded and alive existed within the quarter-mile radius the drone was currently covering. Donovan just received word the FBI and SWAT teams were ten minutes away. Coleman felt helpless and pitied anyone inside who might have been shot and needed assistance.

However, whoever shot them also had to either escape or face down the formidable assets of the FBI when they breached the security wall and forcibly entered the home. And if they planned to escape, her drone might be the only line of defense they had to prevent it.

Coleman's eyes kept bouncing back and forth between the split screen, scanning for anything that moved or was detected by infrared. Then, in the blink of an eye, she saw two objects light up the infrared screen. Switching to visual, she couldn't make them out under a set of palmetto trees, oleander bushes, and other thick brush. But she saw something rustling; infrared didn't lie. There were two people who appeared out of nowhere, about two-hundred yards northeast of the security wall.

"Captain," the excitement in Coleman's voice was palpable. "Two bodies detected, northeast of the home."

Donovan was on the phone with the FBI at the moment, and told them, "Hold on," then turned to Coleman. "What do you got?"

Coleman pointed to the two bodies on the infrared, now making their way through the vegetation away from the house. In the next second, the visual cleared and two people emerged from under the canopy, a man and a woman. The woman had her hands tied behind her back.

"Holy Shit!" shouted Donovan. He turned on the radio. "All hands, all hands, we have two bogies headed away from the house. A man and woman. Woman's hands are bound behind her back. Their twenty is two hundred yards northeast of the main gate. We have a track on them. Can anyone there give chase?"

A few seconds with nothing. Then Adam Davis from McClellanville PD came on the radio. "Sir, there's nothing but heavy thicket between here and there. No good way to cut through it quickly. See if they're going to a road nearby."

"Ten four," replied Donovan. "Standby for update." Donovan put the radio down and peered at the drone footage. "What's going on, Liz? Where are they headed?"

"They're walking down what looks like a path right now, Sir." Coleman kept her eyes glued to the screen. She saw the two figures, now only partially obscured, work their way through the thick brush.

"And where the hell did they come from?" Donovan asked rhetorically. "That's what I want to know."

"I don't know, Sir. They just appeared. There's no way they came from the house above ground without me knowing it."

Donovan grunted. "Son of a bitch must have a tunnel out of the house. This guy's a real piece of work. And the woman tied up. Had to be the girl the sheriff said was with the guy whose car is out front. Which means—"

"The guy who drove there is probably in the house, shot," Coleman finished Donovan's sentence.

Donovan shook his head. "What a cluster fuck. I swear."

Coleman interrupted, "Sir, the two are coming out into the open. They're in a vehicle now, looks like a jeep. They're coming out onto a dirt track — right there." Coleman pointed on the visual screen to the jeep, now moving to the east.

Donovan got back on the radio. "Sheriff, we have visual of the two bogies in a vehicle now, driving away. Looks like they're in a Jeep 4x4. Headed east. Can you get out of there and cut them off? Hold on, let me see what's out there."

Before the Sheriff answered, Donovan asked Coleman, "Where does that track lead? Pull up a map."

"Yes, Sir." Coleman's heart pounded as she zeroed in on their prey. A few keystrokes and a road map appeared on the drone visual. "Ok, there they are. They're on a dirt road here," she pointed her finger at the jeep, "which runs about five miles east. Comes out on Dupree Road. From there, they have a couple of different ways to get to Highway 17. That or go down a road that dead ends at the South Santee River."

Back on the radio, Donovan shouted, "Sheriff, get two cars out to Highway 17, northbound, and block off the roads before you get to the South Santee River. From there, we'll close the noose on them."

"You got it," came the reply from Sheriff Keating.

"Pulling out," said Davis.

"I'll update FBI and have some of them send some resources that way as well."

"Ten four."

Donovan put down the radio and watched the jeep work its way down the dirt road. He put his hand on Coleman's shoulder. "Great work, Lieutenant. Outstanding."

Coleman smiled and felt a surge of warmth course through her body. This was what she had always dreamt of. This was why she did what she did. All the training, all the experience, everything seemed to lead to this pinnacle of what she was hired to do. "Just doing my job, Sir."

******

Leroy was flabbergasted upon hearing the information come over the radio. "That's got to be Sweeney he has as a hostage. What in God's name is she doing out here?"

"And Petrino?" queried Tony. "My guess is he's lying dead in that house."

Leroy peeled his squad car from the area outside the gate and floored it back to Highway 17. "That would be my guess as well. I don't know how this whole shit show got put together, but I'll be damned if I have to go back to that hospital and tell David Sweeney his daughter was killed this morning after everything that happened yesterday."

Tony stayed silent and shook his head.

Five minutes later, they reached the highway. "So, what's between here and the Santee?" Leroy asked. His geographical knowledge of the area dropped sharply once they were out of Georgetown County, south of the river.

"A whole lot of nothing."

"And plenty more places to hide out — that little shit."

"We've got eyes in the sky, Leroy. We'll track them down."

Leroy grunted and sped on to 17, heading north. "And then what, Detective? A cornered snake is the worst kind of snake."

Tony tried to sound reassuring. "FBI is coming right behind us. They'll take the lead in a few more minutes."

Leroy turned to Tony and said, "And that's supposed to make me feel better? We need to cover the intersections at 17. Which one first?" Without waiting for an answer, he got on the radio and asked for Davis, the lead deputy from McClellanville.

Davis answered back right away. "We're right behind you, Sheriff, heading north."

"How many intersections before the river need to be covered, and what are they?"

"Three roads, Sheriff. South Santee Road loops around and is the first and third juncture. Seven Mile Road is in between. Why don't you take the first one, it's coming up soon, and my two cars will cover the other ones."

"Got it. The first road is coming up now. We'll stand guard and wait for command from the FBI."

"Ten four, Sheriff. We'll get this guy soon."

Leroy ended the radio call and slowed down to enter South Santee Road. He parked the squad car on the shoulder facing south with the lights flashing, then sat back and took a deep breath. "Well, Tony. It's out of our hands now. Let the FBI finish this thing off."

As if on cue, a voice came over the radio. "Calling all squad cars. This is Special Agent in Charge Charles Gossamer. I am taking command of this operation effective immediately. I want to know who is out there and what your current position is. Let's start with the Georgetown County Sheriff."

Leroy got back on the radio and gave the new boss his location. Gossamer then went through the other police cars involved. When he finished and told everyone to wait on his command, Tony asked Leroy, "There, you feel better now?"

Leroy rolled his eyes and answered without emotion, "No."

CHAPTER 46

Amelio felt like he had beaten the odds and that damn Coast Guard drone which had to have tracked him ever since he was at the wreck site. He had a brief reflection about Diego and the fate of the divers, but he brushed it quickly aside. Not his problem. His problem now was to figure a way out of McClellanville and out of whatever dragnet the cops undoubtably had set for him. All he knew for certain was the Coast Guard vessel on the creek prevented any water escape. He didn't know how many cops were waiting outside the security wall, waiting for him to show up.

He assumed more help would be on the way, probably the FBI, and they'd have the resources to breach the wall and enter the house. But they wouldn't find him. Unfortunately, however, they'd find loads of incriminating evidence. Evidence implicating him with the drug running, the salvage operation, then throw in a couple of murders to boot. It would also point the finger at Constantine, which may jeopardize the entire organization. Again, not his problem, at least for now it wasn't. Down the road, Amelio pictured himself freed from the US authorities and disavowed from the organization. Perhaps a cozy, secure retirement in Venezuela or maybe Mexico, where some of Constantine's rivals might offer sanctuary. But that was in the future. Right now, he had to get out of McClellanville safely to even have a future.

The dirt road which enabled his escape ended. He planned to take South Santee Road up to Highway 17, and then turn north. Once he got to Georgetown, he'd turn inland and eventually make his way back to Miami. Perhaps. Maybe not. He couldn't think straight with everything else going on.

Amelio suffered an acute paranoia he had never before felt. It was the drone. An eye in the sky he couldn't detect but could see everything he did. Surely it still hovered above his home, waiting for something to happen. No way could it have detected him and the Sweeney girl leaving the tunnel. Right? He questioned himself but couldn't be sure.

Amelio took a left onto South Santee Road and began the three-mile drive to the highway. He glanced skyward every few seconds, searching for the drone but saw nothing. Getting on 17 without detection was crucial. It would get him out of whatever dragnet the cops may have set. Then he'd be free to cross the Santee River and go anywhere to the north undetected.

This hope faded as soon as he saw the highway a half mile ahead. Flashing red lights lit up the intersection. Amelio knew they were for him. The Sweeney girl saw them as well and started moaning through her gag. Ok, he thought, as he struggled to maintain his composure. He half expected that. It was a precaution, that was all. It didn't mean they had spotted him or knew he was in a jeep. They just had their dragnet out surrounding McClellanville. Still, this was not good news.

Amelio abruptly pulled into a gas station and turned around, hoping he wouldn't be detected. He kept his eyes on the rear-view mirror and headed back south on South Santee Road. The flashing lights didn't move and were soon out of sight. Amelio breathed a sigh of relief, but realized his options were even more limited. He was sure the other roads leading out to 17 were also being monitored. This meant he was trapped, yet again. But he had a long history of escaping traps, and he wasn't about to be caught in this one.

There was one other way out. A few miles south was another road, the Santee Gun Club Road. It was a dead-end leading to, naturally, the

Santee Gun Club. But it wasn't the club itself that interested him. It was the dock on the Santee River outside the gun club. He had passed it several times before on the river when he explored the area prior to buying the McClellanville property. The dock always had a few boats tied off. His escape would be a simple matter of taking one boat at gunpoint, then make his way out to the ocean from there. Sure, it was a long shot, but he was running out of options.

Amelio turned left onto Santee Gun Club Road. He looked across at the Sweeney girl. She continued to moan and squirm. But she wasn't going anywhere with her hands tied and secure in the seatbelt. Her usefulness was nearing an end. Assuming he'd get on a boat and out of the dragnet they had set for him, he'd dump her in the Santee River before he made it to the ocean. Without the use of her arms, she wouldn't last two minutes before she went under. The alligators would handle it from there.

Once more, Amelio cursed his fate. But he also admired his own resourcefulness. He would get out of this jam. He always did, and he would again. And just like all the other times, he knew his life depended on it.

******

Emmy knew her life depended on staying cool; that and a lot of luck. Staying cool she could do. She did it yesterday, stranded in the middle of the ocean, death all but certain. She kept her cool then and got lucky. Now, as fearful as she was, Emmy stayed focused, breathing slow and steady through her gag, and not panicking with her arms immobile.

She knew the authorities were tracking them down. When she saw the flashing lights at the Highway 17 intersection, she understood the situation had turned dire for Amelio. Why doesn't he just give up, she thought, but knew he wouldn't. His type doesn't give up. They fight to the death. His death, she hoped, and not hers.

The jeep turned around after seeing the flashing lights and was now headed back to where they came from. Then it turned left onto another road. Emmy wasn't familiar with the geography here, but she knew they were still south of the Santee River and the only way to cross it was on Highway 17. Heading south on this road had to lead to a dead end. Then what? One last stand? A murder / suicide? Maybe he'd just leave her and set off on foot by himself. Emmy tried her best to maintain her composure.

The road was sandy dirt, and the jeep kicked up a ton of dust. There were signs saying the area was some kind of hunting ground. Tall pines were spaced out among a mostly cleared floor. She noticed a few elevated deer stands. Emmy wondered what kind of game was hunted there. Deer for sure, among other animals. Today's menu would feature humans. Emmy gulped at the morose thought.

Whatever the endgame, it was about to happen. Up ahead, she saw the road end at a building with a small parking lot in front. She could see the river behind it. Now what?

Emmy saw some men come out of the building. They appeared to be holding rifles. She scooted down in her seat as low as she could, closed her eyes, and said a quick prayer.

CHAPTER 47

Special Agent in Charge Gossamer took control of the operation immediately upon his arrival. He set up a command post outside Amelio's front gate and quickly put all local law enforcement, the Coast Guard, and his own forces together on the same radio frequency. With lightning speed, he laid out a plan of action.

Two SWAT units under his command set to work breaching the security gate wall. With no motion detected or sound coming from the house since the initial two gunshots, and the two bogies spotted outside the perimeter, Gossamer felt the risk of further violence in the house was minimal. He wanted to know as soon as possible who'd been shot and what their condition was.

He also wanted access to the drone feed. At first, Lt. Coleman was either reluctant or didn't realize how that could happen, but Gossamer also had an IT expert with him and within a few minutes, he enjoyed the same feed on his iPad that the Coast Guard saw from their command center.

Gossamer had a detailed map of the area spread out on the hood of his cruiser. He referenced the drone feed and demanded, "Where are we looking at?" He could see the jeep moving down the dirt track, which didn't appear to lead anywhere.

Lt. Coleman said, "The track he's on will come out on South Santee River Road in a couple miles."

Special Agent Christoff Dunne, never more than a few feet from the SAC, pinpointed the jeep's position on the map. Gossamer followed the road and saw the three intersections with Highway 17.

"Do we have assets at these intersections?" He barked into the radio. "Tell me who is where."

Each police patrol declared their affiliation and their position. Dunne marked the map with each. Gossamer asked, "And what do we know about this woman he's got with him?"

At first, no one offered an answer. Leroy realized he was the only one who knew her. "SAC Gossamer, this is Sheriff Keating from Georgetown County. The woman's name is Emmy Sweeney. She was involved with the shipwreck incidents yesterday. At this point, we don't know why she was at the suspect's home. But I'm certain she's being held hostage."

"Thank you, Sheriff." Gossamer studied the drone footage as the jeep neared the end of the dirt road. "He's going to have to make a choice here soon." Then they saw the jeep turn left, headed toward the highway. Back on the radio, Gossamer said, "Sheriff Keating, suspect is heading north on South Santee Road. Heading your way, ETA two minutes. Sending backup now."

"Ten-four, Sir. We'll be waiting."

******

"Looks like we're in the right place at the right time," Tony said as he readied his service pistol. Both he and Leroy rolled their windows down, exited the patrol car, and took defensive positions behind the open front doors. They peered down the road, looking for any sign of a jeep. None came.

"They should be here by now," said Tony.

Then their radio crackled. "Sheriff Keating," shouted Gossamer. "The suspect jeep has turned around. Pursue down South Santee Road. I'll keep you posted."

Tony looked across the car. "He must have seen the lights. Can't be far."

The two jumped back in the patrol car and added siren to the lights. Leroy peeled out and raced down South Santee Road, feeling the rush of the hunt. He didn't give one shit about this Amelio guy. He just prayed the Sweeney girl would come out of it all right.

Gossamer came back on the radio. "Sheriff, the suspect has taken a left turn on Santee Gun Club Road. Continue pursuit. The road ends at the gun club by the river. Backup is right behind you."

"Ten four," replied Leroy. He turned and smiled at Tony. "A gun club, huh? This might get interesting."

******

Gossamer kept his eyes on the drone feed as the jeep took its turn down Santee Gun Club Road. As soon as he gave Keating his instructions to follow, he radioed the McClellanville PD.

"Davis, you there?"

"Yes, Sir. I heard."

"What can you tell me about this gun club at the end of the road?"

"Not much to it, Sir. It's got a gun range and a dock on the Santee River. Mostly a bunch of good ole boys who shoot guns in the morning and drink beer in the afternoon."

Gossamer smirked briefly and hoped it wasn't ever the other way around. "Can you get a hold of them right away? Tell them what's coming at them."

"I'll do that, Sir."

"And tell them to stand down. I don't need any non-law enforcement personnel involved."

Davis chuckled over the radio. "I'll do that, Sir, but I'm not sure they'll listen."

This got under Gossamer's skin. "Goddamn it, Deputy. I don't want anyone killed out there today."

No response other than, "We're on our way, Sir."

Leroy interjected over the radio, "And tell them not to shoot the girl."

Gossamer pinched the bridge of his nose and shook his head.

CHAPTER 48

Rex Stanton ended the surprise call he just received from Deputy Davis of the McClellanville PD. At first, he thought the small gun club he ran had somehow run afoul of the law. He'd had several visits from the deputy over the course of the last few years. Mostly minor violations. Nothing that ever warranted more than a warning. Some of the guys were experimenting with various illegal bump stocks lately. One of them was firing out there right now. But nothing could have predicted this urgent message.

Rex pocketed his phone and called out to the three other men at the range. "Hey, y'all. We got ourselves a situation. Grab your guns and meet me out front."

"What's goin' on, Rex?" Buster Donald, always eager for any new adventure that involved firearms, asked.

"Just got a call from our local deputy. Seems there's a drug runner fleeing from the law, headed our way."

Buster scratched his head. "Why the hell would a —"

"I don't know, you idiot," Rex interrupted. "Guy probably wants to hijack a boat and escape."

"I got the only boat here," chimed in Ronnie Dawson. "I'll be damned if he thinks he's going to take my boat."

The four men formed a straight line outside the front door. Each had a loaded rifle in their hands and an itchy trigger finger. The excitement they felt was like nothing they'd ever experienced before. Shooting at targets was nothing compared to live action. Whatever was coming their way was up to no good.

"Think he's gonna run tail when he sees us?" Buster asked the group.

"Hope to hell not," said Ronnie. "I ain't never had the chance to shoot a real ass drug runner."

Rex saw the jeep first. It came around the bend and headed straight towards them at a high rate of speed. All four men raised their rifles. Fifty yards away, the jeep screeched to a halt. For a minute, nothing happened. Rex saw a Hispanic-looking man sitting at the wheel and a young white woman sitting beside him. To Rex, he felt like Wyatt Earp at the OK Corral. If the man made a move, it would be the last thing he'd ever do.

"I need a boat," the man suddenly yelled. It wasn't a request. "I'll pay you for it."

"You ain't gettin' no boat," Rex stated without hesitation. "Now get your ass out of my gun club before you get the business end of this here rifle."

The man didn't respond, and the standoff continued.

Buster whispered to Rex, "Can we shoot him now?"

"No. Wait and see what he's going to do."

Then they heard a siren coming from up the road. A few seconds later, flashing lights appeared and closed in fast. The man in the jeep turned around and saw what was coming his way.

"Give it up, Mister," Rex hollered. "You ain't going nowhere."

But instead of going nowhere, Rex couldn't believe his eyes when the jeep took off and accelerated straight for them. In an instant, Rex realized the man meant to run them down.

"Give it to him, boys." And before he finished 'boys', four simultaneous rifle blasts deafened the parking lot.

******

Amelio realized he had reached the end of the road. Not just the end of the Santee Gun Club Road, but the end of everything. Everything he had worked for; all his dreams, hopes, and desires were staring down the barrel of four long guns aimed right at him.

At first, he thought he might bribe his way out of the mess. Payoff whoever owned the boat out back. He had a stash of $5000 cash in the glove compartment of the jeep. But they didn't bite. Then he put the blame on the girl. The God-damned bitch who had stuck her nose in his business too many times for him to count.

He turned to Sweeney and screamed, "You stupid cunt! You've fucked everything up. Now you're going to get us both killed." But she had her head buried and turned away from him. It didn't matter. At this point, it seemed nothing mattered.

Amelio heaved in breaths, hyperventilating, his heart pounding in his chest, trying to think of another way out. There wasn't anything else he could think of to get out of this jam. The gun club men weren't going to get him a boat. He knew the drone that had been tracking him would see him here at the gun club. It was only a matter of minutes before who knew how many law enforcement rained down upon him.

He thought about making a last stand with the girl as a hostage. And just how would that play out? Even if they somehow let him go with her as a hostage, they would continue to track him. He'd never escape, he'd never taste freedom again.

He continued to breathe heavily, his rational mind slipping from its precious hold on sanity. He couldn't think anymore. Everything around him turned into a blur. Then he heard the sirens. A quick turn of his head confirmed what he already knew. Now he was in a trap, and there wasn't any way out of this one. One final semi-rational thought pushed into his fried mind. Get to the boat. It was his only escape route. And there was only one way to it— through the men with the guns. Amelio screamed "Aaaaarrrrrgh" and the top of his lungs and slammed the accelerator to the floor. He made it halfway.

******

Emmy knew in her heart; this time she was going to die. Amelio kept screaming at her, this was all her fault; that if she hadn't had stuck her nose where it didn't belong, none of this would have happened. And if he was going to die, so would she. When the jeep came to a stop in front of the men with the rifles, she knew it was curtains for both of them.

Amelio wanted a boat. Oh, wouldn't that be great, she thought. Then she'd end up as his sex slave or something even more grotesque. But the one man with the rifle shouted he wasn't about to give Amelio his boat. Then she heard the sirens behind her. It had to be the same cops they saw at the highway. They must have spotted the jeep and followed them. This entire ordeal was about to end, one way or another. Emmy felt certain she'd die in a hail of gunfire.

Then Amelio did something even more crazy. He gunned the jeep and drove straight at the men with the guns. Emmy screamed and ducked down even further. Just as her head dropped below the windshield, an enormous blast of gunfire deafened her. Glass shattered everywhere and she, for the second time in less than an hour, felt warm blood splatter over her face. But she wasn't hit, and she wasn't dead.

Emmy raised her head and peeked at the driver's side. Amelio slumped in his seat, with half his head blown off. Emmy quickly closed her eyes and shivered with shock and fear. She heard voices. It sounded like they were closing in on her. The passenger door opened, and she heard a man's voice. "Miss, are you Ok? Miss, are you hurt?" She couldn't open her mouth. More men arrived. She heard muffled sounds. "Is she hit?" "I don't know." "Let's get her out of the jeep."

More footsteps came. Emmy continued to stay in the fog of shock. What happened? Was she shot? Would she even know if she was? Then she heard a voice she recognized. "Miss Sweeney, are you hurt?" She knew that voice. It was a voice she had just heard recently, a comforting voice, a safe voice. It was the sheriff. The Georgetown County Sheriff. For a split second, she thought, oh shit, am I ever in trouble now. But it brought her back to reality, and with that, the realization that she was in fact, still alive and safe.

Emmy raised her head and turned to the passenger side window. "Yes," she said, barely croaking out the words. "Yes, I'm all right." Then she began to cry.

******

As Leroy raced down the Santee Gun Club Road, he envisioned a final fateful end to this travesty. He knew it would end badly and fatally for the idiot drug runner. He had fooled too many law enforcement for too long and his time was about up. It was the Sweeney girl that had him worried. The scenarios in which she could come out of this unharmed, or even alive, were few. Leroy feared either she would die in a hail of gunfire from that gun club, or the drug runner would shoot her first, and then die himself.

When he came around the last bend and saw the jeep in the parking lot, then four men in front of the building holding rifles aimed at the jeep, he knew the chase had ended. He thought maybe there would be a standoff. Emmy might be held hostage, then there'd be some kind of negotiation. He'd let Gossamer arrive and deal with it.

But none of that happened. Suddenly, the jeep took off and drove straight towards the line of men with the guns. Before he could even blink, not believing his eyes, all four guns exploded.

"God-damn it! Why'd they do that?" Leroy screamed. He screeched the squad car to a halt in the back of the jeep and he and Tony raced out of the car. Two of the gunmen reached the jeep first. Leroy arrived a few seconds later. His first glance was at the driver. The drug runner slumped over the steering wheel, most of his face blown off. Then he looked at Emmy. She lay dead still, crouched on her side. No obvious wounds were apparent. He gently shook her and called her name. When she finally raised her head and said she was all right, Leroy felt his heart stick in his throat. It was a feeling unlike any he had ever felt before — ever.

CHAPTER 49

Gossamer watched it all unfold on the drone footage. When he saw the gun club boys raise their long arms, he almost choked. After the rifles went off, he held his breath, waiting to see if Emmy was all right. When he saw her raise her head, he exhaled a long sigh of relief. "Sheriff Keating, can you confirm the suspect is dead and Miss Sweeney is unharmed?" He knew the answer to the first one, as not much remained of Amelio's head.

"Yes, Sir," the sheriff replied. "Suspect is deceased. Miss Sweeney appears to be unharmed. We'll need to get her checked out to be sure."

"Roger, thank you. Good work. I'll call an ambulance for Miss Sweeney. More help is on the way shortly."

Leroy confirmed.

Gossamer glanced over to Dunne and said, "This'll be an interesting one to tell the director."

"Yes, Sir," whispered Dunne, still in shock himself. He'd seen nothing like that, ever before.

However, Gossamer wasn't one to dwell on sentimentalism in the middle of an operation. He quickly switched gears to the home in McClellanville, directing Coleman to move the drone back over the home. While the action unfolded at the gun club, he noticed the security wall at the home had been breached. He radioed Special Agent Kirk Thomas, who led the team into the house.

"Kirk, are you in the home yet?"

"Yes, Sir," came the reply. "Just entered. Hold a second."

Gossamer studied the drone feed as the home came back into view. "I assume nobody else has left the house."

"No, Sir," came the reply from several of his operatives.

"Lieutenant Stark, go ahead and enter the home from the back. Nobody's going to leave by boat."

"You got it," responded Stark.

"Sir," Thomas broke in. "We have one male in the living room. Deceased. Shot in the head. We're searching the rest of the home now."

"Shit," whispered Gossamer, away from the radio. "Roger. Let me know as soon as you secure the home. I want to see how this bastard lived myself."

"Copy, Sir. Should be just a couple more minutes.

******

Fifteen minutes later, after they hoisted him up and over the security wall, Gossamer entered Amelio's front door. The department's munitions experts would arrive later to blow the front gate. As soon as he entered, Gossamer realized Amelio lived a life of luxury. The house's exterior implied a modest Creekside home. But the interior was anything but ordinary. The furniture was made from the highest quality Italian leather. The kitchen boasted the most modern appliances available, and the bedroom was decked out to fit a king. They soon found the trap door which led to the tunnel Amelio took outside the wall and to the boat shed.

After a brief tour of the place, Gossamer focused on what mattered the most — intelligence. He received confirmed information on the deceased — one Sonny Petrino, full-time fish store owner, part time two-bit criminal for the Constantine cartel. The brief summary he received from Sheriff Keating was Petrino had taken Sweeney hostage as a ploy to enter the drug runner's home in order to surprise and kill him. Over what was unclear. It would come out in due time. But it was very apparent the homeowner was a major player in the cartel. Most likely the head of the organization's activities in the Carolinas. Gossamer had been briefed on the cocaine capture and the drug runner in question.

Gossamer went to Thomas, who looked over the shoulder of his IT guru, Martin Kittering. Kittering had Amelio's laptop out and was busy tapping keys. "Can you hack in?" Gossamer asked, hoping for a quick entry. Access to the guy's computer network would be a treasure trove of information, the first step in the department's long desired effort to take down the crime organization.

Martin paused and turned around to address Gossamer and Thomas. "It's not the least accessible entry I've ever seen, but I'm not sure I can get in without taking it back to the lab."

"Understood. Keep me abreast."

"Yes, Sir. I will."

Gossamer walked back across the living area. "What else do we have?" he asked Dunne, who had been busy casing the home.

"Well. Sir," Dunne answered with a grin, "we found these. Guessing this was what the hubbub was all about at sea." He handed Gossamer two gold coins with Jerusalem crosses on the front.

Gossamer took the coins and gave them a quick look over. "From that shipwreck, huh?"

"It appears so. Got him just in time. Coast Guard reports the vessel that went out along with our guy brought up bags of the stuff."

Gossamer laughed. "I bet Constantine was banking on millions from a haul like that. Son of a bitch is probably trying to reach his guy right now, wanting to know when his gold is going to show up."

"We'll have his phone as soon as Sheriff Keating is through with the body. That'll be interesting as well."

"Absolutely. I feel like a kid in a candy store. What else do we have?"

"Sir," someone called out from downstairs, "You might be interested in this."

Gossamer walked down the steps leading to an elaborate game / party room. He followed Dunne to a closet in the corner. The door was busted open.

"He didn't lock this down like one would think for something this sensitive. Guess he wasn't expecting company like us."

Gossamer stepped inside the walk-in closet. Inside were wall-to-wall stacks of military grade weaponry. Machine guns, RPG, C4, and boxes upon boxes of various ammunition. Gossamer folded his arms and nodded, grinning widely. "Outstanding," he proclaimed. "It's Christmas in September."

CHAPTER 50

Four days later

Leroy walked down the row of cells holding the various miscreants of his county and arrived at the far end, where he found a much-subdued Dr. Morgan sitting on his cot, arms folded. Morgan's attention perked when he saw the sheriff approach.

"It's time, Doctor. Get up," Leroy told him, his voice even, hiding the animosity he held for his prisoner.

Morgan jumped out of bed and went to the small sink, where he splashed water on his face and ran his fingers through his now filthy hair. "It's about damn time," he grumbled, approaching the bars. "You promised me a hearing on Tuesday. It's Thursday."

"Sue me." Leroy inserted his key and opened the cell door. "I told you the judge is busy. You're lucky you got in today."

"I gave you information. You got what you wanted. You owe me."

"Hah!" Leroy laughed out loud. "I don't owe you shit. We would have found our man with or without your help. Hands out front."

Morgan did as he was told, and the sheriff placed handcuffs on his wrists. "And you're sure I'm going to be offered bail?"

Leroy rolled his eyes. "I'm not sure of anything, other than you're a world class scumbag. Bail is up to the judge."

Morgan mumbled something Leroy didn't catch and didn't care to hear. They walked down the hall and out the door, then across the courtyard, and into the courthouse. Morgan's attorney, Leonard Barry, met him in the lobby, where Leroy gladly handed him off.

"Thank you, Sheriff, for taking such good care of my client," said Barry. "I trust he wasn't a burden to you."

Leroy scoffed. The statement wasn't completely sardonic. After word got around of a rich doctor caught with a cooler full of cocaine, a couple of prisoners expressed their desire to place Dr. Morgan on the receiving end of a homemade shank, if given the opportunity. Leroy made sure such a prospect didn't present itself.

"Dr. Morgan kept to himself," was all Leroy said.

The three of them entered the courtroom. Leroy took a seat in the back, while Morgan and Barry took their places up front, while they waited for Judge Waterson to get to their case. Tony came in and sat next to Leroy. He was in a jovial mood.

"What kind of bail do you think he's going to get?" Tony asked.

"My guess is between 1.5 and 2 mil."

"Sounds about right. What about the ankle monitor?"

"Hmph," Leroy grunted with disgust. "If it were up to me, I'd keep him locked inside his house."

"Think the judge will go for that?"

"Probably not, but we'll suggest it."

Tony changed the subject. "What time is the funeral? I assume you're going?"

"Eleven o'clock. Of course, as are you."

"Absolutely. And how is Miss Sweeney doing? Have you talked to her since Sunday?"

Leroy nodded and smiled. He more than talked to her. He'd seen her each day and by now felt he was almost a nuisance to her. But the events of Labor Day weekend had left an indelible mark on him. His initial irritation with Emmy's independent mindedness had worn off. Ever since she raised her head toward him in Amelio's jeep; a look so pitiful, so lost, and so exhausted, he'd taken it personally to see her through recovery.

Physically, Emmy came out in decent shape, considering what she'd been through. Six stitches to her face from a piece of broken windshield glass was all she needed in the hospital. The psychological wounds would take much longer to heal.

Leroy took it upon himself to assist Emmy every way he could. He substituted for her greeting Jack's family at the Myrtle Beach airport when they arrived on Sunday evening. Then he helped arrange Jack's funeral details. Leroy stayed in close contact with her throughout the week. Just yesterday, he was with her at the hospital, when they released David Sweeney. Emmy thanked him again for probably the hundredth time, but also gently requested that she didn't need so much attention anymore. After all, didn't he have the rest of the county to protect?

"I have," Leroy replied to Tony. "She's doing as well as can be expected."

"Hmm, that's good to hear."

"Case # 384566," Judge Waterson announced. "The State of South Carolina vs. Dr. Paul Morgan. Would the parties please rise."

Leroy and Tony brought their attention to the bench. Gina Ricci, the Georgetown County DA, stood and addressed the judge. "Judge, Dr. Morgan was caught red-handed with over ninety pounds of high-quality cocaine. I'm happy to report his connections to the cartel he worked for have been captured or killed. However, Dr. Morgan remains a high flight risk, and we ask the court to deny bail."

"Your Honor," Barry replied in rebuttal, "Dr. Morgan presents no such risk. He acknowledges the mistakes he has made and understands he will face these charges in court. He simply wishes to return to his practice, where his many patients depend on him for their health care. We request a set bail and will agree to wear an ankle monitoring device while he is free, awaiting trial."

Waterson put her hand on her chin and studied Morgan. Leroy knew the judge had a reputation for leniency on these bail hearings and relied heavily on the monitoring systems, especially now, where they could be customized to specific locations. He expected the same here.

"I'll agree to a monitor placed on Dr. Morgan," she replied. "What areas are you expecting him to be allowed access to, other than his home and the Georgetown Memorial Hospital?"

"Your Honor," replied Barry, "we appreciate the opportunity. We request Dr. Morgan have access to all of Georgetown County, so he can shop for his needs and visit patients as needed."

Waterson rolled her eyes. "Yeah, that's not happening. You better narrow it down."

Leroy noticed Morgan whisper something in Barry's ear. The lawyer nodded and asked the judge, "Your Honor, my client would be willing to restrict his accessible area to his home, the hospital, and his yacht in the Georgetown Landing Marina. He spends considerable time there."

"Seriously," Gina interrupted. "The marina?"

"Your Honor, obviously, Dr. Morgan will not be sailing. The monitor will alert authorities if he's even fifty yards outside his mooring."

Waterson considered the request. "Ms. Ricci, any objection to this?"

Gina cast a glance back at Leroy, who slightly nodded his head. "No, Your Honor, the state can live with this."

"Very well. Bail is set at 1.5 million dollars. The defendant will be restricted to the areas discussed." She slammed her gavel down and announced the end of the hearing.

Leroy took a deep sigh. He turned to Tony and asked, "How long do you think he'll last?"

Tony grinned and replied, "I'll give him a day."

******

One hour later, Morgan was a free man. At least, free to roam the limited access space he was allowed. Didn't matter, he had no intention of staying put. Everything with the judge went as he expected. The fact he was out on a million-and-a-half-dollar bond phased him not in the least. Of most importance, he was allowed to visit the marina area. That way, he could get a head start on his escape.

First things first, however. He had to get home and pack. Pack for a trip which had no return. He knew that much of his belongings would stay in DeBordieu forever. He debated what he would take. Anything that looked like an extended trip may draw attention. Particularly from that nosy dockmaster, Robbins. Morgan suspected Robbins was involved in some aspect of his capture. Not that he could prove anything. It was just a hunch. Morgan decided on one small suitcase, but he thought even that may arouse suspicion. Did Robbins know about his arrest? How could he not? Finally, Morgan decided on a single backpack. A few light clothes and toiletries would suffice until he got to the Caymans.

The plan was quite simple. Once on *Doctor's Orders* with a full tank of gas, he'd make a beeline east past the twelve-mile territorial limit and out of the reach of the US authorities. Sure, they'd know he was making an escape, thanks to the problematic monitor secured tightly to his ankle. Before he arrived home, he thought a pair of bolt cutters would take care of the nuisance once he got on the boat, but the damn thing was too tight to fit the blade end of the cutter under it. It would take some more doing, maybe not until he reached the Caymans, where he could hire discrete professional help. Morgan presumed, hoped, and prayed that the tracker had a relatively limited range. He knew they would notice he was headed out to sea and might try to chase him. But he'd soon be out of their detection range and safe within an hour.

Safe, however, was a relative term. The fact was, Morgan felt less safe than at any time in his life. He knew the organization was capable of many unappetizing ways to kill him. From the moment he stepped out of the courtroom, fear consumed him, and he saw danger around every corner. He was first driven to the compound lot to pick up his truck, where it had been towed from the marina. Could Constantine's people have placed a bomb in his truck and blown him up when he turned the ignition? It didn't happen. Still, Morgan felt the cold sweat of panic run down his neck.

When he arrived home, he feared snipers were hiding in the bushes. Or maybe they had broken into his home and were waiting to ambush him inside. Again, only silence surrounded him.

By the time he finished packing, Morgan felt somewhat more confident the organization wasn't waiting in the wings to kill him. When the cops gave him back his personal items, including the burner phone he used to communicate with Amelio, he saw five calls in the few hours after his arrest. Nothing after that. Morgan wasn't stupid. He knew Amelio would be after him, but couldn't predict when or where. Surely, Amelio found out what had happened. But did he know he was out on bail yet? If he didn't, Morgan knew he would soon.

Assassination attempts aside, Morgan's next biggest concern was getting out of the marina and reaching the territorial limit before the Coast Guard, or whomever, tracked him down. With the ankle bracelet locked down, they'd be alerted as soon as he left the marina. A straight shot east at full speed would take him less than thirty minutes, top, to reach the limit. Would it be enough? He'd soon find out.

CHAPTER 51

Emmy woke on Thursday morning to what she knew would be another trying, emotional day. At least she was in the comfort of her own bed, Sandy by her side, wishing for her to get up and be fed. This was the day of Jack's funeral. Thank goodness Sheriff Keating had stepped in like he did and met Jack's family on Sunday night, then also took on the lion's share of the funeral details.

Something about his attitude toward her had changed from the cool reception she received after the near drowning on Saturday. It seemed only moments after the ordeal ended in that tucked away gun club parking lot, with Amelio shot in his jeep, glass flying everywhere, that the sheriff appeared out of nowhere. And he was so kind.

He arrived at the hospital shortly after she was admitted. Stayed with her the whole time she was there. It was almost as if he felt indebted to her, as opposed to the reality where she was indebted to him, and all the other men and women of the Coast Guard, the FBI, and the local police departments.

Whatever it was, she was beyond grateful. Everyone had been so nice and generous to her. News of the ordeal made all the headlines. It seemed every newspaper, news station, and podcaster in the Southeast wanted to interview her. Sheriff Keating made sure none of them got close to Emmy until she felt ready for them. And wasn't she thankful for that? Emmy was still trying to grasp what happened to her, herself. It all seemed so surreal. Jack, the coin, the wreck, the rescue, the ploy with Sonny, and the final chase — it was still such a blur.

Poor Sonny. He didn't deserve what happened to him. Not that she condoned his association with such a ruthless band of criminals. She preferred to remember him as the kind and compassionate fishmonger she and Jack had gotten to know over the past three years. Now, both he and Jack were gone. And there would be no funeral for Sonny. The sheriff told her they sent his body back to Italy, where his only family still lived. More than once, she felt saddened by the cruel irony. He got to go back to Salerno, just not the way he hoped.

She had her own family to worry about as well. Dad came home from the hospital yesterday. Always grouchy, he was particularly ornery about the recuperation period he faced. The PT therapist assigned to him was a man who, in his words, treated him like a butcher tenderizing a slab of beef. Why couldn't he have any of the several attractive female therapists at the rehab center? Mom rolled her eyes and shook her head, then called him a disgusting old man.

At least dad was thrilled that Amelio was gone. When he received the entire story from the sheriff about what Emmy had been through at the end, his face reddened and the language he used embarrassed everyone in the room. Then he wanted to know about the rest of the bastard organization responsible for what happened. We're working on it, the sheriff assured him. We're close. Finally, dad wanted to know about Dr. Morgan. He knew about the arrest and the cocaine. When the sheriff told him Morgan would most likely be out on bail Thursday morning, it upset him even more. Emmy and her dad were glad to hear about the ankle monitor, but still — really? Dad preferred Morgan meet a fate similar to Amelio.

Emmy gave Sandy a big, good morning hug, then rose to feed him and made her coffee. Since she came home, everything around her seemed enhanced. The morning sunshine felt warmer, the coffee tasted fresher, the bed was more comfortable than she had ever remembered. Emmy supposed near death survival did that to people. Twice no less.

But today would be another emotionally draining day and she had to prepare herself for it.

Even though Jack had never been religious since she'd known him, his family was Catholic and insisted on a service in a Catholic church. There weren't any in Georgetown, so they would need to travel up to Pawleys Island to the Precious Blood of Christ Church. The service was scheduled for 11:00 AM.

After that, the burial would be at the small cemetery out on Morgan Point, past East Bay Park in Georgetown. Emmy insisted on this place, as Jack had previously mentioned it in passing. It made sense, since Jack sailed past the point every time he set out to fish. Jack's family wanted him to be buried at the cemetery by the church, but Emmy put her foot down on this one. It was Jack's request, not mine, she insisted on them. His mother didn't want her son buried in some out of the way tiny cemetery with no religious affiliation.

The test of wills ended with Mrs. Abromski's conciliation. She reluctantly agreed after a few choice comments. Emmy let it pass. She doubted she'd ever see them again once they caught a plane back to Boston later that day. If she could just get through this, she could spend the next few days relaxing and recharging before returning to work on Monday. It was something she more and more looked forward to.

Emmy opened her wardrobe and tried to decide what to wear. The only black dress she had was a long gown. The forecast was still in the upper eighties. She settled on a black skirt and white blouse. Somebody didn't like it — tough. She was truly on her own now and wasn't afraid to make her own decisions. Emmy winced at the thought of some of the horrible decisions she'd made in the past week. There was nothing wrong with making bad choices, if you learned from them. Emmy felt she had learned more about her recent poor decisions and their consequences than anything else in her entire life.

CHAPTER 52

Constantine seemed to be in a perpetual state of rage. It had been four days since he had had any contact with Amelio, and he had no other way of knowing what was going on in South Carolina. As if losing forty kilos of cocaine wasn't bad enough, he could only suspect the salvage operation of the *Concepcion* had also gone to shit. He assumed Amelio had been captured or killed.

With no contacts on the ground in the area, Constantine had to rely on public media for any news about what happened. And there wasn't anything coming out. He'd seen the articles in the Charleston papers about the cocaine bust. Nothing in them connected the seizures to his organization. Whether that would continue was anybody's guess. But the collapse of the salvage operation would be even bigger news, if indeed it had happened. Or the authorities were keeping it under wraps for other security reasons. The worst possibility of all was the authorities had compromised Amelio's home in McClellanville. If that happened, and the FBI went through the place; confiscated his laptop with all that sensitive information on it, captured the arsenal he kept downstairs, the consequences would be mind-boggling. It might mean a fatal blow to his organization, as well as himself.

He needed to find out what happened in South Carolina. The uncertainty gnawed at his mind like a termite feasting on a rotted old home. As if on cue, his trusted assistant, Carlos, entered the living area with a grim look on his face.

"What is it?" demanded Constantine. He could tell the news was not good.

"It's Amelio, Sir. I just heard from one of our operatives in Charleston. He hadn't been able to get anywhere near Amelio's home since Monday. The road into his house has been closed. Today, the road reopened, and he went outside his house. The police have it roped off. He said there was much activity going on, lots of flashing lights outside. I'm afraid he's been compromised, Sir."

"Yah think!" Constantine shouted back. "Fuck! I wonder if that idiot is dead or in jail." Constantine rose and walked to the bar and poured himself a shot of tequila. He downed it, then glared at his assistant. "Got any suggestions?"

Carlos shook his head.

"I thought not. We're going to have to freeze all operations until this thing blows over. Have you —" Constantine's question was interrupted by the sound of a loud bullhorn from out front.

"Sebastian Constantine, this is the FBI. I am Special Agent in Charge Charles Gossamer, and I am under orders from the Director of the Federal Bureau of Investigation. I have a warrant for your arrest. You are ordered to open your front gate and exit the house with your hands up."

All the blood drained from Constantine's face. No more reason to speculate what damage may have been done in McClellanville. He knew once they penetrated Amelio's laptop, all the secrets would fall out. And now they have. Constantine looked around as if there were something or someone to save him. He had only Carlos and a couple of servants in the house at the time. Even if he had his best men around and chose to fight, he knew it would end in disaster. They might have been able to hold the FBI out front at bay for a while, but then the freaking Army would probably be right behind and down this throat.

So, in deciding whether to fight and go down in a blaze of gunfire or surrender, Constantine considered discretion the better part of valor. He had good lawyers, but so did the US government. Maybe he could fight the charges and live to see another day of freedom. Or, perhaps more likely, he would end up like Noriega or El Chapo and spend the rest of his life in some miserable prison.

The bullhorn blared again. "Constantine, this is your last chance. If you don't open the gate and surrender, we will blow it and take you by force."

Constantine cast a wary glance at Carlos. "I'm afraid this is the end, my friend. Go ahead and open the gate."

Carlos did as he was told. Within a minute, half a dozen heavily armed agents stormed through the front door. Constantine remained silent as the agents spread throughout the compound. Before they hauled him out in handcuffs, Constantine had one question for the lead agent. "What happened to Amelio?"

Gossamer looked him straight in the eye and said, "He's dead."

Constantine scoffed and thought, lucky him.

CHAPTER 53

Emmy took her place in the receiving line in the front lobby of Precious Blood of Christ's elaborate church. First time she'd ever been there. First time she'd ever been in any catholic church. The place had a certain unmistakable solemnity about it. Large stained-glass windows brightened with a kaleidoscope of color from the late morning sunlight. Emmy felt glad she agreed to hold the service here. The many mourners now streaming through the front door brought a sense of warmth that tempered her sadness.

Emmy stood in the middle, with Jack's family to her right and mom and dad to her left. Dad was still in a wheelchair, much to his displeasure. Doctor's orders, he lamented; the irony of Morgan's yacht's name not lost on his ill humor. Mom made sure he stayed seated.

The agenda was straightforward. They would greet the guests as they arrived. Jack's body lay in the sanctuary in an impressive-looking coffin, covered with an assortment of lilies, carnations, and chrysanthemums. The service would be short. Neil agreed to speak as well as Jack's father and brother. Emmy declined. The emotion of the day, on top of everything else that happened, was plenty enough for her. A small group of friends and relatives would attend the burial immediately afterwards. Tom had offered to provide a spread at Coastal Catch following the gravesite service. Emmy graciously agreed.

The attendance of well-wishers was impressive. The parking lot looked almost full, and the line extended out the front door.

Sheriff Keating was one of the first to arrive and continued to show his support and empathy. Emmy got the feeling he felt guilty somehow. He as much as apologized earlier for his failure to protect her from harm.

That's my job, he had told her, to protect. Emmy was grateful but knew her misadventures were completely her own doing.

"How are you holding up, Miss Sweeney?" the sheriff asked her, holding both of her hands.

Emmy gave him a bashful smile. "I'm doing well, thank you. I'm so glad you could make it here. And I want to apologize again for the trouble I caused." It must have been the tenth time she had told him this over the past few days. She felt like she needed to do it every time she saw him.

"Please, Emmy, please. No more apologizing. We're all happy to have you safe."

Emmy raised her eyebrows at him. It was the first time he addressed her by her first name. It put her at ease. "Thank you," she said in a whisper.

The sheriff asked, "Would it be all right if the detective and I attend the gravesite ceremony?"

Emmy shrugged. "Sure, if you'd like to. That would be fine." She knew the space would be tight at the small cemetery, but who was she to say no to the county sheriff. If Jack's mother had an issue with it, she could deal with him herself.

Dad overheard the question and pulled her arm down so he could whisper in her ear. "Good, I have some questions for him."

Emmy could only imagine what that might entail.

The next mourner was Theresa Jenkins from the Rice Museum. Emmy's eyes lit up seeing her, the first time since last Friday when she learned the whole story of the lost treasure fleet.

"Ms. Jenkins, it's so good to see you." Emmy gave her a hug, but not too tight, given Theresa's frail build.

"You too, Emmy. I heard about what happened to you. I'm so glad you're safe."

"Me too." Emmy cracked a smile. She knew she'd be saying that a lot today. "Will you be coming to the reception at Coastal Catch later? I'd love to catch up some more with you."

"Of course, dear. I wouldn't miss it."

"Did you hear that the ownership of the wreck site with the treasure is headed to court soon?"

Theresa smiled. "Remember what I told you? If the treasure was real, there'd be a bruhaha about the ownership like you've never seen before."

"And I believed you," Emmy said emphatically. "We'll at least protect the site from the criminals."

Theresa chuckled. "Yes, dear. You took care of that, didn't you?"

Emmy blushed. "Well, sort of, I guess. I'll see you later."

Next in line was Jordy Gorman. Emmy gave him a broad smile. "Well, hello there, boss. Have you missed me?"

"Missed you?" Jordy hugged Emmy before answering further. "Why, the place has practically come to a standstill without you. Everyone wants to know when the hero of Georgetown is coming back to work."

Emmy's cheeks deepened a further shade of red. "Yeah, some hero. I did nothing except get myself into trouble. But I'm planning on coming back on Monday. I'm ready. I need some normalcy in my life."

"Well, I'm glad you're doing well. We'll talk more at the reception."

Right behind Jordy was Tom Boswell. Emmy took another deep breath, realizing how many people in her life she was indebted to, and felt a special bond with.

"Thank you again, Tom, for offering your restaurant. Jack would have wanted it that way."

"Emmy, you know it's my pleasure and honor and the least I could do. You both have meant so much to me."

"I'm sorry your investment didn't pay out in the end. As it turned out, it worked — too well."

"Emmy, you have nothing to be sorry about. I'm just thrilled you could find the wreck site and the treasure. It's truly a historic find."

"It is, it is. But don't forget, I didn't find it. Jack found it, with your help."

"Yes and look where it got him. I don't want to hold you up. We'll talk more at the restaurant."

"Absolutely, Tom."

Emmy continued to greet the well-wishers. The sanctuary was nearly full, and the line finally subsided. There was one person whom she hadn't greeted yet — Neil. Surely, he wouldn't miss this. She had had no contact with him since the hospital last Saturday. Was he avoiding her? Did he feel responsible in some way? She knew him too well and knew how much he was hurt by what happened to Jack and with her and dad.

She peeked toward the back of the line. There he is. He showed up. Two minutes later, Neil approached. It appeared he'd already been crying. His eyes were red and swollen.

"Hello stranger," Emmy said. She gave him a reassuring smile and then hugged him. "I was beginning to worry about you."

"Hello, Emmy. Thanks. It's been a tough week. How have you been holding up?"

"You know, I'm struggling too. Need to get through today. Tomorrow will be a new start."

"Yes, I suppose. I still, I still —"

Emmy thought, oh jeez, he's going to cry right here. How is he ever going to give a eulogy? Dad came to the rescue.

"Neil, how the hell are you? Where have you been, lad?"

"Hello, Mr. Sweeney," Neil said weakly. "I've been around. I just —"

"This man's a hero," Dad called down the receiving line towards Jack's family. "He saved my life and Emmy's as well." Then back to Neil. "You know that, son. I mean it."

"Thank you, Mr. Sweeney. Thank you."

"Neil," Emmy interjected. "Go in and save seats for me and mom and dad, upfront. You need to sit with us."

Neil looked at Emmy with brighter eyes. This seemed to cheer him up. "I'll do that, Emmy, sure. See you inside."

Emmy watched him stroll into the sanctuary, wondering again what he'd been doing the last few days. And what he was going to do with his future.

She greeted the last few guests. It was time. Dad looked up and asked, "Are you ready, darling?"

Emmy looked down and smiled as best she could. "I'm ready as I'll ever be."

CHAPTER 54

Morgan arrived at the marina fully paranoid. He didn't know exactly where the outer limit of his allowed area lay. He was just told he could go to the marina, but no further. The plan was simple enough. Back out of his dock. Get a full tank of gas, the pumps were still on the marina property, then get the hell out of the dodge. He'd take it at full speed east until he was outside the territorial limit. Then he'd head due south and throttle back to conserve gas. He had enough fuel to reach Freeport in the Bahamas by early the next morning. After refueling there, he'd sail around Cuba and reach Grand Cayman by the following day. Then he'd regroup; take out some cash, get the damn ankle monitor removed, and plan his new life. Surely, he felt, surely the monitor signal will drop off soon after he was out to sea.

At 1:00 PM, Morgan walked past the dockmaster's office, grimacing at the memory of being nabbed at that exact spot. He didn't even risk a glance into the office, just walked straight down the pier, one modest backpack on his shoulders. But he feared every step. Were the cops waiting for him? What about Amelio? Was he watching him? Morgan wouldn't relax until he was well out to sea.

Wasting no more time, he started the engine and backed out of his mooring for the last time. Although his apprehension was still palpable, Morgan saw the shining light of freedom draw ever closer. He constantly looked all around for any sign of trouble. Other than a couple boats coming and going, the place was quiet. He veered around the main docks and settled into the marina gas pumps. He knew he had to have one last personal interaction. Joe, who ran the marina's pumps and small store, walked out to greet him.

"Afternoon, Joe. Fill it please."

"Yes, Sir, Dr. Morgan."

Morgan glared at the man with suspicion. Did he know what happened? He saw Joe glance down at his ankle, but Morgan wore long pants for the trip. No sense advertising your greatest humiliation. Joe raised his eyes to Morgan's face and smiled. "Fine day, Sir. Seas should be calm today."

Morgan breathed a sigh of relief. Joe didn't seem alarmed. One more stress point behind him. "Yes, it is. Looking forward to a pleasant cruise."

"Where you headed today, Dr. Morgan, if you don't mind my asking?"

And just like that, the paranoia was back. Morgan gulped. Was Joe going to go straight back inside and tell Robbins what was going on? He knew Robbins knew about his arrest. Probably played a role in it. He forced himself to remain calm and replied, "Going up to Murrells Inlet today. Meeting some friends for dinner on the boardwalk." Simple, to the point, nothing extra. Let the cops poke around Murrells if they want.

"Enjoy your day, Sir. Stay safe."

Morgan smiled. Stay safe, like it was as easy as waking up in the morning. "Thanks, Joe. You too." Morgan wanted to get away as soon as possible but was afraid if he went back on the boat, Joe would alert Robbins. So, he stayed in the vicinity but avoided any further small talk.

Five minutes later, with no other interference, Morgan paid Joe in cash for the gas and climbed back onboard. Now for the next step. He was certain, as soon as he moved away from the marina, he'd be outside the monitor zone. The sheriff would get an alert and they'd be after him. Morgan itched to push the throttle all the way and speed out of the bay as fast as he could, but before he could do that, he still had to sail past the damn Coast Guard station. The last thing he needed at that point was to have the Coast Guard detect a speeding vessel in the channel. They enforced a strict ten knot limit for any boat coming and going in the channel. In the past, he pushed that limit, except, of course, on one of his drug-running missions.

Oh, did he ever miss the cocaine. Fortunately, he still had a small stash at the house and had enough to enjoy the trip ahead. There were contacts in Grand Cayman where he could restock. The five days in the county cell had sent him into some serious withdrawals. The line he snorted as soon as he got home made him feel physically better, but in no way helped his apprehension. Now, pulling away from the marina, before he reached the Coast Guard station, he dipped his spoon into the small bag of coke in his pants pocket and took one more snort. It helped, but until he got out to sea and cleared that territorial limit, he couldn't relax.

Morgan steered through to the center of the channel and kept his speed at ten knots. Every few seconds, he turned and peered back to the marina for any sign of trouble. There was none. The marina disappeared for the last time. The Coast Guard station approached on his right. Were they looking for him? Had they been alerted yet? There wasn't any sign of activity he could see.

Soon he was past it as well. Up ahead was East Bay Park, leading to Morgan Point, the last spit of land before the bay widened, then led out to the sea. He passed it every time he came in from the ocean. No, it wasn't named after him. It was named after some long-ago mayor of Georgetown. Should have been named after him, as much as he'd contributed to the community. No more though. He was done with the city, the county, the state, and the good old USA. The Caribbean awaited him, and he couldn't wait to get there.

Morgan glanced over to his right and noticed a group of people gathered near the end of the point. They seemed to be watching him closely. He couldn't tell who they were or what they were doing. One guy looked to be in a wheelchair. Morgan paid them no mind but turned his attention to the open bay ahead of him. It was time to get a move on. The excitement welled up inside of him as he pushed the throttle to full speed. *Doctor's Orders* responded in a flash and Morgan felt the thrill of his yacht's acceleration. Suddenly, he felt as free as he'd ever been in his life. Looking up to the sky, the warm sea wind in his face, he shouted to the Gods, "I'm king of the wor—"

CHAPTER 55

Emmy, her family, Jack's family, along with Neil and the sheriff and detective, stood around Jack's grave. Emmy felt like she was holding on by the thinnest emotional thread. She'd made it through the church service and the eulogies. Thank God she decided not to try to speak. Neil blabbered for a couple of minutes then broke down. He had to be helped off the stage. Now, the brief gravesite service was almost over. They were lowering Jack into the ground, his final resting place, close to the bay and the ocean he loved so much.

It all seemed so much a blur. Not just the funeral, but everything that had happened from the moment she first worried about Jack not returning a week ago Monday, to right now. Mom and dad stayed by her side the whole day and they promised her their continued support with anything she needed.

What she needed was peace. Peace and a return to normalcy. And what exactly was that? What would the 'new normal' be, as people like to say? Wouldn't life return to as it was before? Everything as it was, except for Jack? Her job, her friends, Sandy, all will still be there and in a few weeks, the world will be the same as it ever was.

Except it wouldn't. Not even close, and it was way more than Jack. Emmy now realized she viewed life completely differently. It was more than an altered perspective, more than appreciating what she had to a higher degree. It was something spiritual. A bond with God she'd never felt before in her life.

Emmy told her parents earlier that day that she wanted to go back to the church and asked if she could join their congregation at the Pawleys Island Community Church where they attended services. Of course, dear, mom told her. Then mom smiled at dad. Emmy hadn't attended church since her confirmation almost twenty years ago. Perhaps she would find more answers there.

One more task lay in front of her. While the priest continued to recite his prayers, Emmy and the others took turns throwing a small shovel full of dirt on top of the casket once it was lowered into the ground. Emmy cried again. This time the tears flowed as strongly as they had all day. "It's over now," she whispered to herself. "It's over now."

******

As the group began to make their way out, David thought to ask Leroy, "By the way, Sheriff, what's the status of Dr. Morgan? I trust he's still in jail and not out on bail."

Leroy grimaced. He had hoped the subject wouldn't come up. And he had almost gotten away with it. He took a deep breath and told David, "Actually, I'm afraid to say that Dr. Morgan made bail this morning. The DA did her best to deny it, but the presiding judge is fairly liberal in bail hearings and agreed."

David appeared flabbergasted. The others stopped and listened to this shocking news. "You have got to be kidding me!" David shot back. "You mean he's out — a free man?"

Leroy held up one hand. "Not a free man, Mr. Sweeney. He has an ankle monitoring device. He's limited to his home in DeBordieu and the hospital. That's it. I'm sorry I didn't tell you earlier in case you run into him near your home." Leroy had forgotten that David and Morgan lived in the same development.

"I still can't believe it. I heard how much cocaine you found him with. There shouldn't have been any bail."

Again, Leroy frowned. It was all over the media this week, once news got out of the biggest drug bust in recent memory taking place right here in Georgetown. "I can assure you, David, Dr. Morgan isn't going anywhere, anytime soon."

Just then, Leroy received an alert on his phone. Tony simultaneously got the same thing. The others looked on with interest. Leroy's eyes popped wide open when he saw what it was.

"Oh, for the love of Christ!" Leroy shouted, then turned to Tony. "You get the same thing?"

"I did. Can't believe it."

David's curiosity intervened. "What is it, Sheriff? Something wrong?"

"Police business, Mr. Sweeney. Tony, come over here." The two officers stepped away from the group until they were out of earshot.

"Looks like that son-of-a-bitch is making a run for it." Leroy watched the location of Morgan's monitor. The alert went off before Morgan was a hundred yards from the marina.

"I really can't believe he thinks he's going to get away," Tony said.

"Oh, he's not." Leroy got on his radio. He kept OIC Duvall on his frequency for just such a possibility. "Alex, are you there?"

After a couple seconds, the radio crackled back. "Yes, Sheriff, what can I do for you?"

"Looks like we got a runner. Dr. Morgan's ankle monitor just went off. He's in his yacht heading out of the channel. Should sail past your station any second now."

"Hold on, let me look."

Leroy waited impatiently. It would be up to the Coast Guard to track him down.

"Yes, Sheriff, I can see him now. We're on it. He's not going to get far."

"Thank you, Alex. I appreciate your help. Keep me up to date."

"Yes, Sir, I will."

Leroy ended the radio call and turned to Tony. "Of all the most obtuse, arrogant bastards I've ever met. This guy takes the cake."

"He'll be coming right by here before long."

Leroy realized they were only a half mile east of the Coast Guard station. The two walked over to get a better view of the bay. The others must have realized something was going on and eased over near the shore as well.

In another minute, *Doctor's Orders* appeared from the left, keeping a slow but steady pace down the channel. David was the first to recognize it.

"That's Morgan's boat!" he shouted and pointed. He turned to Leroy and said in a disgusting tone, "I thought you told me that bastard wasn't going anywhere? He's trying to make a run for it."

"David," Leroy retorted, as calm as possible, "he's not going to get far. I just alerted the Coast Guard. I assure you they'll catch him very soon."

All six watched in awe as *Doctor's Orders* came into view directly in front of them, only three-hundred yards away. The boat suddenly accelerated, its wake widening. For a split second, Leroy was concerned about the Coast Guard's ability to catch up.

The fireball shocked everyone. At first, it nearly blinded them in its intensity. In the second and a half it took for the sound wave to reach them, there was nothing but stunned, incomprehensible silence. Then the explosion rocked them backwards, nearly knocking them off their feet.

Leroy watched as the smoke rose over the bay and the remaining bits and pieces of what was Dr. Paul Morgan and his yacht fell back into the water. Nobody said anything. Leroy tried to grasp what his eyes and ears had just perceived. He had never seen or experienced anything like it before.

Finally, David said one word that encompassed it all. "Wow."

******

Emmy slowly regained her senses. Once again, she had witnessed unimaginable violence. When would it ever end? She stood there, shaking, at the water's edge, Jack's new grave behind her, and tried to get control over her emotions. It was futile. Mom and Neil came over and hugged her. Dad held her hand from his wheelchair.

"Why?" she whispered to no one in particular. "Why do people around me keep dying?" She looked skyward, as if God himself would answer her. No one deserved to die like that. Dr. Morgan may have been a dishonest man. Amelio was certainly a hardened criminal. Sonny got mixed up in the wrong business, and Jack's curiosity and greed led him to his end. But nobody, she didn't care how unsavory or evil they were, nobody deserved to die like these men did.

Sure, she'd been lied to, deceived, mistreated, and abandoned and for that, punishment was warranted. Was this God's will? Is that all it is? Emmy wanted answers, but knew she'd receive none. There really weren't any. No good ones, no straight and easy ones, at least. Maybe she'd figure it out — in time. She had plenty of that. At least she hoped she did. She still had her life, her health, her family and friends, and Sandy. These were the things most important to her. These were the things that made life worth living. She'd pick up the pieces and make a new start. Look forward, she told herself. Not back. The past held too much pain. But the pain would ease with time.

The sheriff and detective had left in a hurry right after the explosion. There was nothing else to do at the gravesite. Emmy snapped out of her musing and told her parents, "I'm ready. Let's go."

ACKNOWLEDGEMENTS

I wish to thank the following for their invaluable input and feedback towards The Lost Fleet. Thank you again to the folks in the Surfside Chapter of the SCWA. Your feedback over the last three years has been so wonderful. Thank you, Bob, for a great tag line. Thanks to Anica for your edits and insight. Thank you, John, for sharing your boat knowledge. A big thank you to Cmrd. Matt Kroll and Officer in Charge Adam Witt of the United States Coast Guard for their generosity and technical assistance in the portrayal of the USCG. And a very special thank you to Melinda for her terrific help in producing yet another fantastic cover.

ABOUT THE AUTHOR

The Lost Fleet is Marvin Levine's sixth novel and his fifth in print. Retired now six years after his career in Manufacturing, Marvin continues to enjoy the laid-back lifestyle of the South Carolina Lowcountry in Pawleys Island. He loves to write his stories set in the beautiful geography the area provides. He enjoys biking and kayaking when he isn't travelling with his wife Margaret to visit his three children and six grandchildren.

You can learn more about Marvin at www.marvinlevine.com

You can contact him at mr20.levine@yahoo.com